Loving the Rain engages the reader from the first page. Through sports, mystery, an array of emotions and even bits of romance... combined with an unpredictable ending...makes this book difficult to put down.

Lori Rathbun, Amazon.com Reviewer

Loving the Rain is a must read for anyone who loves well written, suspense-filled stories with plot twists/turns and heartfelt emotions.

Jessica Carroll, Amazon.com Reviewer

•••••●•••••

An engaging and delectable mystery with more layers than most natural onions, *Skeleton Key* keeps the reader riveted right through to the end.

Mallory Anne-Marie Haws, Amazon.com Reviewer

Skeleton Key is an intriguing story that keeps you turning the pages to find out just exactly what Clay and Tanner Thomas have gotten themselves into.

Ashley Fontainne, Bestselling Author of "Number Seventy-Five"

•••••●•••••

Bulletproof is heart-warming, compelling, unforgettable—a novel which never loses its hold on the reader...

Books4Tomorrow

It's like seeing a jigsaw puzzle come to life. It was so awesome, as the book progressed, finding out little nuggets that would then send your theories on a totally different path. *Bulletproof* kept me guessing until the very end.

Melissa Pearl, Author of the Time Spirit Trilogy

ALSO BY JEFF LaFERNEY

Loving the Rain

Skeleton Key

Bulletproof

JEFF LaFERNEY

JUMPER

TOWER
PUBLICATIONS

Cover, interior book design and eBook design
by Blue Harvest Creative
www.blueharvestcreative.com

JUMPER

Published by
Tower Publications

ISBN-13: 978-0615809137
ISBN-10: 0615809138

Visit the author at:

Website:
www.jefflaferney.com

Blog:
www.jefflaferney.blogspot.com

Facebook:
www.facebook.com/authorJeffLaFerney

Goodreads:
http://www.goodreads.com/author/show/4121665.Jeff_LaFerney

To my two amazing kids: Torey and Teryn

ACKNOWLEDGEMENTS

I'm extremely appreciative of the many people who aided me in this final product. Thank you to my wife, Jennifer, first of all, for her patient support and listening ear. She was also one of my many helpful readers who gave comments and advice, asked questions, and spotted errors. Thanks to my Aunt Linda Smith, who I think encourages me as much as she helped me by reading my manuscript. My teacher friend, Jodi Ely, has been a great supporter, but for this book she also added some honest comments, some helpful questions, and among the errors, caught a glaring content mistake that everyone else missed. Thanks to Renee LaRocque who actually read *Jumper* twice, once at the beginning and once after a thorough editing and revision was done. Her friendship and abundant help is appreciated. Thank you to Autumn Perry, area news anchor and one of my former students, who helped me with my news reporter character. Special thanks go to authors Eliott McKay and Suzanne Purewal who didn't just read the manuscript for errors but dared to be truthful and challenge me to improvement. Their honesty, suggestions, and words of affirmation meant a lot during the considerable revision process. Finally, Angie Edwards cannot be thanked enough. She's such an insightful reader and kindly, openly honest friend, that she stretches me. She does so many things for which I'm grateful to promote my writing career, but mostly she encourages me to keep getting better.

PROLOGUE

• • • • • • ● ● ● ● ⬤ ● ● ● ● ● • • • •

"No! I will not so much as *consider* signing a treaty giving you control of decisions relating to the national security of Israel!" shouted Binyamin Edelstein, Israel's prime minister.

Edelstein spoke with such force of emotion while in the inner office of Jordanian King Akmal-Adnan, that the three private security personnel who sat warily outside the doors rose to their feet, ready to aid their leader. Jordanian Special Operations Command forces (SOCOM) also stood and met the security unit's concerned looks with intimidating glares. No one possessed a weapon; however, all of the men were highly trained in hand-to-hand combat and were confident in their skills.

Inside the Bosman Palace, King Adnan had a self-satisfied smirk on his scarred face. The King's prime minister, his head of

Jordanian Royal Special Forces, and his personal assistant—a man trained during eight years in the military—sat stone-faced as Edelstein flew into a rage. It was as if they presumed such a response and were entirely unsurprised. Israeli President Elias Shalom, the foreign affairs minister, and a man who was Edelstein's most-loyal staffer and personal secretariat silently stared at the Prime Minister. President Shalom reached over and grabbed Edelstein's arm, pulling him back into his seat where he simmered silently, glaring at King Adnan.

The lighting in the plush office appeared to dim, and the air seemed to thicken with a mixture of gloom and anxiety. While Edelstein seethed, Elias Shalom observed the office. On the walls were mounted trophies of the heads of a buffalo, a moose, a lion, and a brown bear. Swords from various ages and cultures crisscrossed on the walls in a museum-like display.

The king stood on his prized bear rug and ran his fingertips along the disfiguring scar on his face while confidently perusing the room. *Interesting*, he thought. *They are all uncomfortable except for President Shalom, who seems much surer of himself than the prime minister.* His laughter resounded in the office with a reverberation echoing madness. "I had no doubt that you would reject my proposal, so I shall simply warn you that my plans *will* move forward. I will forge treaties or invade countries if need be, but I *will* unite the Middle East under my leadership. The other nations would prefer to invade your land, destroy your temple, and subjugate or kill your people. I had hoped that you would see the futility of your rejection and join with me in the early stages of my plans so that I might protect you from destruction."

"We've done just fine protecting ourselves, and we'll continue to do so," Edelstein spat out.

"Occasionally throughout history, that would be true, but do you believe it to be true if all of your neighbors are encouraged to destroy you?" King Adnan slid a piece of paper to the prime minister, who began reading.

"Have no mercy on the Jews, no matter where they are, in any country. Fight them, wherever you are. Wherever you meet them, kill them. Wherever you are, kill the Jews and the Americans who are like them—and those who stand by them—they are all in the same gutter, against the Arabs and the Muslims—because they established Israel here, in the beating heart of the Arab world, in Palestine. They created it to be the outpost of their civilization, the vanguard of their army, and the sword of the West and its crusaders. This is the truth, oh brothers in belief. From here, Allah the Almighty has called upon us not to ally with the Jews or the Christians, not to approve of them, not to become their partners, not to support them, and not to sign agreements with them. Oh, brother believers, the criminals—the terrorists—are the Jews, who have butchered our children, orphaned them, widowed our women, and desecrated our holy places and sacred sites. They are the terrorists. They are the ones who must be butchered and slaughtered like animals, as Allah the Almighty said: 'Destroy them: Allah will torture them at your hands and humiliate them, and he will help you to overcome them, relieving the minds of the believers.'"

After reading the document, Edelstein angrily stared up at the king.

"That was from an Arab cleric," informed Adnan. "Those are words that are being preached to the Muslims. They are the words that will motivate the Islamic nations to destroy your people, ransack your nation, and tear down your temple. I will encourage them to do what they desire to do unless you agree to follow me. Only then can I spare your people and your country because, Prime Minister, as I've already stated, I *will* be moving forward with my plans. Will you be *for* me or against me?"

Something rustled in the corner of his office—an unseen presence that temporarily distracted the king.

"Are we there?"

"I'm not sure *where* we are."

"*Shhh!*"

Heads turned toward the sound of the voices, but there was no one in the room except for those seated at the table. King Adnan hesitated and then refocused his attention on Prime Minister Edelstein. He roared, "*For* me or against me?"

Shaking with anger, Edelstein stood and directed his political team to follow. "As I said before, I will *never* sign a treaty. A pact with the devil…that's what it would be, and I refuse. Excuse us. We will be leaving now." He ripped the treaty in two and let it flutter to the floor.

●●●●● ● ●●●●●

FRIDAY, JUNE 15
One Day Before the Discovery

A ray of light appeared on the rock face. Gradually, the light source grew and began to materialize into a human form. Cassiel stood on a rock outcropping in the Northern Swiss Alps and gazed down at the Rhine River flowing in the Ruinaulta Gorge below. From forty-six hundred meters (about fifteen thousand feet) above sea level, the U-shaped river flowed silently, well below the snow-covered Alpine peak where Cassiel waited patiently for his companions, the frigid breeze stirring his hair.

Cassiel and his friends were three of the many guardians of the nations of the world. They concerned themselves with political, military, and economic issues, including occasionally interfering with those among humanity who would become rulers. Additional projections of light appeared as two more angels materialized as solid bodies of a man and a woman. First Uriel and then Perisa stood in their human forms before Cassiel.

"Greetings, Cassiel," Uriel said as he nodded at his companion.

"Good afternoon, my friend," stated Perisa with a grin.

"Welcome, my fellow principalities. Thank you both for coming as I requested."

"You pick the most-lovely settings for our meetings, Cassiel. This view is breathtaking," noted Perisa as she observed the wonder of the Alpine valley below. The green foliage and sparkling, blue river contrasted beautifully with the rocky crags and snowy Alpine peaks.

"Cassiel, I've learned after thousands of years that our mountaintop meetings indicate a plan is in the works," remarked Uriel. "What are you scheming now?"

"I was about to ask the same thing," added Perisa.

Cassiel seated himself on a rock ledge, his back against the frozen limestone and shale wall. He inhaled deeply, expanding his barrel chest before slowly releasing a plume of wispy vapor. With a serious expression on his square-jawed face, he answered, "We're looking at the Rhine Canyon...sometimes known as the Swiss Grand Canyon. From our vantage point, all we see appears to be at peace. But while we're amazed at the serenity and beauty, trouble is brewing in this world. We're meeting today because it's time to put step one of our plans in place. The girl is now of age, and there is no more time to waste."

Perisa's curiosity changed to excitement. "I assume you're talking about the time travelers?" she asked.

"I am. There are evil forces at work as we speak, setting the stage for chaos in the Middle East and beyond. We are being allowed to interfere and manipulate circumstances to attempt to put leaders of integrity into place. We've been assigned three immediate tasks. Each of us will complete one task. Then we are to watch over and guide the girl and the time traveler until step one is completed.

"Just tell us what to do," Uriel said. He was an angel of action, impatient at times but determined in his execution of orders. Taller and leaner than Cassiel, he had a twinkle in his eyes and an easy smile that inspired confidence in others as he manipulated situations. "This has been something we've foreseen since the new time travelers were born…but why are we starting with the girl?" Uriel inquired.

"Because she is the one to influence Jordanian King Akmal-Adnan. He has been possessed by the demon, Hoaxal, and his strength and power are growing quickly. Hoaxal's influence has already spread to Egypt and Turkey."

"How will such a young girl affect such a powerful, demon-possessed man?" Perisa asked.

"Hannah Carpenter will possess power and strength that is greater than any that Akmal-Adnan possesses. She is the one to expel the demon, so we can defeat him. His influence has reached beyond Jordan and into Israel. And the time traveler, Cole Flint, has been selected not only to help her but to assure the proper leaders are set in place."

Perisa's alert eyes opened wide at the revelation. Her cute but fiery personality was usually evident. "I've been watching him, Cassiel. He's still unaware of his ability."

"He is about to learn what he can do," remarked the leader of the trio. "Perisa, when it happens, you will go back six years to meet him and to extract him from his troubles. Prepare him to encounter the girl on Mount Nebo in two days." Cassiel glanced down the mountain, causing his comrades to follow his gaze. There in a forested, river valley was a large, brown bear in search of food. "Four years ago, you temporarily relocated the young grizzly from the ranch in Montana to this valley, Uriel. Move him today to the Smoky Mountains in Tennessee where Cole will bring the girl."

"He's adjusted to the other habitats. What's one more?" Uriel replied. "Anything else?"

"Yes. After that, make sure Hannah and her family visit the Byzantine Church of Moses at the top of Mount Nebo in Jordan in two days."

"What will you be doing, Cassiel?" asked Uriel.

"I will place the Staff of Moses firmly in the mosaic at the entrance to the church and make sure that its discovery makes the world news. We shall all meet at Mount Nebo in two days. A new era of time travelers has begun. Evil forces are at work. Use all caution in the spiritual realms, friends," Cassiel warned, "and may the Most High be with you."

•••••●•••••

ONE

· · · · · ● ● ● ● ● ● ● ● ● ● ● ● · · ·

SATURDAY, JUNE 16
The Day the Staff Is Discovered

A small but boisterous crowd had gathered inside the training gym in Port St. Lucie, Florida, for an illegal, unsanctioned, extreme cage-fighting event. Eight fights among training members at the gym were scheduled, but the enthusiasm was from the preliminary events. A fighter with the ring name of Vehemence challenged members of the crowd to fight for one five-minute round.

Cole Flint, a strong but wiry man of just twenty-four years observed the attraction emotionlessly. He was barely five feet eleven inches tall, and his slim, muscular frame carried no more than 185 pounds. Three large, strapping challengers had been dispersed in less than two minutes each. Two of the burly competitors were carried from the ring unconscious, while the other left nursing a separated shoulder. The crowd was in the mood for additional violence.

"We're paying out ten to one. Pay fifty dollars for a chance at five hundred. For a hundred dollars, you can win a thousand!" the ring announcer shouted into his microphone. "Who can last five minutes in the ring against Vehemence?"

Leaning against the back wall, Cole waited patiently for the crowd to get restless. The stench of sweat and beer filled the training gym. The temperature escalated, yet he remained calm and cool while analyzing the champion's strengths and weaknesses. The familiar feeling of sadness and despondency began rising to the surface, yet Cole shook it off, not caring much for his own well-being.

"Hey, sexy, are you lookin' for a good time?" asked one of two sexy ladies who had strolled over to flirt.

"No thank you. I'm not here for fun."

"Well, what other reason would you be here?" teased the second of the two. "We can show you a good time, I'm sure."

"I'm sure you could, but no thank you. I'm here for *him*," Cole revealed as he pointed toward the ring.

"Vehemence?" flirt number one asked incredulously. "He never loses."

"Hopefully, he will this time. Excuse me, ladies."

While he fixed his attention on the cashier's table as he moved toward the ring, he passed another attractive woman whose smile seemed vaguely familiar, but when he curiously turned, all he saw was a dissolving ray of light. When he refocused on his destination, he found that incredibly, he was somehow already standing at the money table at the foot of the cage, wondering how he had negotiated his way through the crowd so quickly.

"You?" laughed Vehemence, who had grabbed the announcer's microphone. "You think you can last five minutes against me?"

Members of the crowd initially laughed and jeered but eventually became uneasy as they saw the intensity and determination begin to flame in Cole's eyes. The ring girl caught a glimpse, gave a slight gasp, and scurried to the opposite side of the ring to share her impression that Cole was terrifying. Two men who had been howling for another challenger only a moment before glanced into Cole's eyes and backed away from the front row, struck by an unintelligible fear. He casually counted out five one-hundred-dollar bills and set them in the cashier's hands.

"Five hundred dollars!" shouted the microphoneless ring announcer as he watched the challenger sign his name to the transaction receipt. The announcer commandeered the microphone from Vehemence's hand and peered through the wire fence of the octagonal cage in an attempt to see the name of the fighter. Finally, as he read the signature, he called out, "Our challenger is Cole Flint! For the chance to win five thousand dollars, Cole must survive five minutes in the cage with our champion, Vehemence! Move aside people and let the man into the cage!"

Cole casually but confidently climbed his way into the cage. While sporting his sleeveless white T-shirt, the crowd could see his tattoo of the American flag displayed on his right shoulder and the word *Flint* tattooed on his left. His shoulders, biceps, and triceps flexed as he applied hand wraps to his wrists and knuckles. He momentarily knelt on a tattered knee of his boot cut jeans in what appeared to be a minute of serious, focused meditation, his fists clenched and his jaw set in determination. He rose and slid an ill-fitting mouth guard in his mouth before making his way to the center of the ring to stand opposite his mammoth opponent. The quieted crowd began to settle into the idea of another massacre at the hands of Vehemence, and the clamor rose once again.

A female voice yelled out, "My money's on Flint! Any takers? Place your bets now! I'll pay two-to-one!" Perisa, a giddy radiance to her angelic face, collected bet money that poured in for the bout, including several steep wagers from some broad-shouldered bouncers who were drawn to her physical attractiveness but also her obvious naïvety for betting on what they saw as a sure loser.

The fighters were steered to the center of the ring for instructions. Vehemence outweighed Cole by more than a hundred pounds. Tattoos covered his gleaming, shaved head and continued down his neck and over his entire upper body and arms.

"It's mixed martial arts," the referee explained. "Anything goes except for eye gouging, hitting in the groin, kicking when your opponent is down, hitting in the back of the neck or the spine, and throwing your opponent from the cage." The referee smirked at the challenger, recognizing the absurdity of that last prohibition.

"So I can bust his ugly face?" Cole asked.

"You'll be lucky to last a minute, little man!" Vehemence countered.

"I'd be surprised if you could tell time….Do you even know what vehemence means? If it means stupid and ugly, you've chosen well."

"It means I'm gonna kill you is what it means!"

Vehemence raged and scowled in fury as ring aides pulled him to the side opposite Cole. The crowd noise escalated, and the bell sounded.

The crazed giant wasted no time in charging at Cole with an obvious strategy of overwhelming the smaller man with his size and weight. As he was about to make his tackle, Cole dropped flat on his back, bent his knees, and planted his feet squarely in the ribs of his opponent. Using the madman's momentum and the wiry strength of his own legs, he kicked his feet into the air, sending Vehemence soaring into the metal cage behind where he dropped to the canvas with a thud. The crowd roared wildly, shouting for additional violence.

Vehemence staggered awkwardly to his feet, enraged that Cole had gotten the best of him. One of the bouncers caught his attention and fed the end of a chain through the fence. Once Vehemence gathered the chain into his hand, the crowd cheered wildly. "Anything goes, Flint! You heard the rules!" he howled, swinging the chain in circles above his head as he slowly approached, a throbbing vein in his temple threatening to implode his miniscule brain.

Cole had too much pride to flee his attacker, so he took him head-on. The chain lashed out, but Cole raised his left forearm to block it. As it deflected around his arm, the end link nicked him slightly above his left eye, causing a minor cut that dripped crimson. Vehemence jerked the chain back and swung again. Cole blocked it again. He leaned his head to the side to avoid more damage, but the chain wrapped solidly around his arm. Vehemence gave it a pull and hauled his adversary forward where he kicked Cole in the ribs. When he doubled over, Vehemence elbowed Cole in the side of the head, spinning him away but also releasing him from the hold of the chain.

As Vehemence approached again, twirling the chain like a lasso, Cole didn't move a muscle. Though his head spun from the elbow blow and his breathing labored from the kick in the ribs, he calmed himself and stood his ground. From the perspective of the raging crowd, he looked as relaxed as could be while never taking his eyes from his opponent. When Vehemence got within striking distance, he attacked, aiming the chain once again at Cole's head. But Cole did an unexpected thing…he leapt up into the air toward the raging giant. The chain wrapped harmlessly around his body before he landed back on the floor. In one fluid motion, Cole yanked the chain, pulling a surprised Vehemence toward him. He lowered his head and slammed it into the hulking giant's chin. The muscle-bound fighter's front teeth chomped onto his tongue, and his jaw cracked audibly.

Vehemence dropped his weapon and held his jaw as blood dribbled from his mouth. With a crazed expression on his face, he spit the severed portion of his tongue onto the cage's canvas floor, howled in anger, and attacked. "I'm gu..uh ki' you!" he yelled with half a tongue. He swung his huge fist like a madman, but Cole coolly dodged it and jabbed a hard left into Vehemence's jaw. The giant swung again, but Cole blocked the punch with his left forearm and sent a hard right jab once again into his opponent's chin. Eyes watering from the pain, Vehemence swung again for the third and final time. Cole ducked, and with the strength of his entire body behind his left hook, plowed a third bone-jarring punch into the goon's jaw, completely dislocating it from its socket. Vehemence fell unconscious to the canvas, his jaw hanging grotesquely from his ugly head.

The crowd shouted in appreciation, but Cole simply stepped out of the cage before the referee could even raise the winner's hand in victory. The underlying sadness replaced the intensity in his eyes. He spit out his mouth guard, dropped his hand and wrist wraps to the floor, and stopped at the cashier's table as the crowd noise diminished in confusion. Cole extended his hand while the cashier counted out five thousand dollars. Wordlessly, the new champion pocketed his money and exited the training gym.

●●●●●◉●●●●●

SATURDAY, JUNE 16
The Discovery of the Staff of Moses

As the first tourist group of the morning continued, they approached the stone that marked the entrance to historic Mount Nebo in Jordan. The tour guide, Haneen Urduni, had made the tour hundreds of times using memorized words and often paying little attention to what she said. "This engraved stone," she explained, "is a memorial to Moses, the great prophet of the Old Testament who delivered the Israelites from bondage in Egypt. It is here at the top of Mount Nebo that God gave Moses the opportunity to view the Promised Land, though he was never able to enter it with his people. Legend says that Moses died on this mountain, but his grave was never discovered. As the sign states, this memorial to Moses is considered to be a Christian holy place."

A boy of roughly ten years of age read, "And Moses the servant of the Lord died there in Moab, as the Lord had said. He buried him in Moab, in the valley opposite Beth Peor, but to this day no one knows where his grave is. Deuteronomy 34:5-6."

"What did you just say?" Haneen asked as she took a look at the sign. "What is going on here?" she asked. "This sign is supposed to say 'Franciscan Custody of the Holy Land...Mount Nebo Siyagha...Memorial of Moses...Christian Holy Place.' The sign is missing."

Cassiel melded into the tour group and smiled to himself at his handiwork of the previous night. Haneen took out her cell phone and called her boss, Amed Hakim. "The memorial stone at the top of the mountain has been stolen...or replaced... or altered somehow....Yes, I'm sure. I've been giving tours for over seven years....I don't know. How would I know how it happened? You need to tell someone, Amed. A historical land-mark is missing...."

She ended the call and turned back to the tour group. "I apologize. This stone is not the one that's supposed to be here. I don't know what to say." She hesitated. "I guess we should simply continue the tour."

Somewhat shaken, Haneen led them up a road, but she composed herself enough to continue. "Mount Nebo is a one thousand meter or thirty-three-hundred-foot-high mountain, located ten kilometers or six miles northwest of Madaba in Jordan, opposite the northern end of the Dead Sea. If the Holy Scriptures are correct, you will be walking the same steps as the prophet Moses before he died." Cameras flashed as people climbed over rocks and caught breathtaking glimpses of the biblical Promised Land.

The view became even more spectacular as the group reached a viewing platform erected for Pope John Paul II in March of 2000. "This summit is slightly over eight hundred meters or twenty-six-hundred feet high and provides a panorama of the Holy Land. To the north, you have a partial view of the valley of the Jordan River. The West Bank city of Jericho is visible this morning from this summit, as is Jerusalem." She pointed and waited patiently as several people commented and snapped pictures.

They next made the climb to the peak at which Moses was believed to have stood while regarding the Promised Land. Several of the tourists bowed their heads in prayer as they considered the probability that they were standing on the exact spot where Moses stood with God Himself, overlooking the Holy Land. At the site stood a brazen serpent statue, "commemorating the bronze serpent Moses made in the wilderness to halt the plague of snakes that was killing complaining Israelites," Haneen recited. "On the platform at the summit is a modern sculpture by an Italian artist representing Moses's staff and Jesus's words in John 3: 'As Moses lifted up the serpent in the wilderness, so must the Son of Man be lifted up,'" she quoted.

When she finished her narrative, that same young boy called out again. "There's nothing here about a serpent in the wilderness, lady. The words say, 'But even the archangel, Michael, when he was disputing with the devil about the body of Moses, did not dare to bring a slanderous accusation against him but said the Lord rebuke you! Jude 1:9.'"

"What is this?" Haneen asked. "This too is new."

Standing amongst the group, the angel, Cassiel interjected. "Maybe it's a sign of something. Both signs are about the death and burial of Moses." Cassiel smiled, knowing the real surprise was yet to come. "Maybe we're being prepared for something amazing that's about to happen."

Excited speculation broke out among the tourists as Haneen called her boss for the second time, explaining the newest strange occurrence. She was told that authorities had been contacted and were on their way. Haneen concluded her call and raised her hand to quiet the crowd before inquiring whether the tour group still wanted to see the Byzantine Memorial Church of Moses. The group excitedly agreed, wondering if something amazing really *was* about to happen.

Haneen continued her well-practiced narrative as she led her group to the church. "Because of the connection to Moses, Mount Nebo is an important place of Christian tourism. The Franciscans own this site and have excavated important remnants of the early church and its stunning Byzantine mosaics. The modern additions to the Church of Moses are very simple, consisting of little more than a shelter over the excavations and ancient mosaic floors." The group gathered in front of the entrance to the old, stone church.

"Just inside the entrance to the left," Haneen continued, "you will see the excavated baptistery, which includes some of those ancient mosaics. The baptistery and mosaic can be precisely dated to August 531 thanks to a Greek inscription which also listed the names of the three workers who created it." She began to lead the tourists inside the building.

Walking backward, Haneen faced the group. "You will find the mosaic to be in remarkable condition because it was overlaid merely six decades later in 597. The original mosaic remained hidden for nearly fourteen hundred years until it was discovered in 1976 when the one on top was removed for restoration." Haneen smiled as she noticed the awe on the faces of her tour group who were all gazing toward the mosaic she had been describing. She dramatically rotated, leading with her hand. "Behold the awesome animal mosaic from the Church of Mo…"

Her words were cut short as she beheld the reason why the others were gawking. Her jaw dropped open as her wide eyes beheld an incredible sight. There, planted in the mosaic, was a pure sapphire staff. It gave the impression that it was glowing, giving off a source of light, yet it cast no light rays at all. It was a deep but nearly transparent blue—flawless and clear. Though it was an inanimate sapphire rod, it bestowed the sense of life and power and strength. Hebrew engravings marked the precious gem from which the staff was formed, adding to the sense of purity that seemed to emanate from the priceless, vivid-blue object. The hush that had fallen over the crowd demonstrated each person's awareness that he or she was in the presence of something holy and powerful—something that unquestionably was embedded solidly in the stone floor.

Cassiel exclaimed, "It's the Staff of Moses!"

People spun to look briefly at the enthusiastic speaker and then turned back with the realization that his words left little doubt as to their truth. As they resumed their admiration of the breathtakingly stunning staff, Cassiel's human form dissolved into light, and he disappeared from sight an instant before Amed Hakim, Haneen's boss, and two public security force officers entered the building. The Staff of Moses had been discovered.

●●●●● ● ●●●●●

TWO

· · · · · · · · · ● ● ● ● ● · · · · ·

SATURDAY, JUNE 16
The Day the Staff Is Discovered

Up and at 'em, honey. Your sister has already showered, dressed, and eaten breakfast."

"But it's just a shiny, blue stick," Hannah Carpenter mumbled nearly incoherently.

"I'm not sure what you're talking about, but it's time for you to get up, honey."

"He appeared right out of the sky," she mumbled again, eyes still closed and curly blonde hair strung across her face.

Kristina, Hannah's mother, walked into the bedroom and shook her daughter awake.

Hannah pushed the covers from around her head with a moan. It was 9:00 a.m. on Saturday. She was far too tired to be expected to climb out of bed.

"We still have lots of cleanup to do from last night, Hannah. Your father has a list of things we need to accomplish before my writers' club comes over this afternoon. Did you have a good time at your graduation open house last night?"

Hannah moaned again, but at least her answer made sense. "My feet still hurt from standing in those crappy shoes, and if it's possible, I pulled a muscle in both cheeks from fake smiling. I'm glad it's over. Can't I sleep in a little longer, Mom?"

"No, honey. You've *already* slept in."

"Mom, I'm eighteen years old...I've graduated from high school. When're you gonna start treating me like an adult and let me make my own decisions? Like what time I want to get up."

"That's a wonderful idea, Hannah! So after we clean up the house and yard this morning, I'll let you borrow the car, and you can go out and find a job. Community college starts in the fall, and you'll need some tuition money."

Hannah sat up quickly, realizing immediately that her mother was one hundred percent serious. She sighed in resignation before plopping back onto her pillow.

"You might want to get up now...before I start to get cranky," her mother added before turning and exiting the room.

Hannah immediately hauled herself from her bed and headed for the shower. When she finished, she toweled away the steam from her mirror and groaned about her wavy, strawberry-blonde locks. She observed her tall, slim, five-foot-nine-inch frame, wondering what her future had in store for her, but immediately recovered from her daydream when her mother called, "It's time to eat, Hannah!"

She put her hair in a ponytail and dressed hurriedly, respectful of her parents' expectation that she make a timely appearance for breakfast.

Her mother had scrambled eggs and buttered toast for her. As she sat at the table, Hannah's dog, a twelve-pound shih tzu, began licking her toes. "Good morning, Teddy," she said as she scratched his ears and lifted him onto her lap. The dark-brown dog sniffed her face before licking her directly on the lips. "I love you, Teddy. You're such a good boy." She held him closely and kissed him on the nose.

"I remember when I was little," remarked Sarah, Hannah's fourteen-year-old sister, "and you would always say one day you were gonna have a big pet bear of your own that could hold you in *his* lap every morning. Instead, you have a dog that looks exactly like a teddy bear."

"I only said that because you liked to hear it, Sarah. My little teddy bear makes me happy enough. Thanks for breakfast, by the way, Mom."

Richard, a well-known historian by trade, walked into the kitchen, whistling a tune and carrying a piece of paper. He tossed it on the table and walked to the refrigerator in search of orange juice. Kristina set down *To Kill a Mockingbird*, the novel she had nearly finished, picked up the paper, and read the list of activities he'd written. "What's this, Rich?"

"I have the next week off—no classes, no projects, no research—so I figured I'd do some things around the house. That's my list."

Hannah leaned over and looked at it. There must have been thirty things jotted down. "The only thing you left off the list, Dad, is save the world. Are you sure you can't accomplish that in the next seven days too?"

"I was thinking I'd leave that for you to do, Hannah," he replied with a smile of confidence as if he believed it could happen.

"Yeah, well, first I have to eat breakfast, do my chores, and get a job. Maybe I'll save the world at a later date. I'm not quite the overachiever that the rest of you are."

Kristina, who was on the last chapter, returned to the book she had been raving about while Richard perused some pictures that the family had displayed at the graduation party the night before. "I love this picture," he acknowledged. "There you are practicing your heart out on the swim team. You're the only one still in the pool."

"Dad, that was the qualifying race for the conference meet. The reason it looks like I'm the only one in the pool is because everyone else is already finished. I came in last by a mile. Thanks for reminding me."

"And speaking of reminders, Hannah," cut in her mother, "you have to return your color guard props to Mr. Hankins today—the flag, rifle, and sabre we borrowed for the open house. I promised you'd bring them back to him right away. He has a flag corps group practicing today."

"Here's a picture you can't complain about," Richard said to his daughter. "Marching band color guard. You received the award for best of team. The way you handled those props was a joy to watch."

Hannah regarded the picture closely and grimaced. It reminded her that she joined the squad simply so she wouldn't have to try out for volleyball like her father wanted. She feared getting cut, so she picked something easier. "It's not as much fun as watching Sarah dribble circles around everyone on the basketball court or catch grounders and throw like a boy in softball. Face it, Dad. I'm nothing special."

"No, honey," her mother interjected, "we love you precisely the way you are, and take my word for it…you'll make your mark on the world someday. You just wait and see."

She rolled her eyes and was saved from further pep talks by the ringing doorbell. Teddy rushed to the door, barking his tiny head off, followed closely by Mr. and Mrs. Carpenter. The girls also pivoted their chairs in curiosity to see who it was. When Richard opened the door, Teddy started jumping all over the tall, smiling man in the Federal Express uniform brandishing a delivery envelope.

"May I help you," asked Richard.

"I have a package…next day air for a Mr. Richard Carpenter."

"That's me. What is it?"

"I might be able to tell you if I had X-ray vision, Mr. Carpenter, but since I don't, you'll have to open it. I *did* notice it says right on the package 'Open Immediately,' so it could be something important. You just need to sign here," Uriel stated.

Richard scribbled his signature and tore open the package as the Federal Express man began petting Teddy. "Look at this!" he exclaimed. "It's four round-trip tickets to anywhere in the world! Wait, there's a note. It says, 'As one of our frequent flyers, we chose your name in our random monthly drawing to reward some of our most-loyal customers. Congratulations, and enjoy your trip compliments of American Airlines!' Can you believe it, Kristina? I can't think of the last time I won something. We could go someplace this week. How about it? We're both off…the kids are out of school…"

While everyone focused on the letter, Uriel dissipated into light before moving unnoticed into the house and turning on Fox News on the family television with the volume blaring overly loud.

"Where would you want to go?" Kristina asked as the television popped on and the words "…Staff of Moses" resounded throughout the house.

A photo of the translucent-blue staff filled the television screen and preceded a video clip of a huge crowd of people gathered in front of the excavated remains of the Byzantine Memorial Church of Moses at the top of Mount Nebo. The area was roped off, and armed security stood with guns ready in front of the tourist attraction.

The video switched to the on-air reporter, the young and very attractive Lauren Molina. "What we've discovered is that a sapphire shepherd's staff is embedded in the mosaic stone at the entrance to the Basilica of Moses, the memorial church at the top of Mount Nebo. Historians, geologists, church leaders, and more have inspected the staff which somehow appeared overnight, and the consensus of opinion is that it very well might be the legendary staff of the biblical prophet, Moses. According to Deuteronomy 34, Moses came to the top of Mount Nebo to view the Promised Land, but God didn't allow him to make the trip with his people. He died on the mountain and God Himself or His angels buried Moses in a sepulcher somewhere on the mountain. Ironically, the verses that give the information that I just shared were engraved overnight on the Memorial of Moses at the entrance to the tourist site. Also, the words of Jude 1:9 were somehow engraved in the sculpture which represents Moses's staff on the platform at the mountain's summit. Jude 1:9 talks about how Satan and the archangel, Michael, fought over the body of Moses. Historians and treasure hunters have been interested in the Staff of Moses for thousands of years, believing that it holds the power of miracles. The staff might truly belong to Moses, but no one has yet been able to remove it. Currently, security and Jordanian government leaders are filtering in people who, one at a time, are trying to pull the staff from the stone mosaic. So far, it remains firmly entrenched in the rock."

Richard Carpenter was immediately intrigued. He lowered the television volume and spoke to his family. "I know what to use these tickets for. Who's for a trip to the Holy Land? We can visit the memorial church while we're there. Maybe they'll let us attempt to pull out the staff. I'd love to see it and take some pictures....Who knows, maybe we'll get to touch the actual, mighty Staff of Moses."

"I know the drill, honey. I'll make arrangements for the tickets and pack for the both of us while the girls get ready and you do some research. It appears we'll be spending your week off in the Holy Land….I'll do it as soon as I finish this amazing book," she added with a smirk.

Uriel, feeling pretty good about what he'd accomplished, let his light fade completely as he headed for his next destination.

●●●●● ● ●●●●●

THREE

SATURDAY, JUNE 16
The Day the Staff Is Discovered

Cole exited the building into the blazing hot Florida sun and squinted as his eyes adjusted. While stuffing the five thousand dollars he'd won into his jeans pocket, he approached his parked motorcycle beside the stone wall of the training gym.

"Where do you think you're goin', Flint?" asked the irritated voice of one of the bouncers he'd seen inside the building.

Cole noticed four other muscle-bound gorillas fanning out and coming to a stop beside the bouncer who had asked the question. Casually, he responded to the talking ape, "Well, looky here. It's Moe, Larry, Curly, and Shemp...and I'll call you Stooge. I was thinking a bank, maybe...to make a deposit."

"You ain't goin' nowhere. Least, not before you hand over your cash winnings."

"So that's how it works, Stooge? If someone bests your champion, five comedians are sent to retrieve the cash? Go back and tell your boss that next time he should send someone more competent." Without responding, the five men took a couple of steps closer. "Oh, I'm sorry…competent means capable, skilled, adept. It means you won't succeed."

"We lost money bettin' against you. I figure takin' yours is an easy way to get it back."

"Well, that's where you've made a mistake because figuring takes brains, and clearly all you stooges are short on brains." As Cole spoke, the intensity sparked in his eyes once again, causing each of the men to sense the danger and hesitate briefly. "Turn around and go back to the television studio you came from, and no one will get hurt," he warned softly.

Though his confidence was shaken by the ferocity in Cole's eyes—that mercilessness that he saw in the cage fight—the lead bouncer wasn't about to back down, at least not with four large friends at his side. "The only one who's gonna get hurt is you if you don't hand over the money. I got me four friends that'll help me make sure of that."

Cole shook his head slowly—almost sadly—and said, "It's not enough."

Stooge made the first punch. Cole tossed his head aside at the last instant and Stooge's fist slammed into the stone wall, breaking three knuckles and cracking his wrist. Cole kneed him in the groin, and he toppled over in pain. The second bouncer took a swing that crashed into Cole's left cheek turning him sideways and to his right. Cole coiled his strength behind his elbow and recoiled, smashing it into the man's temple and knocking him unconscious. As the third man leapt forward, Cole stepped in, turning his head to soften a blow and then jammed his fingers right into the man's throat. He fell away, gasping for breath.

The last two men each pulled out knives and advanced much more carefully, one from each side as their target stood sideways to them. Cole eyed both with his peripheral vision. They charged simultaneously, knives extended like spears in an attempt to impale their victim. Cole stepped back slightly and demonstrated an amazing exhibition of hand-eye coordination. With his left hand, he grabbed the wrist of the attacker to his left while at the same time using his right hand to push the arm of the attacker to his right up into the air. With his left arm, he jerked the wrist and the knife across his body and directly into the neck of the man to the right. Then with his right hand, he grabbed the knife and the hand that was extended into the air and brought the blade down to stab directly into the other man's skull. The attackers slumped to the ground, dead, each still holding the knife which had killed the other.

Cole stepped away from the two dead bodies as he heard a siren in the distance. The entire fight had lasted less than a minute, yet five men lay on the ground either dead or injured severely. His intensity began to simmer, replaced by sorrow. It reminded him of the spring of 2006, when he had wreaked similar havoc on a group of his high school peers who had started a fight. All of a sudden, Cole disappeared from the present and found himself sitting in the principal's office being interrogated by the principal and two police officers.

●●●●●◉●●●●●

Six Years Before the Discovery

Shocked, Cole found himself in the principal's office at his former high school with the principal, the assistant principal, and two police officers. His left cheek felt bruised and swollen, and his right cheek felt as if it had been scratched or scraped. His ribs throbbed, his left forearm ached, and the cut above his eye was tender, though the bleeding had subsided. Confused, he found himself in the exact situation that he'd been in six years earlier, a situation that changed his life completely.

"So explain to me, Cole...what started the fight?" asked Mrs. Foster, the principal, who eyed him curiously as if she barely recognized him. One police officer glared at him with his arms crossed. The other had a notebook and pen ready to write down his response.

It had been six years earlier, but Cole remembered it perfectly. Five bullies from the power-lifting team had been harassing a helpless ninth grader in the boys' restroom. Cole intervened and spoke to Russ Smallock, the leader. "The girls' bathroom's down the hall. Maybe you should take your skirt and panties to the right restroom." Smallock took an aggressive swing at Cole, missed, and was struck in retaliation with a pointed second knuckle jab above the lip and slightly below the nose, dropping Smallock to his knees in agony. Cole escorted the rescued freshman into the hallway as Russ fought tears of pain from running down his cheeks.

Later the same day, Cole liberated an innocent sophomore girl in the cafeteria. Russ and a friend wouldn't let the girl pass with her tray to get to a table. Cole walked past the friend, bumping into him before he reached the girl to escort her away.

"Got a date with your girlfriend, Flint?" Russ smirked, his upper lip swollen to an embarrassing proportion.

"Exactly," he replied. "So now that you see she's taken, you can get back to that boyfriend of *yours* and leave my girl alone."

Anger seethed in Russ Smallock, but the cafeteria apparently hadn't been the place to take his revenge on Cole, so he waited until after school where he and four friends tried to even the score.

But now they were in the principal's office after school, and Mrs. Foster asked again, "What started it, Cole?"

Cole rubbed his hand on his face, surprised at the feel of the rough, whiskered growth that he never had while in high school. "I was walking to my car in the parking lot after school when all five of them jumped me."

"She asked you, young man, what started the fight," the officer with the notebook reiterated.

"I interfered with their bullying a couple of times. I guess they didn't like it."

"So who started the fight, Cole?" Mrs. Foster questioned.

"They did."

"'They' meaning…?" the officer asked. "They all jumped you at the same time?"

"I'm not sure who hit me first. Russ, I think."

A third police officer entered the office. He whispered something to the cop with the notebook and then left.

"You're in big trouble, Cole," the officer alleged. "Four of the boys were carted off in ambulances to the hospital. The other—Russ Smallock—is dead. The boys say you started the fight."

Unexpectedly, the door swung open again. Perisa entered the room in a professional-looking suit and stood next to Cole. "What's going on here?" she asked.

"We're questioning this young man about a fight he was involved in," Mrs. Foster stated.

"Not any more, you aren't. He has a right to council in a situation like this. Have you called his father? Have you charged him with any crime?"

"We're just trying to get to the bottom of what happened in the fight," the quiet officer with the folded arms explained.

"He doesn't have to answer any more of your questions. He's coming with me. And the next time you interrogate him, it will be with advocates and legal representatives present. Is that clear?" She grabbed Cole by the arm and steered him toward the door. "Good day," she said as she swung the door shut.

Once they made their way from the office and headed out the doors of the school, Cole asked the obvious question. "Who are you? I saw you at the cage fight, didn't I?"

"I'm a friend, and we need to talk. Can you think of anywhere on the planet that's private enough to go where we don't have to worry about other people?"

Cole hesitated before finally saying, "Up north, maybe— Gaylord, Michigan…at my grandpa's cottage. But that's a long way away. We can't…"

"Yes we can if you picture it in your head. Can you think of a time when you were alone in that cottage?"

He nodded in the affirmative.

"Good. Hold my hand. Think about the cottage—picture it—and tell yourself you want to go there."

●●●●●◉●●●●●

Twelve Years Before the Discovery

Cole did as instructed. He closed his eyes as he visualized. He felt a whoosh of air on his face, and then the solid, hard pavement under his feet felt softer. When he opened his eyes, he stood with Perisa on the living room carpeting of his grandpa's cottage. "What the heck? What's happening to me? How did we get here?"

Perisa ignored his question. "Why did you choose this place?"

"I don't know. Probably because it's where I have my last good memory of my mom and dad back when I was only twelve years old. That would make the second half of my life pretty sad, don't you think?"

"Come over here, Cole, and sit down. We need to have a chat."

He sat on the couch, still trying to figure out what was going on. "I want to know how we got here, and how did I end up back in the office of my high school?" He stood and began to pace the room.

Perisa smiled. "Listen, Cole. Please sit down. I've got some things to tell you, okay?" He nodded and sat back down. "What happened was that you time traveled with me. But you can do more than that. You can also teleport—that's how you got to the cashier's table so quickly. You're what is often called a jumper." She paused to gage Cole's reaction. When he didn't say anything, she continued. "There are different kinds of time travelers, but what *you* can do is you can move in time to anywhere you can visualize. You can also jump to any place you can visualize."

"That's just *awesome*," he verbalized sarcastically. "And I can fly...and make myself invisible."

"Well, no...you can't. But you can fight, and you seem to consistently help other people."

Cole tilted his head and sort of glanced at Perisa out of the corner of his eye. "Uh, yeah, I guess I have multiple super powers...so let's get back to that visualizing thing. You're saying that because I pictured the cashier's table, I traveled there? And because I thought about the fight in high school, I sent myself back in time?"

"Yes. And this is the time that you remembered for your grandfather's cottage."

"That's crazy. How is that possible?" Then, as if an idea came to him, he asked, "If what you're saying is true, I can go back and change the fight, right? I can go back and change things so I don't end up in prison, right? Can I go back and not have to kill Mo and Curly?"

"Not so fast, Cole. No...you can't. You could try, but it wouldn't work. Well, it might, but then something else would happen to create the same result. It's very difficult to change history that's already played out, and there would be consequences if you managed to do it. Russ Smallock is dead. If you went back in time and tried to change that, he'd end up dead anyway. The bouncers died. It was their destiny, and it cannot be undone."

"So if I went back to the three years after the fight, no matter what, I'd still be in prison?"

"It would seem like that's true, but minor details can be altered because they don't throw off history. For those three years, you were off the grid, so to speak. You served time for manslaughter in a fight that you didn't start—one in which you were defending yourself. But I've managed to take you away from that. I've now made a minor alteration. The problem is that by doing that, I've created some consequences."

"Like what?"

"You won't go to prison, but you'll be a fugitive of the law… just like you're also now a fugitive because of the parking lot fight in Florida. When the police show up after your fight outside that gym, there will be two dead men, and the three injured ones who you left behind are going to lie about what happened. You're a fugitive in the present too. They know it's you. Three living witnesses…your motorcycle…a signature inside the training gym. And they'll connect you shortly to the killing outside your high school. By time traveling from Florida back to your high school in Michigan, you've changed your life completely."

Cole lowered his head and took a deep breath. When he looked up, only a few seconds later, focus came into his eyes. "If I go back to Florida, I'll end up in prison again, won't I?"

"I can't know something that hasn't happened. All I know is that the perception is that you fled the scene of the crime in Florida twelve years from now, and six years from now you disappeared after a violent fight at school. You have a record of violence, and there are witnesses in both fights that will lie and testify against you. Starting at your high school fight, you're a wanted man."

"And if I go back to high school, you're saying I can't change what happened, right?"

"There are minor alterations you could make in the past... maybe change some of the details...but the strands of time are already ingrained in history. Historical results are very unlikely to change no matter what you do in the past."

"But I can change the future, right?"

"Yes, Cole, you and your abilities can have a great impact on the future."

"So while I'm running from the police the rest of my life, you're saying you have a plan for me?"

"Yes, I already have a purpose for you, Cole Flint. It involves a girl. She's been selected to do something great. And she will need your help in less than forty-eight hours."

●●●●● ● ●●●●●

FOUR

· · · · · · ● ● ● ●　●　● ● ● ● ● · · ·

MONDAY, JUNE 18
Two Days After the Discovery

As the American Airlines Boeing 777 taxied down the runway, the pilot's voice sounded through the speaker system. "This is Captain Royce Martin. We are arriving at Amman Queen Alia International Airport in Amman, Jordan. It is currently 1:30 p.m. It's sunny, ninety degrees Fahrenheit—thirty-two degrees Celsius—and forty-nine percent humidity. Please keep your seatbelts fastened until we come to a complete stop. I hope you enjoyed your flight and choose American Airlines to meet all your future flying needs."

Hannah roused herself from her seventeen-hour stupor, the last eleven of which were in the uncomfortable coach seat on the flight from Orlando, Florida, to Amman, Jordan. With the eight-hour time difference from her home near St. Louis, it felt like

5:30 a.m. after a night of very little sleep. She was wedged between two larger-than-average-sized men but was still grateful to be far enough away from her father to miss out on his excited prattling. At least a week in the Middle East would delay the inevitable job search her mother was sure to demand.

She peeked across the aisle and watched Sarah as she continued to carry on a conversation with a cute college-aged guy—a conversation that more than likely lasted most of the flight. No one had spoken to Hannah the entire flight except the female attendant who had spilled Coke on her white T-shirt about nine hours before.

The two-hundred-foot-long jet airplane contained a full-to-capacity 247 seats with passengers hurriedly accumulating their items for debarkment. Hannah caught sight of her father whose excited grin practically made her groan out loud. When she exited the plane, Sarah was waiting barely outside the exit doors, and together they waited for their parents.

"What happened to your shirt?" her mother asked when Hannah took off a hoodie that she wore on the plane to cover the pop stain.

"Good morning...or afternoon...to you too. Attila the flight attendant thought I'd rather wear my Coke than drink it. I would've changed but I don't have another shirt in my carry-on."

"You can change as soon as we pick up our bags," her father said optimistically. "What time can we check into our hotel room, Kristina?"

"I was told 4:00, so we'll have to wait around a little while," she replied as the family walked up the exit ramp.

"I have a better idea," Richard suggested. "Let's pick up our bags, get our car rental, and head right for Mount Nebo before they close down the tourism for the day. Maybe we can see the staff today."

The luggage carousel went round and round and round. All of the luggage for the Carpenter family was removed—except for Hannah's. Hers didn't arrive, so Richard impatiently filed the lost luggage claim with an attendant who spoke very poor English. The airport employee could see the discouragement in Hannah's eyes. He held up a finger which seemed to signify "one minute please" and left his post for a moment. When he returned, he handed Hannah a small toiletry bag.

"What's this? You're giving me a shaving kit? What is it?" she asked the claim attendant. "It can't be the clothes I need."

"Essen..chals" is what she thought he said. His accent was strong enough that she wasn't sure.

"Essentials?" she asked.

"Essen..chals keet." He spoke slowly.

"All the *essentials* are loaded in this small shaving kit? Are my clothes in there?"

"Shu kran," he said, but he pointed at Hannah and then back to himself with a smile.

"I think he wants you to say thank you, Hannah," Sarah suggested. "He seems to like you."

"For giving me a toothbrush and shampoo? Okay...sure... shoe crayon," she mimicked.

By then her father had finished filling out the form, leaving the hotel address and his phone number. "Oh, good," he said as he noticed the kit. "At least you'll have the essentials." He was so excited that he failed to notice his daughter roll her eyes.

The attendant smiled crazily, and to say goodbye, he waved his arm off at Hannah while repeatedly saying, "Ma'assalama... ma'assalama."

"Myuh salami, sir...goodbye," Hannah repeated.

All Hannah had when they exited the airport was the essentials kit and what she had in her backpack and tote bag. "I can't even change my stupid shirt," she complained. In the rental car on the way to Mount Nebo, Sarah handed Hannah a shirt to wear—a green army camouflage T-shirt which said, "I kick butt and take names later."

"Nice."

"But it's so *you*, Hannah." Her sister laughed.

Hannah finished stuffing the kit into her backpack and announced, "I'm getting a bad feeling about this trip."

"Now, girls," Richard interrupted, "I want to tell you about the staff." He was so excited that he'd already forgotten about Hannah's luggage issue. "People have wondered for centuries if the staff was wooden or if the Jewish mythology was true about it being made of sapphire. From the picture we saw on TV and the articles I've already read about the discovery, it's clear that the staff we're going to see is pure sapphire."

"Besides it being an expensive gem, what's so special about it?" Sarah asked.

"The story behind the staff was that it was created at twilight shortly before the very first Sabbath at the end of the creation week. The Jewish Sabbath Days are on Saturday, and the staff that we're going to see was discovered by the first tour group of the morning...on a Saturday. Apparently, it was placed inside that church sometime near twilight on the Sabbath Day...which might be coincidence or not. Anyway, the story is that Moses's staff was first given to Adam in the Garden of Eden. The staff was then passed along from Adam to Enoch, Methuselah, Noah, Shem, Abraham, Isaac, and Jacob. Then the story gets interesting. Jacob took it with him to Egypt and gave it to his son, Joseph, who had become the Prime Minister of Egypt. Upon Joseph's death, all of his possessions were removed to Pharaoh's palace, including his sapphire staff. Jethro, one of Pharoah's advisors, stole it and made off with it to the desert. One day, he thrust it into the soil of his garden in Midian, but from that moment, it became permanently secured in the ground, and Jethro was unable to pull it out. When Moses fled Egypt after killing an Egyptian, he met Jethro's daughter, Zipporah, and asked her father for her hand in marriage. It's said that Jethro would only give his approval if Moses was able to pull the sapphire staff from the ground. Jethro was a prophet who declared that the one who could remove the staff was the chosen one and would be allowed to marry his daughter."

"So all this excitement is about a girl?" Sarah asked naïvely.

"Oh, no. It's much more than that," her father replied. "Moses used that staff to perform many, many miracles: the ten plagues on the Egyptian Pharaoh…the dividing of the Red Sea…calling forth water from a rock…and many more. According to the bible and Jewish tradition, when Moses died, he was buried by God Himself—or possibly His angels—on what is now known as Mount Nebo. Most historians believe that he was buried with his staff and his grave has been hidden and protected by angels ever since. Even Satan himself fought with the archangel, Michael, over the body of Moses, according to Jude 1:9. Moses's staff held power from God, and even the forces of evil recognized that. In theory, Satan and his demons have been searching for that staff ever since."

"How would anyone know for sure that the staff we're going to see is the actual Staff of Moses?" Kristina asked.

"First of all, there's no historical record that the staff had a crook in its neck similar to most shepherds' staffs. All indications are that the one Moses carried was comparable to a walking stick. What we saw on TV was more like what we would think of as a rod than as a staff. Secondly, it would surely be the purest of sapphire if God created it for Adam in the garden. Any gemologist or dealer of sapphire would be able to evaluate the purity. Third, there would be engravings—Hebrew abbreviations for each of the ten plagues and engravings signifying names of God. Anyone who gets close enough could identify them."

"But, Dad," wondered Hannah, "isn't the staff stuck in a rock? How valuable is it if it can't be moved? Unless King Arthur or Moses himself shows up, it's nothing more than an attraction at a museum."

"You never know," he said with a smile. "Maybe one of us will be able to pull it out."

• • • • • ● • • • • •

Six Years Before the Discovery

Perisa and Cole traveled together forward in time to the College Bike Shop, a motorcycle dealership in Lansing, Michigan, on the day of the high school fight. "You have five thousand dollars in your pocket," she said. Cole patted the pocket with the money, remembering that his fight winnings were there. "Here's another $9,450. I won it betting on you."

"Seriously? You knew I was going to win, didn't you?"

"Of course. You're Cole Flint, and the other guy was an overconfident, steroided-up, muscle-bound ape. Money in the bank, if you ask me."

"So I walk in, pay cash, and ride off to the wild blue yonder, fleeing the law for the rest of my life?"

"Pretty much. Pick a ride you're happy with and go off and practice jumping—teleporting. Here's a picture of the Church of Moses on Mount Nebo so you can visualize it when the time is right. When I let you know, you have to rescue the girl." She handed him another picture. "Take her there. It's a forest in the middle of the Great Smoky Mountains in Tennessee. It is there that you'll protect her and prepare her however you can for the time she's needed most."

"Prepare her how?"

"To fight…survive. To know herself. To believe in herself. You have your work cut out for you," she declared with another easy smile.

"How will I recognize her?"

"Here's her picture, Cole, but you'll recognize her because she'll be the frightened girl with armed soldiers closing in. Get her out of danger immediately."

Cole studied the picture. She was an attractive but ordinary-looking teenager, petting what looked like a tiny teddy bear, though he guessed it was some sort of dog. Whatever would make her something special wasn't obvious in the picture, but he figured there must be something or there would be no reason to protect her. "She'll be safe in the mountains?"

"Maybe…maybe not. There will be people searching for her, and there are spiritual forces at work as well that will likely find her eventually. But you can take her anywhere, and you can take her anytime. There is no one better equipped to protect her." She hesitated, noticing the curiosity on Cole's face. "What is it?"

"This is a lot to take in…even to believe. How is it possible?"

"Time on earth is perceived linearly. But that's not how time really works."

"Then how does it work? If all I have to do is picture where and when I'm going, I want to be able to visualize how it works too."

Perisa smiled and stretched out a wire—where it came from was a mystery. "Do you recall how people once thought the world was flat?"

Cole nodded.

"They couldn't comprehend how it could be round. But it was, regardless of what they thought. Well, people think of time like a timeline," she explained as she stretched out the wire.

"But it's really round?"

With a hand on the end, somehow Perisa fashioned the straight wire into a perfect circle. "Like this?" she asked Cole.

"Yeah…no beginning, no end. It sort of makes sense to me."

Perisa giggled. "Well, that's not how it is, Cole." With a quick couple of twists of her hand, the wire formed into a coiled spring. "Time is more like this. No beginning or end, but all time is piled on top of each other. In the spiritual realms, past, present, and future are all happening at the same time." She then pressed the spring with her thumb and compressed it into a solid piece of metal. "It's not *really* a spring, though. Everything that happens on earth is happening on a linear timeline—at least it is to the people living here—but in the spiritual world, it's all happening at the same time…except to you. *You* are the spring…sort of like a slinky. You rise out of time, stretch in whatever direction or time you want, and then settle back into the metal." As she spoke, the "slinky" she mentioned rose out of the metal and dropped back into the visual aid, theoretically into a different time or place.

"I don't know how you're doing that, but thanks for the visual. You gonna give me the magic wire in case I have to explain things to the wonder girl?"

"What wire, Cole? There's no wire," she said as she held up her empty hands. "I know you have questions, but I need to say goodbye for now. I sense your anxiety…and sadness. You must deal with that in your own way, but please know that I will be watching…and please be careful." She opened the dealership door and stepped outside. When she didn't walk past the store window, Cole opened the outside door, but she had disappeared.

He turned around to step back onto the sales floor. There in front of his eyes stood a brand new Kawasaki Ninja ZX-14 street bike. Its bright-blue paint sparkled on the showroom floor. Cole walked slowly up to the bike, touching it as though he couldn't believe his eyes. A salesman with the name "Blake Morrish" on a nametag walked up beside him.

"It's a beauty, isn't it?" When Cole didn't respond, he continued. "It's the most-powerful street bike in the world. Four cylinder…six speed transmission…474 pounds of pure power and magnificence. The 200-horse-power engine will easily attain 180 miles per hour. It can cover a quarter of a mile from a standstill in just nine seconds."

"I'll take it," Cole stated as he stepped forward. All of a sudden, he had a sense of purpose which brought a feeling of confidence.

Blake Morrish laughed. "The ticket price is $11,999, son. You'll have to fill out loan papers, and we have to check your credit history. Do you even have a credit history? And I have to tell you, though she's a beauty, this bike's not for everyone."

"My credit history doesn't matter. I have cash, Blake." Cole peered squarely into Morrish's eyes. "And this is the bike for me." The salesman felt a chill run down his spine. There was something dangerous about the soft-spoken young man.

"Let me get my manager," he said, grateful for the opportunity to escape the blazing eyes of his customer. When the manager arrived, Cole had already counted out thirteen thousand dollars in cash. Thirty minutes later, the purchase price, taxes, and fees were paid and a temporary license plate was installed. Cole rolled out of the dealership with the Ninja, two helmets, and about fourteen hundred dollars still in his pocket. He accelerated onto the street and shot up to fifty miles per hour in about three seconds. As he quickly approached a delivery truck in his path, he thought of the Golden Gate Bridge and found himself speeding over the bridge from Oakland to San Francisco.

●●●●● ● ●●●●●

FIVE

· · · · · · · · ●●● ● ●●● ● · · ·

King Akmal-Adnan of Jordan arrived with his entourage at 2:27 p.m. Escorted by General Jibril Marid of the Jordanian Royal Special Forces, Akmal-Adnan and his prime minister, Ghazi-Hazim, stepped out of the armored vehicles to much fanfare. Cameras rolled while the Jordanian national police, the "public security force," moved the crowd away from the church. News reporters stood before various network and world news cameras to give their takes on the arrival of the most-important national figure in the nation of Jordan.

Unknown to the camera crew and the curious crowd, it was the King's second trip to the mountain. On his first trip, in the evening two days before, after much concerted effort, he resigned to leave without the staff. It didn't budge from the rock. This time, a soldier carried a large duffle bag, loaded with tools in case the king was still unable to pull the staff from the stone. He determined that he would remove it, even if it meant damaging the relic.

King Adnan made a show of waving to the tourist crowd, most of whom had already stepped inside the church and given his or her best effort at pulling the staff from the mosaic. People, many of whom were not native Jordanians, waved out of respect and curiosity. A pall fell over the entire area as demon spirits arrived in faithful watchfulness and expectation over the King. In the background in invisible angelic form, Cassiel, Uriel, and Perisa tranquilly watched the proceedings.

The king spoke to General Marid. "After years of fruitless searching for that staff, I will do everything in my power to remove it from the rock floor and make its power my own."

The security detail had spread out after backing the crowd away from the king and stood with firearms visible and ready. Demons circled the church entrance and skittered on invisible, taloned feet around the rocky terrain of the mountain. Only a single reporter from Fox News, Lauren Molina, continued to prattle on about the King's entrance. All others somehow felt the atmosphere change from one of excitement to one of unease.

"Please follow me, my King," replied the general as his officers protected him and led the way to the church entrance.

"A hush has fallen over the mountain," reported Lauren, "as King Adnan of Jordan makes his way into the church. There's a disquieting feeling that has pervaded the mountaintop…."

"Ahhh," the king said softly to the general as his eyes settled upon the sapphire staff. "Its beauty is nearly unimaginable." He hesitated. "With the Staff of Moses, my plans are sure to come to fruition."

Cameramen converged on the doorway as the king stepped circumspectly toward the relic, but the security force kept everyone back, closing the door and giving the king the privacy he desired. The inner glow that pulsated from the gem seemed to be weakening and becoming duller. It could have simply been a trick of the eyes, for all the "experts" had already confirmed that the staff was not glowing as it appeared. Instead it just *seemed* to be radiating light because of its purity and possibly its holiness. Akmal-Adnan approached the dulling relic. The demon spirit, Hoaxal, greedily licked his lips upon seeing the staff. King Adnan mirrored the action, licking his own lips and voraciously rubbing his hands together in anticipation. He believed he was chosen for that very moment.

Anxiety radiated within the shelter that covered the excavated walls and mosaic stone floor. When he removed the rod from the stone in King Arthur fashion, he wondered what would happen. Would lightning strike? Would he perform some otherworldly miracle for all on earth to witness over their television screens? Would he regain youth and vigor and be filled with wisdom and power? As Akmal-Adnan gripped the staff with both hands, it seemed that all breathing stopped. He had done his prayers and felt that the staff *would* be his. He wrapped his hands around the gem and tugged at it gingerly, expecting the rod to slide gracefully from the rock. It remained firm. In a second more strenuous effort, he strained skyward, but again the staff remained solidly entrenched in the rock. Finally, with a puff and a concerted groan, he, with all the possessed united strength that Hoaxal could include, yanked a mighty tug, and yet the rod remained embedded in rock. It did not budge in the slightest.

Ghazi-Hazim inched toward the King, and in a low voice asked, "What should we do, Akmal?"

"Use the sledgehammer," he angrily replied.

Hazim motioned toward one of the soldiers who stepped forward nervously. The general nodded and the soldier grabbed the handle, raised the tool above his head, and slammed it into the flora and fauna crafted into the mosaic stone floor. The first swing cracked the floor about a foot from the staff, but the stone in which the staff was embedded held firmly. Four more powerful blows caused no damage to the stone.

King Adnan stepped forward and tried one last time to yank the staff from its foundation, but it held firmly. "Cut it!" he demanded.

Another soldier stepped forward with a saw, fitted with a blade made of a metal matrix, impregnated with exposed diamond particles. The small cutting edge was "guaranteed" to saw through sapphire.

Ghazi-Hazim swallowed nervously and asked, "Do you know what might happen if the staff is damaged?"

"I must have it," he proclaimed greedily, ignoring the question. "Without it, my planning is for naught. Cut it!" he demanded once again.

The soldier plugged the saw into a portable generator and started it. He bent to the floor and touched the blade to the staff. Sparks sprayed into the air and the blade ground into the stone. A full minute passed as the blade rotated and scattered sparks. Eventually, the flashes of light decreased. King Adnan stepped forward and the soldier shut down the saw. He bent to the ground where the sawing occurred and examined the stone. It looked exactly as before. The saw blade, however, was destroyed.

The king angrily yanked once again on the staff, but of course, it didn't move in the slightest. The tools were replaced inside the duffle bag while the king composed himself to face the media waiting outside the church. They made their way to the doors, and King Adnan forced a gracious smile as he waved to the cameras that taped his embarrassed, unsuccessful exit from the building.

As the fallen demon angels prowled around the top of the mountain, dark rainclouds began to accumulate. Reporters, looking heavenward, nervously chattered about the king's failure to procure the staff. Lauren bluntly stated, "He entered the church confidently, but his exit was no different than anyone else's on the mountain. King Akmal-Adnan is empty-handed and the rock floor has maintained its firm grasp on the historical relic. Security is not allowing reporters near the discomfited king as he heads back to his vehicle."

Winds picked up while the Carpenter family parked their car in the designated tourist parking area and hiked the short distance to the top of the mountain. Hannah, backpack in tow, eyed the darkening sky.

"You should have left your backpack in the car, Hannah," her mother stated.

"Are you kidding? I'm not losing sight of the thing. I'm already missing my luggage; I'm not taking a chance on losing everything else."

"Like your essentials kit?" Sarah joked.

Hannah faked a grin in return. She didn't find her sister amusing.

Upon coming within sight of the church, the family witnessed the king and his entourage re-enter their vehicles. News reporters and cameramen were hustling to their news vans. When the anxious crowd was finally released by the police force, the tourists quickly headed back down the mountain to the lot where their cars were parked. Lauren had her photographer point his camera to the sky as they watched the dark clouds gather and felt the wind picking up.

"As King Adnan of Jordan re-enters his government-owned vehicle, it appears an unusual and unforcasted storm is quickly approaching. The crowd of tourists is making its way off the mountain after having waited uneasily before the military-like protection of the Jordanian king."

"Excuse me," Richard Carpenter impatiently interrupted the reporter. "Could we see the staff inside that church?"

Lauren moved the microphone from in front of her mouth. "Yes, but people are evacuating the mountain to avoid the storm that's coming."

The engines of the state vehicles and police vehicles all began to roar to life while Richard motioned for his family to follow him into the church.

As the king's car shifted into gear, Akmal-Adnan caught sight of the Carpenters making their way *into* the Church of Moses rather than back down the mountain. "Wait," he ordered. "That girl…it's her." The order to hold was passed to the other drivers.

"It's going to storm, Rich. Don't you think this can wait until tomorrow?" Kristina asked.

"It'll only take a minute. I'm dying to see it with my own eyes…photograph it. Don't you want to touch it?"

Deafening thunder exploded, but Richard wasn't to be denied. He withdrew his camera as the family entered the door to the historic stone church. There it was…with an increased, bright-blue hue. "Can you believe it?" he asked excitedly. An incredible bolt of lightning could be seen through the open remains of the uncanopied portion of the Basilica followed almost immediately by another tremendous explosion of thunder.

He slid his hand along the staff reverently as he shot picture after picture. It possessed breathtaking beauty. Purity emanated from the polished gem, and again, it seemed a living entity. The family, in awe and reverence, gathered around the staff in admiration. Another brilliant flash of lightning and a horrifying peel of thunder broke them from their trance.

"We need to go," Sarah begged. "I'm scared."

"Okay, you're right. Let's each give the thing a heft and get out of here."

"It's time," Cassiel ordered Perisa. "Go to Cole Flint, and send him now."

Perisa disappeared as Richard gave the staff a yank. It stood firm. Kristina tried next. Still, no movement occurred. Sarah nervously glanced to the sky as she gripped the staff and another thunderclap, louder than any other, shook the mountain. She gripped, yanking on the gem with no luck and then ran, her father and mother following closely behind her. They exited the church as huge drops of rain began to fall. Richard put his arms around his wife and daughter before realizing that Hannah wasn't with them.

Hannah seemed under a trance. Her family fled before she could try to dislodge the staff herself. Slowly, she reached forward and grabbed hold with her right hand. She felt peace as her palm gripped the radiant gem. The staff was warm to the touch, as if it flowed with energy and power. It felt right in her hand, like a comfortable tool—as if it belonged to her. Only a mere few seconds passed, but Hannah felt as if time wasn't of any essence. This rod that once divided the Red Sea beckoned her to lift it. She felt relaxed as she tightened her grip and wasn't surprised in the least as it slid out of the rock without any resistance at all. The Staff of Moses balanced comfortably—delicately—in her right hand. In a sort of dazed wonder, she walked with it to the church exit, and right as she stepped out from the church, her father glanced back to look for her. Hannah Carpenter possessed the Staff of Moses.

King Adnan saw Hannah exit the church with the staff and gave a quick order. "Take it! Take it *now!*" Within seconds, doors flew open and Royal Special Forces, amidst a torrential rainstorm, aimed their weapons at Hannah.

Lauren caught a glimpse of the girl from her news-van window at precisely the time she exited the church. She quickly took out her cell phone and began recording the scene as the Jordanian military police surrounded Hannah and the Carpenter family. Lauren could see the fear in the girl's eyes despite the driving rain as guns pointed menacingly at her.

Out of the pouring rain, a bright-blue motorcycle appeared, its muscular driver in a blue, sleeveless shirt and dark, blue jeans materializing from thin air. The machine landed on the stony, muddy ground with a sideways skid and slid to a momentary stop right before the girl. Hannah's attention diverted from the gunmen to the stunning, dark-haired rider. With no hesitation, Cole Flint, the time traveler, stood quickly, lifted her, set her facing him on the seat, and accelerated in an incredible burst of speed toward the stone church. From the viewpoint of the Carpenter family, the government entourage, and Lauren Molina, it appeared that he drove right through the stone wall. The girl, the staff, and the mysterious rider had simply vanished.

●●●●● ● ●●●●●

SIX

• • • • • • • • • ● ● ● • • • • • • •

WEDNESDAY, JUNE 13
Three Days Before the Discovery

Hannah stood in the downpour, staring into the barrels of guns too numerous to count when a flash of blue appeared out of nowhere. Strong arms lifted her onto a motorcycle, and driver and passenger sped off back toward the church and into…a forest. The bike bounced once and then skidded along a mountain path before coming to a halt. Hannah's arms were wrapped around the driver's waist, the sapphire staff still in her right hand. Her right cheek rested against the right cheek of the man who had apparently kidnapped her and driven miraculously out of a storm and into a forest where the hot sun sprinkled through the leaves.

She leaned back far enough to get a glimpse of her kidnapper. His dark hair was wet and raindrops trickled down his face, one stopping and dangling off the tip of his nose. He had a small cut healing over his left eye. A puffy, yellowed bruise on his left cheek and the thin line of a scab on his right were both apparent despite a scruffy two or three days' growth of facial hair. She studied his alert, brown eyes speckled with emerald, and her first reaction was to feel self-conscious. She was basically on the lap of the man who had taken her from her family, but she found herself worried about the mass of curls plastered to her head which always seemed too red to her when they were wet. She wore a backpack, a camouflage T-shirt, and nonmatching blue shorts which exposed her creamy complexion in comparison to his dark, even tan. His muscular arms and shoulders flexed as he lifted the slender girl from the motorcycle.

"Who are you?" she asked.

"I'm Cole Flint. Who are you?"

"You kidnapped me and you don't know who I am?"

"I *saved* you...and you're 'important' for some reason," he explained as he made little quotation marks with his fingers.

"I'm not important. You made a mistake kidnapping me, so why don't you take me back to my parents?"

"I can't do that. I was told to bring you here."

"By who?"

"By *whom*. By a really nice-looking lady who explained to me that I could teleport and time travel. She also told me I needed to save you...and she told me two days *before* you stole that blue pole. She told me again a few seconds before I saved you."

Hannah rolled her eyes. "She told you that you can teleport and time travel, and then you just went out and *did* it? And it's not a blue pole—it's the Staff of Moses...and I didn't steal it. You seem to know so much—including proper grammar—why don't you know I pulled it from a rock?"

He laughed at her. "Your story is harder to believe than mine....
You're staying here. I have to protect you...and prepare you."

"Protect me from what? Prepare me for what? A career as
a kidnapper?"

"You ask a lot of questions."

"*What?*

"See?"

"Can a girl hate a guy after like five minutes, even if he has the
coolest motorcycle she's ever seen?"

"I suppose it's possible. I'm already tiring of *you* and all your
questions...whatever your name is."

"Take me back to my parents!"

"You don't remember the guys with guns? You wouldn't be
safe there."

Hannah stormed off down the path for a good fifteen steps
before turning back in frustration. "What would make me special?
I'm *not* special. Who would ever expect *me* to do anything exceptional?" She started walking back toward Cole who had settled
back comfortably onto his motorcycle, his muscular arms folded
across his chest. Her aggravation peaked as she walked back. "I
think I had a dream about this!" She sat on a fallen log and started to cry—a soft cry of frustration and anxiety and fear of the
unknown. A single tear rolled down her right cheek.

Cole climbed off the bike, sat down beside her, and wiped the
tear from her face. "I was told to protect you, and I was told you
needed to be moved here, away from Mount Nebo. I don't know
why, but that's just the way it is now. So...are you planning on
telling me your name?" he asked gently.

She forced herself to smile—like she did at the graduation
open house—and pretended to be stronger than she felt. "It's
Hannah...Hannah Carpenter." After a short pause, she asked,
"What's gonna happen to my parents and sister?"

"Do you want my guess? My guess is that they'll be taken away by the guys with guns."

••••• ● ••••••

As the rain poured down and the police and soldiers closed in, a man on a dazzling blue Kawasaki motorcycle swooped in and took Hannah to the unknown. After the bike and riders appeared to vanish through a stone wall, Richard ran into the church in hopes of finding his older daughter, but she was nowhere to be seen, and when he exited the church, he found his wife and younger daughter in the grips of two soldiers. Several guns were pointed his way.

The thunder and lightning ceased and the rain fell in a light drizzle, but the ground was pooled and muddy. A man of obvious importance exited the car as two men in public security force uniforms each grabbed one of Richard's arms and dragged him toward King Akmal-Adnan. "Who are you?" Richard demanded.

"My name is Akmal-Adnan. I am the King of Jordan. The land we stand on belongs to me, and therefore any relics discovered upon it belong to me. The girl has stolen my staff, and I demand that she return it."

Richard bowed his head in respect before replying. "The land we stand upon, sir, is owned by the Byzantines." He was a historian, and he'd done his research.

"Yet I am their king, and it is *my* kingdom. If I claim it, it is mine. The staff belongs to me."

"My daughter didn't steal the staff. Somehow she pulled it from the mosaic stone inside, but she certainly had no intention of keeping it. Someone who wanted the staff must have kidnapped her. If you want the staff, you need to find the man who kidnapped my daughter."

Lauren, the sole reporter on the scene, and Sam, her photographer, were back on duty and were taping the entire interaction.

"You will be detained until we find this daughter of yours. Until we find her, you and the rest of your family will be held in custody....Arrest these people, General," he ordered Jibril-Marid, "and dispatch your men to make a search of the mountain. Close down all means of escape for the man on the motorcycle. When you find him, arrest him and bring me the staff."

The Jordanian police cuffed the prisoners, and they were led to separate security vehicles. Lauren continued to record the proceedings from her cellphone inside the van. She recorded King Adnan as he pointed to the van and watched a policeman confiscate the video equipment of her photographer before she shut down her phone and stuffed it inside her bra. The police did a casual search of the van for other recordings and then sent the Fox News employees on their way.

●●●●● ● ●●●●●

MONDAY, JUNE 18
Two Days After the Discovery

In Givat Ram, Jerusalem, Israeli Prime Minister Binyamin Edelstein met with the Knesset—the legislature of Israel—in the Ben Guyon Government Complex. The extra session was to discuss current events relating to King Akmal-Adnan of Jordan. Evil spirits, emissaries of Hoaxal, skittered around the room on taloned feet, spreading confusion, deceit, and fear with their whispered messages. A call to order was made, and then Prime Minister Edelstein got right down to business.

"Thank you for meeting this evening," he said to the elected Knesset members and the appointed cabinet of ministers, representing each of fourteen different political parties. "It has reached our attention that King Adnan is presently discussing his alliance treaties with the Prime Minister of Turkey and the President of Egypt. Though we have no *true* friends, Jordan, Turkey, and Egypt are all our current political allies. Any pact they sign which doesn't include Israel is worrisome...and we will *not* be signing King Adnan's treaty."

"Why would Turkey and Egypt do such a thing?" asked Ibrahim Swartz, the minister of defense.

"I don't fully know the answer to your question, but I'm confident that each nation currently has reason to withdraw from us. An alliance, therefore, doesn't seem out of the question."

President Elias Shalom was supposed to be no more than a figurehead with minimal political clout in the country he loved so much, but he was a man of experience, wisdom, and sound political judgment which made him highly respected and admired. After listening patiently to the discussion, he asked, "Please explain to the others what would motivate our allies to distance themselves from us, Binyamin."

"Certainly. For the third consecutive year, with the help of United States President Stonehouse, we have successfully blocked potential suppliers from selling nuclear power generating reactors to Jordan. As we already know, Jordan has accumulated over eighty thousand tons of uranium and has phosphate reserves containing as much as another one hundred thousand tons. King Adnan claims to want to start a peaceful nuclear energy program in Jordan to offset its total dependence on other nations for oil. But we persuaded President Stonehouse to convince the United Nations that the spread of nuclear power could open the door to the spread of nuclear weapons. We're grateful for his help and support, but as we in Israel are also well aware, King Adnan has been attempting to build a nuclear armament for years. Our determination to block his supply channels simply slows the development of his armory. But after his attempt to force us to unite with him, we can easily recognize how dangerous he would be with a nuclear arsenal."

Minister of Defense Swartz interrupted. "I understand what Akmal-Adnan has against Israel, but why make an alliance with Egypt and Turkey?"

"Geographically, it makes sense," answered President Shalom. "With Jordan to our east, Egypt to our south, and Turkey to the north, we are somewhat protected from our Middle Eastern enemies. Our enemy neighboring nations—Iraq, Syria, Lebanon, Saudi Arabia, and Palestine—are in a sense, walled out. But if King Adnan forms an alliance with Turkey and Egypt and he has a nuclear arsenal, he may believe he can subjugate Israel, and then he can turn his attention against the oil suppliers. King Adnan has his sights set on taking over the entire Middle East."

"We have our own nuclear armament and the best-prepared military in the world. He would never threaten us with nuclear war or any other kind of military action," imparted Minister Swartz.

"Maybe not, but if given the proper motivation, our enemies might declare war in an attempt to take back the Promised Land."

"If Adnan were to somehow gain control of the world's oil supplies, it would have worldwide ramifications. Do you believe Adnan has his sights set beyond the Middle East?" asked Speaker Daniel Argowitz, head of the Knesset foreign affairs and defense committees.

"The *better* question is why would our allies, Turkey and Egypt, turn their backs on Israel while helping a lunatic become so powerful?" asked Foreign Affairs Minister Moshe Litzman.

"It's quite ironic that you would ask such a question, Moshe," replied Prime Minister Edelstein. "It is *you* that has stirred the ire of both countries. Not only have you publicly criticized the Turkish Ambassador and told the Egyptian president to, quote, 'Go to Hell,' but you've accused both men of anti-Semitism. It is you that has stirred the pot. It is you that has created animosity from leaders who were once willing to stand with us against our enemies."

"You're suggesting they would follow a madman simply because I've hurt their feelings? That's absurd," responded Minister Litzman.

"You may personally feel as such, Moshe," imparted the wise President Shalom, "but we in Israel have learned throughout history that we have no true friends. We may have made some political allies in the United Nations, but there are no countries that are totally *loyal* to us—not even the United States. Your big mouth and lack of wisdom may have shaken the balance of power in the Middle East. You may have provided King Adnan the 'in' that he needed. You may have thrown our country in grave danger. Akmal-Adnan is determined to become very powerful very quickly, and if he has nuclear weapons, we may soon have another war on our hands."

An uncomfortable fear continued to circulate the room as Prime Minister Edelstein added, "It may not only be a nuclear armament that we need fear, Elias. We also must worry about the Staff of Moses that has appeared on Mount Nebo. If he manages to take possession of the staff, who knows what power he might wield."

●●●●● ● ●●●●●

SEVEN

· · · · · · · ● ● ● ● ● ● ● ● ● ● ● · · · ·

Hannah peeled off her backpack and removed her cellphone. When she made a move to turn it on, Cole yanked it from her hand. "A phone call would be a bad idea."

"Give me that back!" exclaimed Hannah. "I need to call my dad. How do I know if everyone's all right if I can't call them?"

Ignoring his warning, she reached for the phone. Cole grabbed her wrist and held it tightly. "When we teleported here, I also moved us five days back in time. I figured GPS tracking wouldn't work on you because...well...if someone is searching for you, they'll look for a signal five days from now." Cole smiled at his ingenuity. "But it also means that if you make a freaked-out phone call to your dad, he'll find you safe and sound in your own home five days before you disappeared. It won't do you any good, and you won't learn anything about what happened to your family because they're not there yet."

"Seriously? That's freaky. So there're two of me now?"

"Well, I'm not sure. I'm pretty sure there's only one of me because I'm the jumper, but I really don't know. I never thought to ask that question. It's kind of weird to think that if we went back, we might find ourselves if we happened to be in the same place at the same time."

"You've really got this time-travel thing down, I see."

"I did learn that time is comparable to a squished spring, and I'm kind of like a slinky."

Hannah raised her eyebrows. "My kidnapper's a slinky, and I'm some second Moses or something."

Cole shrugged his shoulders. He sat, regarding Hannah, keeping his thoughts to himself.

"What are you thinking?" she asked him.

"I can't help but wonder about the outfit you have on. Camo-green and royal-blue are an odd combination. Either you're color-blind, a geek, or your fashion sense for a sixteen-year-old is entirely out of whack."

"So you pull off a kidnapping, leave my parents to a Middle-Eastern army, tell me you're a time-traveling slinky, and now you're a fashion guru?" Her voice rose in frustration. "And I'm *eighteen*. And my luggage was lost and the stewardess on the plane spilled coke on my shirt." Her eyes started tearing up again. "While you've been analyzing my ability to color coordinate, *I* was thinking that we need to go warn my family to not go to Jordan. We can do *that*, right? *I'll* believe me, won't I?"

"We could try, but from what little I know, they'd probably all end up there anyway. I don't think I can do much to change what's already happened. But I believe we can change the future, and somehow *you* must be the one to do it...I have no idea how," he said incredulously. "You're obviously gonna need a lot of help from me."

"From you? The guy who doesn't seem to know what's going on and who happens to have a beat-up face? What happened?"

Cole touched the slightly swollen, tender bruise and considered the scabs over his eye and on his cheek. "Happened in a fight." Sadness filled his eyes as he remembered the bouncers from the Florida parking lot.

"My protector got beat up?"

"Not exactly."

"You were only sort of beat up? I can't wait for you to start teaching me things," she stated sarcastically.

"You understand less than I do. I know you don't know me, but for whatever reason, I was told to bring you here. I found a place for you to stay temporarily, and I put some provisions there. I'll take you to it and get you settled in, and then I have some things to do."

"You're gonna leave me here by myself? Seriously? How about I put in an order for a new protector?"

Cole ignored her. "What do you have in your backpack?"

Hannah opened it. There was a small pillow she used on the plane. There were some snacks, sunglasses, a hooded sweatshirt, headphones and a charger for her iPhone, her coke-stained T-shirt from the plane, a paperback book, some gum, and her essentials kit from the airport which contained a toothbrush, toothpaste, soap, deodorant, shampoo, conditioner, a wide-toothed comb, and a small tube of hand lotion.

"Well, what else could you possibly need?" Cole joked. "I found a cave a short hike from here that overlooks a waterfall. You'll stay there until we figure out what to do next."

"So while you're time-traveling and teleporting all over the world, I'm to sit in a cave and wait?"

"You can wash that dirty shirt," he grinned. "Listen...I still don't know who or what I'm protecting you from, and I don't know what to prepare you for. And I can't be here and out helping your family at the same time. I need to figure out what to do next." He hesitated, and then he said, "I knew you weren't sixteen...and the coke-stained shirt? It matches your shorts okay." He smiled again.

●●●●● ● ●●●●●

MONDAY, JUNE 18
Two Days After the Discovery

The Carpenter family was taken to the Jordanian SOCOM Center in Amman, Jordan, a newly constructed facility housing the command center for the Jordanian king and the Jordanian armed forces. It was a fifty-seven-hundred square foot facility used for training the "Arabian Secret Weapon"—the number two ranked, most-well-trained Special Forces on earth after the United States Navy Seals.

King Adnan was ex-commander and a former major general of Jordan's Special Forces, which he reorganized and named the Special Operation Command. It was there, in interrogation room number one that Richard, Kristina, and Sarah Carpenter were being interviewed by General Jibril-Marid.

After slapping Richard across the face, he said, "I ask you once again...*where* is your daughter?"

"And I tell you once again...I don't know. A man on a motorcycle kidnapped her before our very eyes."

"When did she get possession of the staff?"

"Just before she disappeared. What kind of question is that? We all tried pulling it out of the rock before running from the church to escape the storm. When I turned back, it was in her hand. I didn't see her pull it out, but clearly, she'd only had it a matter of seconds."

"You are lying. How did the staff come to be placed in the church, Mr. Carpenter?"

"How would I know that? Someone must have placed it there."

"Was it your daughter who sealed it in the rock?"

"That's a crazy question! Two days ago, we were in Missouri eating breakfast. We saw a news report about the staff and came to the Holy Land for our family vacation."

"I don't believe you, Mr. Carpenter. Who is the man on the motorcycle?"

"I keep telling you that I don't know. I don't even know where he came from. Find that man and you'll find my daughter."

"Tell us where she is! And how she's been hiding the staff!"

Richard closed his eyes and let his head fall back in frustration which angered the general who struck him in the face with his fist. "If you choose not to cooperate, we have ways of making you change your mind. We could start with that pretty daughter of yours."

"Sarah? She's just an innocent girl! She doesn't know any more than I do! You're asking questions that don't make sense. We looked back…" he declared in desperation. "Hannah had the staff, and then she disappeared aboard a motorcycle. Hannah didn't even want to be here. We brought her here for a vacation. We don't understand what happened any more than you do."

General Marid was angry. Richard seemed absolutely perplexed, but he had to be lying—he simply *had* to know more about what happened with his daughter. He had to know far more than he said. "Take them to cell C," he instructed a soldier, "and let them settle in. If they don't cooperate, they could be here a long time."

●●●●● ● ●●●●●

MONDAY, JUNE 18
Two Days After the Discovery

Lauren burst into her hotel room and called the Fox News producer immediately. "I have a huge story, Liz," she proclaimed.

Her producer, Elizabeth Desmond, diverted her attention from her computer in her New York office. "What was with the storm on the mountain?"

"Unexplainable, to say the least, but the storm is nothing in comparison to what else I have."

"You have my undivided attention."

"We managed to upload a digital feed of the arrival of King Adnan and his posse and email it to you before they stole our video camera. They cleared away the crowds and made quite a spectacle of trying to pull the staff from the rock. But they were unsuccessful. Then the thunderstorm arrived in a flash—pardon the pun. Once the king was safely in his car, his police force let people scramble back to their transportation, but one family of four just arrived. Other news crews packed their equipment and started leaving, but I stayed for the sake of the lone family who headed straight for the church."

"What happened, Lauren?"

"After a few of the loudest thunderclaps I've ever heard, the family ran out into the driving rainstorm...all but one, at least. When the fourth, a teenaged girl, emerged, she was carrying the sapphire staff!"

"I thought it was embedded in rock?"

"It was. I even tried pulling it out, as did everyone else who arrived in the last two days. It didn't budge, but the girl had it in her hand."

"So you got video and an interview, I assume."

"No. The king's whole entourage poured out of their vehicles, guns raised. Then out of thin air, a man on a motorcycle appeared. He grabbed the girl and vanished as he drove through a solid stone wall."

"You say you didn't get video? No one'll believe a story like that....I'm not sure *I* do."

"Did I say that? I got it all on my cell phone. Between the raindrops on my window and the driving rain, it's not the best quality, but I've watched it, and I have evidence that what I'm telling you is true."

"Send me the video. Our tech wizards'll sort it out."

"I've no doubt. But there's more. The father ran into the church to find his daughter. The rains slowed down to a drizzle almost immediately. By the time he came back out, his wife and younger daughter were in custody, and then the Jordanian Security Force arrested the man too."

"You're kidding! Do you know who the family is?"

"After security confiscated Sam's camera and searched our news van, they left with the family. The only car remaining in the tourist lot was a rental. I'll forward the information to you, and maybe you can figure out who rented it."

"Great job, Lauren! Be ready for a live report as soon as we work through the video and sort the information."

●●●●● ● ●●●●●

EIGHT

· · · · · · · · · · ● ● ● ● ● ● ● ● ● ● · · · ·

The cave was across a river—not an impassible one, but one which resulted from a scenic, flowing waterfall. Rocks protruded temptingly at various leaping points, but danger from the jutting, jagged rocks lurked below the swift current. Though the whole setting was gorgeous, Hannah observed the obstacle course that Cole pointed out and determined he was crazy. Once—if—they could navigate the jumping off points in the river, they had to scale a rock wall to reach the cave opening.

"You've crossed over to that cave before?" she asked skeptically.

"Well, no. I teleported."

"So grab 'hold of my hand and do your thing."

"I could do that, but then, if I wasn't here to do it again, how would you cross when I'm gone?"

"I could go with you, and then it wouldn't matter."

"Not to Jordan—no, you couldn't. Let's go across....It looks easy." He winked and took a leap, balancing precariously on a slanted rock in the river as water swirled all around it. The next jump was at least five feet onto a rock platform of about a square foot. Somehow he balanced without falling forward and into the rushing water. "Come on, Hannah. The water's only two or three feet deep. If you miss, you'll just get your feet wet."

"And my head concussed."

"Good word. But you'd more likely break an ankle or crush a hip." He made a third leap in which he had to balance one foot on one rock and one foot on another. Cole was slightly more than halfway across, but his next jump would have to be to a side-slanting rock, covered with moss. He made the jump, and somehow he balanced himself on the narrow peak, not even taking a chance that the moss might be slippery. A boulder was next—large and curved. If jumping on a giant, rounded slab was safe, so was his next jump, which he actually made with ease. He traversed the two steps across the boulder, and then he sat down to watch Hannah cross the river.

Hannah watched with amazement as Cole routed himself over an obstacle course she saw no chance of repeating; nevertheless, she held her staff securely and took her first leap as Cole sat on the smooth boulder. Her feet landed firmly on the slanted rock, but her body decided that momentum and gravity outweighed her strength and balance. She splashed in the frigid water all the way up to her thighs. It was obvious that Cole watched her, but he gave no reaction to her mishap. Hannah saw no way to get up on the next small rock from the rapidly-flowing river, so she waded back to the shore to try again.

Her second attempt was more disastrous. The shoes she wore were not athletic shoes—they were simple, soft-leather, casual tennis shoes—and since they were wet and gritty from the shore, they had very little traction. On her second jump, she slipped, fell on her hip, and splashed into the water nearly up to her chin.

"Ow! I think I crushed my hip," she said.

"At least your head isn't concussed," Cole teased.

"You think this is funny? You kidnap me to keep me *safe* and then you force me to hop across a river like you…well, congratulations on your amazing athletic prowess. I can't do it."

"I'm not laughing," he replied. "But I *am* wondering what exactly you're expected to do."

"Apparently to be some sort of entertainment for you."

"Listen, maybe if you try to do it without the giant jewel in your hand, it would be easier."

"It's the Staff of Moses, Mr. Sarcasm. And if I leave it, then it'll be over here when I get over there. I think I'm supposed to have it."

"Well, that assumes you're gonna get here sometime, but just in case, why don't you toss it to me, and then you can try again without it."

Hannah stood up in the river, shivering from the cold water. She hoisted the staff like a javelin and hurled it the twenty feet or so to Cole who casually reached up, caught it in his right hand, and tumbled off the back of the rock out of sight.

"Cole?" Hannah laughed. "Are you all right?" He didn't answer. "Cole?" Still there was no answer. Concerned, Hannah quickly climbed out of the river and jumped to the slanted rock, balancing herself precariously. The next jump of about five feet to the small platform taxed the maximum of her athletic ability, but she stood on the flat, square rock and prepared for her next jump. She landed with one foot on one rock and one on another. From there, she leapt to the slanted, moss-covered rock where Cole somehow balanced on its thin peak. Hannah jumped and teetered unsteadily before regaining complete balance. Next was the arched boulder from which Cole had just fallen. Hannah jumped, slipped slightly on the curved rock, and fell to her knees, but she hung on. She crawled across the rock and looked down.

Cole lay under the staff, unmoving. It seemed as if the brightness of the stone had dulled somewhat. As Hannah jumped to the rock ledge below, Cole's eyes fluttered open. He reached behind his head, feeling a lump that had already developed. "I think my head's concussed," he moaned with a slight smile.

Hannah giggled. "At least you didn't crush a hip."

"Get this thing off me, Hannah. It weighs a ton."

"It's not heavy. What're you talking about?"

Cole tried to lift it while lying on his back, but he could barely move it. "It's too heavy. Help me," he said. Hannah reached down with her left hand and lifted it off Cole as simply as could be. The staff seemed to radiate its brilliance once again. "What the heck? Who are you, Hercules?"

"It's not heavy," she answered as Cole moaned and sat up.

He wobbled a little as he stood. "Give it to me," he demanded.

She handed him the staff, but the heavy rod fell right through his hand and dropped onto the rock ledge below. He bent down, reaching with one hand, but he was unable to pick it up. With two hands and a powerful squat, using the strength of both legs, he lifted it, dangling below his waist with both arms extended. Hannah reached out and took it from him in her right hand. Cole wobbled dizzily again, and sat down, amazement in his eyes.

"Either I just turned into a big wuss or you really are handpicked for something. That stick—staff—belongs to you. Look at it. It even seems alive in your hand." Hannah simply stared wide-eyed at it. "How did you get here, by the way?" he asked.

"Same way you did. I jumped from rock to rock," she said proudly.

Cole regarded at her somewhat differently, a flicker of fascination in his eyes. "You know…if I have my Sunday School stories right, Moses used that staff to divide the Red Sea. Do you think you could divide the river?"

Hannah smiled, raised her eyebrows, and shrugged her shoulders. She walked around the large rock, followed by her woozy partner and reached the flowing river. She warily stretched the staff out and gently touched its tip into the water…and the river stopped flowing.

A wall of water began building upstream while the rest of the water flowed away downstream. And as the water disappeared, all of the riverbed's dampness vanished as well, leaving nothing but dry ground.

••••• ● •••••

WEDNESDAY, JUNE 13
Three Days Before the Discovery

Graham Washburn hid among the bushes—a wild-eyed man with an overgrown, scraggly, black beard; bushy eyebrows that were barely visible from the long hair hanging in his eyes; and shabby, weather-beaten clothes, the sleeves of which nearly covered his overgrown, dirty fingernails. He had been hunting for berries, roots, and even insects to eat when he came upon the stunning blue motorcycle on the path.

"Well, looky here," he cooed. "A motorcycle in the middle of the woods."

Take it, a voice in his head hissed.

Destroy it, another voice encouraged.

The keys weren't in the ignition, so a third fiendish voice of a demon named Abigor said, *Find the driver. He'll have clothes that you can steal and maybe some food…and fresh blood for you to spill.*

The third demon's voice seemed the most-reasonable to Graham Washburn. Destroying the motorcycle served no purpose and stealing it was completely useless to him, but getting food and clothing would be useful. And besides some various animals, it had been oh so long since he had felt the rush of a kill. So he made his way through the trees and brush when, finally, alongside the river, he ran across not one but two riders—a young man and a younger girl. The man hopped from rock to rock across the river before settling on a large, rounded boulder on the opposite side.

"Two of 'em," he whispered to himself as he took out his hunting knife.

Fresh blood, encouraged a demon inside his sick head.

The girl was young and had on shorts and a T-shirt.

"A pretty one," Graham hissed. "Easy prey." The man was a touch more of a concern. Graham decided he would have to take care of the man first, and then he'd have time alone with the girl. She had what appeared to be a blue, glass walking stick. As she tried to cross the river, she fell into the water. She was a determined one, however, and tried again, only to make a worse fall.

He kept to his hiding place while scrutinizing his prey. She cared about him; he could see that after she made it capably across the river when she thought her boyfriend was hurt.

Capture the man and she'll do anything to save his life, he heard in his head. When they left the river to come back for the motorcycle, he could make his move.

As his crazy mind began to formulate a plan, the couple reappeared from behind the boulder, and that is when he saw something that convinced him that his craziness was real indeed. The blue rod was more than a walking stick—it was magic. Graham hunched behind some overgrowth and felt his mouth gape as he watched the girl use it to divide the river in two.

It was a miracle! Graham was an escaped criminal—a genuine savage who had killed so many men and women that he'd lost count, but he had never seen a miracle before—not in his entire pathetic lifetime of misery, despair, violence, and addiction. The three demons who continuously harassed him *had*, however. The demons had witnessed numerous miracles in their timeless existences, and they knew with a demonic certainty that the young lady who wielded the "walking stick" was holding the Staff of Moses. It had been found once again. Immediately, one of the demons disappeared to report the news to Hoaxal.

●●●●● ● ●●●●●

NINE

· · · · · · · · · · ● ● 〇 ● ● · · · · · · · · ·

WEDNESDAY, JUNE 13
Three Days Before the Discovery

Both Hannah and Cole stepped gingerly onto the dry riverbed, stunned and unsure if their senses were working correctly. Cole rubbed his eyes to make sure he wasn't simply imagining things while Hannah stood with her mouth hanging open. No one spoke. The waterfall continued to release huge amounts of water, but it had all miraculously stopped short of where they were standing. A wall formed and water steadily rose on the banks. Cole massaged the back of his head, feeling the bump, and trying to decide if his injury caused a hallucination.

Finally, Hannah acknowledged, "It really *is* the Staff of Moses." The wall of water was more than waist high and rising.

Cole squatted and poked his finger gingerly into the water wall. Four fish had swum up to the water's edge and were trying to figure out what to do when Cole reached in and swiped them out, right onto the dry ground where they flopped around before dying. "Dinner," he said. He took a couple steps away and plucked out four more and then two others a couple more steps over. None of them were especially large, but ten would make a good meal.

"What kind of fish are they?"

"Filets, I think," he replied with a grin.

"Oh…I've never heard of those before, but I don't eat much fish."

Cole smiled and glanced at the cave entrance for a second and then disappeared. He vanished into thin air. A few seconds later, he reappeared with a cooler in his hands. Before he placed them in the container, he picked up the fish one-by-one and rinsed them in the water that had risen to about chest high.

After carrying the cooler to the river's edge and setting it down, Cole walked back out onto the dry ground, tilted his head in thought, and then removed his shoes, socks, shirt, and jeans before diving right into the wall of water and disappearing.

"Ooohh. That was cool," Hannah said to herself before Cole's head popped out of the water.

"I'll bet not too many people have ever done that before," he proclaimed. "Come on in, Hannah. You're already wet."

She giggled, temporarily forgetting the disturbing events she'd experienced in the last couple of hours. Hannah set the staff down, walked into the dry river, removed her shoes and socks, and dove through the water wall and into the lake that formed inside the river banks.

Her head popped out of the water, and she let out a genuine laugh. "That was totally crazy!" she admitted.

"You should've taken off your clothes first."

"Me? Are you kidding? You wish!"

"Whatever you want," he said as he swam over to the waterfall in his boxer shorts and disappeared behind the sheet of water.

Taking her clothes off made complete sense, however, because the water level had risen slightly above her head, and her wet clothes were heavy, so, as Cole had done previously, Hannah shed all but her underwear and threw the clothing over the water's edge onto the dry riverbed.

For several minutes, she swam around lazily in the "lake" that she'd created. When Cole re-emerged, he commented. "You're a good swimmer, I see."

"Yeah, right," she replied as she treaded water.

"Do you have any other talents that we can work with?"

"My sister seems to have gotten all the athletic ability in my family. I was on the swim team. Good stamina...no real speed...no real stroke I was good enough to win with, but it kept me in shape. Only other actual talent I have is I can twirl a baton and a flag and such—a color guard for the marching band." She rolled her eyes, somewhat embarrassed by her limitations.

"That could come in handy."

"How do you figure that? The enemy comes and I distract them with my twirling skills?"

"Sure. You mesmerize them and I kick their butts....Really, though, that staff is a lot like a flag you'd twirl in the color guard. Maybe you could use your skill to protect yourself, and that three-hundred-pound stick could be quite a weapon if you learn to use it right."

"It doesn't weigh three hundred pounds."

"Not to *you*, Miss 'Chosen One,' but to *me* it does."

"Mischosen is the truth. The staff should have come out in someone else's hands. Like you, for instance." Hannah treaded water in bewilderment. Her mind wandered, but suddenly, she noticed that the banks of the river were flooding. The water had risen to probably fifteen feet high. "I think we should get out."

Cole nodded in agreement. "Follow me." He swam to the water's edge where he treaded water for a second. He winked at Hannah before performing several upstrokes and sinking to the bottom of the river where he simply walked out onto dry ground. Hannah followed suit and stepped out beside Cole, who gave her an immediate once over.

Her big smile from her astonishing exit disappeared instantly as she covered up the best she could. Cole vanished and then reappeared with a couple of towels he'd stocked in the cave earlier. Hannah immediately held hers up to wrap it around her body while Cole stood in his boxers and dried his hair. "My gosh, Cole. Your muscles have muscles!" As he rubbed his hair dry, his arms and shoulders flexed. His wet, muscular legs, back, and abs were lean and hard. Hannah stared at her protector for so long and so obviously that she failed to continue covering up with her towel, and eventually, Cole noticed her gawking.

"You don't look so bad yourself."

Immediately, she covered up, her face blushing red as she gathered up her clothes. "I'm hungry. Let's eat." Picking up one end of the staff, she faced Cole with her eyebrows raised, letting him know without saying so that she was about to release the water.

Cole hurriedly grabbed his clothes, hustled over to grab the cooler, and stood beside Hannah as she freed the stifled current and a torrent of water surged like a tidal wave. As the water roared and splashed crazily down the river, Cole grabbed Hannah's arm and they teleported together into the cave.

•••••◉•••••

WEDNESDAY, JUNE 13
Three Days Before the Discovery

King Adnan stuffed papers into a file that he locked away in his office safe in the Bosman Palace. For five long years, he had been searching for that mysterious girl and the Staff of Moses. How much easier his plans would be if he had the power of the staff to wield against Israel and eventually other Middle-Eastern nations. Instead, he found himself considering another meeting with the Egyptian president and the Turkish prime minister. The treaty would have to be signed and the secret Jordanian nuclear arsenal would have to be exposed.

As the king gazed out his window in contemplation, he watched the sixty-by-thirty meter Jordanian national flag flap in the breeze from the third tallest free-standing flagpole in the world—126 meters high. Under the influence of the demon, Hoaxal, he faced one of the demon's minions who skittered into the office. Shaking, the visiting demon bowed fearfully to Hoaxal.

"What purpose do you have to invade my presence?" Hoaxal rumbled from King Adnan's body.

"The staff has been discovered," the minion announced with eyes glued to the floor. He waited in terror for permission to continue.

"Speak up, Abigor," ordered Hoaxal impatiently.

The demon gasped, surprised that an entity of the importance of Hoaxal would know his name. "There was a young girl at a river in the Smoky Mountains in Tennessee, my Lord. She was with a man, and she had a blue, gem-like staff that divided the river in two. I came here immediately with the news," Abigor squeaked out in terror.

"Are they being watched?"

"Yes, my Lord. Graham Washburn is there, inhabited by two of my companions."

"Come to me and show the king where they are," commanded Hoaxal.

Horrified, Abigor crept forward on his taloned claws and entered the body of the King. Akmal-Adnan breathed in deeply as he visualized the location of the girl he was impatiently seeking. Abigor backed out of the King's body, panicking that he had made contact with Hoaxal.

"Go back to Washburn and kill the man and girl if you are able. The king will send men to retrieve the staff." When Abigor hesitated, Hoaxal continued. "You are excused….Now!" he roared.

Abigor screeched a demonic shriek and fled back to Tennessee.

Adnan picked up a phone and called General Jibril-Marid. "I need you to send members of SOCOM to the Smoky Mountains of Tennessee—immediately. I have the exact location. The staff has been located again."

●●●●● ● ●●●●●

WEDNESDAY, JUNE 13
Three Days Before the Discovery

Cole had done a decent job of preparing the cave as a camping site. Two cots, two sleeping bags, two pillows, and a couple of additional blankets were stored. There was firewood stacked and some pots, pans, and dishes. Dry ice, various foods, and drinks were in a cooler. There were other articles in a large plastic container: two water canteens, a couple of knives, eating utensils, a hatchet, some rope, a rifle and pistol with ammunition, and a few items of clothing.

He cleaned the fish and started a crackling fire as a silent Hannah paced nervously back and forth. Her shadow paraded against the cold, rocky wall. Because the sun was setting, the flames created the majority of the light. Finally, to break the tension, he asked, "Where are you from?"

"Just outside St. Louis in a town called Belleville. How 'bout you?"

"Apparently, I'm from nowhere now. Grew up in Michigan and was living in Florida, but now that I'm teleporting and time-traveling, I've somehow lost six years of my life. I haven't existed is basically what I was told."

"That's impossible."

"Yeah, and so is pulling a several-hundred-pound jewel out of a rock and carrying it around like it doesn't weigh a thing…not to mention using it to divide a river and who knows what else you can do."

"It doesn't feel heavy to me," Hannah replied. She paused and then inquired, "So what are we now? Some misfit freaks that can't live normal lives? I mean, I wasn't too excited about a summer job and college, but it's looking pretty good to me right now."

"Come over here and sit down," he suggested, tapping his hand on a flat rock to his left. Cole put half the fish in a pan and balanced it on a couple of burning logs. Silently, he eyed it closely as the meal simmered. A slight breeze entered the cave and smoke blew into her face, so she obliged.

Finally Hannah asked a question that had been nagging her at the back of her mind. "Why do you have guns? Who *are* you exactly?"

"I was told you needed to be protected…and prepared… though I don't really know for what. Seems like it's a good idea to have weapons to protect you and—if it comes to it—maybe to train you."

"But why *you*?"

"I've been thinking about that. First of all, I can teleport you away from trouble. That's already come in handy once. Secondly, it seems like it'd be hard to find you now that I've moved you back in time. Thirdly, I don't have much of a life to go back to, so I'm perfect for the job. And fourthly…well…I have a unique set of skills."

"Which are…?"

"Let's just say I know how to take care of myself. The first batch is cooked, Hannah. You can eat it, and I'll fry up the rest for me."

Hannah took her plate and moved to sit on her cot, wrapping the blanket around her shoulders and hungrily eating her fish. She was deep in thought when she finally posed a question. "Cole?" He glanced up. "What about my parents and my little sister?"

"I've been thinking about that too. There's one serious limitation to my abilities, Hannah, and I'm not sure what to do about it yet. I can only teleport and travel to places I can picture. The only thing in Jordan I can picture is that mountain top, and I'm pretty sure they're not there anymore. I need to learn some things before I can help them. Heck, I don't even know if they're in trouble… but I suspect they are."

"How're you gonna find out what you need to know?"

"I assume I'll have to leave and go back to the future."

"Not without me, you won't. You aren't leaving me here by myself."

"I know, Hannah. Of course not."

But in the morning, when she woke up, he was gone.

Because Cole teleported to his motorcycle, Graham missed his opportunity to make a kill, but his departure left Hannah in the cave…alone.

●●●●● ● ●●●●●

TEN

· · · · · · · · · ● ● ● ● ● ● ● ● ● ● · · · ·

TUESDAY, JUNE 19
Three Days After the Discovery

The taxi arrived at 1211 Avenue of Americas in New York, battling crazy traffic the entire way. Lauren Molina stepped out and headed into the Fox News Studio. Lauren's phone had beeped the moment the plane rolled to a stop, notifying her of a phone message from her producer. Elizabeth's message was short and to the point. "Get to the studio immediately. We have a story to break."

Lauren had taken the first flight out of Jordan on Monday evening at 8:00 p.m. She flew to London Heathrow Airport where she had a short layover and then on to JFK International Airport in New York where she arrived at 6:45 a.m., eastern standard time, on Tuesday morning. When she entered the studio at approximately 7:30, there was excitement in the air.

Elizabeth practically ran up to Lauren, grabbed her, and dragged her into her executive office. Then she stuck her head back out the door and informed her administrative assistant, "I don't want any interruptions." She closed the door, motioned for Lauren to sit, and scurried behind her rich mahogany desk and into her leather executive chair. Lauren's investigative eye analyzed her boss. As she surveyed the woman across the desk, she could sense her producer's excitement, but also that signature focused intensity of hers.

Elizabeth considered Lauren closely. Her dark hair was still somewhat flat from the rains in Jordan, her business suit crumpled from the long trip home. Her eyes seemed to soften some as she said, "You've looked better."

"Thank you," Lauren replied with a smirk. "I've felt better too. Jet lag's awesome."

"Well, you'll get the juices pumping again in a minute. We've got ourselves an exclusive thanks to the video you recorded on your phone, and it's quite a story. Care to hear the details?"

"I'm all ears."

"Okay. First of all, the girl's name is Hannah Carpenter from Belleville, Missouri. We checked out the license plates of the rental car in the Mount Nebo parking lot. It was rented to Richard Carpenter. He's a reknowned historian. Lots of well-known research and journal articles...professor at Washington University in St. Louis, one of the nation's leading research universities. His wife, Kristina, is a best-selling author of historical fiction. They have two kids, Sarah, a fourteen-year-old, and Hannah, who is eighteen and graduated from high school this spring."

"Anything special about her?"

"No. Just a normal teenager," she responded, her excitement showing again. "Once we cleared away all the video interference, we have a priceless shot of her T-shirt. It says, 'I kick butt and take names later.'"

"Tough girl, huh? That'll be a nice angle to play up," Lauren replied. "What do you know about the Carpenter family since their arrest?"

"Not a word. They never checked into their hotel; their car's still in the parking lot where you found it. No money transactions, no appearances, no comments about their daughter's disappearance, and no one from the Jordanian government seems to know a thing about them."

"That'll change when the video goes live and people see that the king himself arrested the entire family."

"It'll make for quite a news broadcast, won't it?" Elizabeth smiled.

"The Staff of Moses pulled from a rock by an ordinary, teenaged girl. Well-known parents and cute, teen sister arrested and held secretly...a motorcycle rider appearing out of thin air and kidnapping the girl....What do you know about him?"

"Now the story starts to get *really* interesting. His name is Cole Flint...." Seriousness replaced the excitement in her voice, and her eyes regained their intensity.

"Flint had a temporary license plate on the back of the motorcycle that we were able to trace. Get this. He bought the bike six years ago. Paid cash for it in Lansing, Michigan, just a short time after a terrible fight in the small town of Goodrich. He was charged with manslaughter after a teen he punched fell and struck his head on a car bumper. He additionally put four others in the hospital. Then he fled town and was never heard from again until three days ago outside an MMA training gym in Florida where he defeated a cage-fighting hero. In the parking lot, he had another fight where two men were killed and three others were put out of commission. This time, he had a different motorcycle, but oddly, there's no record of a purchase, insurance, or registration. As a matter of fact, there are no records anywhere that we can find for the past six years. All our sources could dig up was that there was a journal in the motorcycle seat with some information about some time in prison and a deadbeat father. After fleeing the scene of the

Florida fight, the fact that he's a Michigan fugitive showed up in his records. Now he's wanted for arrest again. He's considered to be lethally dangerous. All witnesses to both fights point at Flint as the instigator, but why would he jump five guys? I think there's more to the story."

"But he kidnapped the Carpenter girl. Don't you think she's in some kind of danger?"

"Don't know…Six years, Lauren, and nothing to show for his life. What's he been doing the past six years?" Elizabeth extracted a photo from a file and stared at it a few seconds before saying, "Here's a picture."

"Oooh. A cutie. Look at those eyes! They remind me of yours, Liz, when you're ready to kill me. Same color and intensity. And those arms! Do you have any background info?"

"Solid B student. Some sports in school. He was abandoned in the hospital by his mother, and there was no known father," she mentioned with sympathy in her eyes. "He was put into foster care, but his foster mother, who apparently was a good person, died when he was thirteen years old. The foster agency was pretty tight-lipped, but they finally admitted his foster father became a deadbeat dad, and Cole practically raised himself throughout his teen years. He beat up the school bullies in the big fight. The rest of his classmates and teachers liked him—he stood up for the little guy. His original contention was that the bullies jumped *him*. An attorney whisked him away, and no one heard from him again until three days ago. I need you to find him, Lauren. I think he's the real story."

"More than a teenaged girl wielding the Staff of Moses whose parents were taken captive by the King of Jordan and who was kidnapped by a murderer?"

"Yes…and, Lauren, he was only *charged* with manslaughter the first time and hasn't been charged at all in the other fight."

"Seriously? That's more interesting to you than the girl?"

"Don't you think that maybe the most-amazing thing of all was the motorcycle and two people disappearing into thin air? When the video hits the news, no one will be talking about anything else."

"I'll get myself cleaned up, Liz," Lauren said with a smile. "We'll go on the air A.S.A.P."

●●●●● ● ●●●●●

THURSDAY, JUNE 14
Two Days Before the Discovery

Graham figured he must have missed something when the water blasted down the river because the two motorcyclists had disappeared, but shortly thereafter, he realized they somehow managed to get into the cave above the rocks and were camping for the night. Agitated, he made his way back to his shelter in the forest with a bag filled with roots and berries for a meal, and he spent the night restlessly dreaming of a cascading river of blood.

He rose in the morning and made his way back to the river where he recognized that the motorcycle was gone. Anger surged through his body when he reached the conclusion that he had missed his opportunity for a kill. He wanted blood. In fury, he drew out his hunting knife and sliced across his own arm. His bloodlust simmered as he watched the stream of red liquid drip from his arm and onto the brush alongside the path where the motorcycle had been.

Out of curiosity, he continued to the river anyway and soon realized he could see camping supplies still in the cave. *They'll be back,* snarled an evil voice in his head.

I see the girl. She's still there, said another.

We should kill the girl now and wait for the man to return, encouraged Abigor, the third of Graham's demons.

Since Graham had been hiding out in the Smoky Mountains, he'd only had a couple of opportunities to quench his human bloodlust, and seeing a pretty young girl was nearly more than he could handle. While licking his lips, he gripped his bloodied hunting knife and wiped it on his leg.

"I cain't climb that there wall, so I'll wait for 'er to come down," he communicated to the voices in his head. He'd been living in the mountains for a long time. Sitting and waiting patiently was no problem, so he settled into the brush to watch and wait.

Hannah awoke groggily. When she realized Cole was gone, however, she jumped from her cot and rushed to the cave opening to see if he was by the river, but there was no sign of him. Immediately, she was angry, but after about ten minutes of fuming, she started to feel uncomfortable and alone instead. What was there to do? The book inside her backpack held her attention for about half a chapter before her anxiety and uncertainty got the best of her. She lay back on her cot and listened to a few songs from her iPhone, letting her mind wander. Only a few days before, she dreaded the preparation for her graduation open house, but ironically, she wished she was back there now instead of being stranded in a cave. Then, she was an ordinary graduate with a bright future to prepare for, and now she was some sort of selected hero with the Staff of Moses, no family, and no protector to watch over her. A job and community college were sounding pretty good to her all of a sudden. The iPhone only had forty-three percent of its charge left, so Hannah shut it off and stowed it back in her backpack.

Graham watched her as she leaned out of the cave to see if it was possible for her to descend to the river. *There she is again,* squealed a demon in his head. *We can kill her when she climbs down.* Graham stood to stretch his cramping legs. "She's *fine* lookin'," he whispered to himself. "And she's *all* mine." He licked his lips and slashed the knife into his thigh, drawing a fresh stream of blood. He could feel his excitement rising as his heartbeat pounded in his ears. His bloodlust drove him crazy with anticipation.

Hannah took out rope from the plastic container Cole had included in their gear and searched for something to which she could tie it. There was nothing that would work, but after searching a couple of minutes, she had an idea. If the staff was as heavy as Cole said it was, she should be able to tie the rope to it and lower herself down. Though it wasn't actually necessary, she placed it behind a couple of jutting rocks to sturdy it some so it wouldn't slide or roll. She only weighed about a hundred and twenty pounds while Cole claimed the staff had to weigh at least three hundred. *Theoretically, it should work*, she thought. She unloaded items from her backpack and replaced them with some soap and a towel and her dirty T-shirt. After hooking it over her shoulders, she dropped the end of the rope out of the cave and tugged on it to see if the staff would hold her. It was sturdy, so she sat down at the cave mouth on her rear end, found a place on the rock wall to position her right foot, and then turned and began to lower herself down. It worked.

Graham concealed himself behind a tree. *She's all ours*, a voice howled in his head. *We'll kill her slowly so we can listen to her scream.* Graham's desire for the girl reached its peak, and he began to make his way back along the riverbank behind Hannah as she squatted on her toes, feeling the temperature of the water. After more than a year of hiding in the mountains, Graham had learned how to move quietly—it often was the difference between getting a meal to eat or not. At a bend in the river, he soundlessly climbed down the embankment out of view of Hannah who was hidden behind the huge, rounded boulder. Graham entered the water and started inaudibly wading upstream, the water slightly above his waist.

Hannah decided to wash her dirty shirt before cleaning herself up, so she dunked it into the water, and then rubbed soap on the coke stain. "Stupid flight attendant," she muttered to herself as she scrubbed the shirt aggressively between her fists. She didn't have a lot of soap to waste, so she was really going at it, oblivious to what was transpiring behind her. "Stupid airline. How do they only lose *my* luggage and no one else's?"

By then, Graham had lowered himself even farther into the water because he was no longer obscured by the rock. *Slice her leg deep, and she won't be able to run. Then we can have our fun with her*, urged Abigor in the murderer's head.

Hannah dunked the shirt back into the water as she balanced on her toes. She splashed water noisily as she scrubbed away at the shirt, rinsing the soap from it. Graham rose from the river behind his target with his knife poised, ready to strike.

"*Grrrrrrroar*!!"

A short scream escaped from Hannah as her heart jumped to her throat. She lost her balance when she jerked away from the noise and stumbled before falling into the water.

Invisible to human eyes, Uriel rode on the back of the brown bear he had teleported from Switzerland. The bear blasted into Graham, knocking him back into the massive arched boulder. With three demons possessing his body, the psychopath was strong enough to survive the crushing blow. His demonic eyes blazed in defiance of the grizzly as he raised his hunting knife in defense. The bear stood on his hind legs more than seven feet tall and bellowed a second deafening roar. Graham swung his knife at the bear whose huge paw slapped it right out of his hand. With a second swipe of his paw, he smashed Graham right across the face, nearly rending his head entirely from his neck.

The escaped killer died before he hit the water, and the three demons invisibly rose from the corpse's body only to find themselves in the presence of the sword-wielding Uriel.

"Uriel," Abigor squealed in mock fear. "There's no need for violence. He's dead. We'll leave of our own accord."

Each of the demons bowed in pretended deference to the angel, hoping to lull the angel into a false sense of security.

Uriel smiled. The grizzly sat in the river, staring curiously at Hannah, who sat in the water in shock, fearing for her life. He slowly shook his head at the demon trio and simply replied, "I don't think so."

At that, the demons sprang forward, their own swords brandished. Uriel slashed his sword to the left and then backhanded a slice to the right, easily slaying the two weakest demons. They puffed into smoke, leaving a faint smell of sulfur, and disappeared for eternity. The third demon, Abigor, was much more careful. He took a deliberate swing at his enemy which Uriel blocked easily. The demon lunged, but the sword was again parried effortlessly. Uriel fended off two more uninspired thrusts, wondering what was up the demon's sleeve.

Hoping that Uriel had sufficiently relaxed, Abigor began spinning in a circle so fast that Hannah could see an actual whirlwind spinning above the river. The bear whined and backed away from the swirling air. Uriel held his sword parallel to the ground, pointing it directly at the whirling dervish. With his sword slicing at a remarkable speed, Abigor began to make his move toward his enemy who stood absolutely still and at ease. His defensive posture seemed wholly inadequate...that is, until a bolt of lightning shot from the sky, through Uriel's sword, and into the demon-made tornado, incinerating Abigor into a puff of smoke.

An attempted murder, a raging six-hundred-pound grizzly, a mini-tornado, and a random lightning bolt strike all before breakfast—Hannah's world had gone mad. The wind stopped as suddenly as it had started, and the bear turned his attention back to the helpless girl while Uriel relocated and sat comfortably with his legs dangling invisibly from the cave entrance, watching to see what would happen next.

Hannah sat in the river with the water up to her chin, Abigor's death leaving a stronger smell of sulfur in the air. She hoped the bear might not see her, but it was no use. He calmly stared at her. "If I stand up, will you slap my head from my shoulders like you did that guy?" she asked. The bear's ears perked up upon hearing Hannah's voice. She slowly stood to her feet while the bear watched her closely. He cocked his head and a cute, whining noise escaped his throat. "Why, you're nothing but a big teddy bear, aren't you?"

Upon hearing the words "teddy bear," the grizzly straightened his head and made a small growl, almost purr-like. He dipped his nose in the water, raised his head suddenly, and splashed water on Hannah.

"Did you just splash me?" Hannah laughed. She put her hands in the water and splashed him back. For the next few minutes, she and the bear splashed and played in the water like old friends. Uriel smiled in appreciation, but he knew something that Hannah didn't. Back in the woods, unknown to the innocent girl, four SOCOM soldiers were making their way to the campsite, and so far Perisa hadn't located Flint.

•••••◉•••••

ELEVEN

· · · · · · · · · · ● ⬤ ● ● ● ● ● · · · ·

The Fox News Studio was in a frenzied state as Lauren had the last of her make-up applied and the camera was prepared. Her earpiece was secured in her ear as the lights were readied and the camera was set for the broadcast.

"Ready in five, four, three, two, one...you're live."

"Good morning. This is Lauren Molina with a special news alert." Video rolled as Lauren reported. "Yesterday, Jordan's King Akmal-Adnan and his political and military entourage arrived on Mount Nebo to view what is believed to be the Staff of Moses that was stuck in the mosaic rock just inside the entrance to the Basilica of Moses. As with everyone before him, he and his party attempted unsuccessfully to remove the staff from the rock. As a storm began to form, tourists, visitors, and most news reporters escaped to their vehicles and drove away. Most, but not all.

I stayed—as did the government entourage and one lone family that still happened to be inside the church."

There was a dramatic pause as the video changed from the king and the storm clouds to Hannah Carpenter with the staff in her hands.

"The young lady you are seeing is Hannah Carpenter, a teenager from a suburb of St. Louis, Missouri. Yes, Hannah is holding the Staff of Moses." The video zoomed-in to see Hannah's startled face as she exited the church. "What you see now," Lauren explained as the video zoomed back out, "is the security force for King Adnan, closing in on the young lady with guns raised as if she was some sort of criminal for holding Moses's sapphire staff." Another dramatic pause was sustained. Then, shockingly, out of nowhere appeared a blue motorcycle in the video with a male rider wearing a sleeveless, blue T-shirt. "The rider," continued Lauren, "is a young man by the name of Cole Flint, a fugitive of the law who is responsible for the deaths of three people in two separate incidents in Goodrich, Michigan, and Port St. Lucie, Florida." Amazingly, the video pictured Cole grabbing Hannah and lifting her onto the motorcycle before riding ahead and disappearing through a solid stone wall.

"I saw it with my own eyes," Lauren narrated as her face appeared once again on the news alert, "and I still can't comprehend what happened. Cole Flint kidnapped Hannah Carpenter and vanished apparently into thin air. The Staff of Moses was stolen before my very eyes."

She continued as the video reverted back to the mountain scene. "What you see now is Richard Carpenter, a well-known American historian; his wife, Kristina, a best-selling historical fiction writer; and his daughter, Sarah, a fourteen-year-old ninth grader. When the staff and motorcycle disappeared, the gunmen from the military attended to the family. They were arrested and taken away. For the past twenty-four hours, there has been no news of their whereabouts, and officials for the Jordanian government have expressed no knowledge of their location.

"The video you are watching came from my cellphone. Officials for the Jordanian government took all video evidence from my photographer, and they searched our news van for any other videos. What they were unaware of is that I had recorded the whole thing and the nation would soon be witnessing evidence of the arrest of an innocent family, an arrest for which Jordan is claiming no knowledge...."

For the rest of the morning, Fox News continued the special reports, bringing in experts on the Jordanian government, the Staff of Moses, and foreign relations. A colleague of Richard Carpenter's was interviewed as well as his wife's publisher. A law enforcement officer from Port St. Lucie was questioned about Cole Flint. Since Fox had the only video of Hannah, Cole, and the arrests, they were experiencing a complete news coup, and families all over the United States and around the world were tuning in... and Lauren Molina became well-known around the world—a world that included the nation of Jordan.

●●●●● ● ●●●●●

Six Years Before the Discovery

After Cole went to his house and scrounged up a spare set of keys, he headed for his high school during the last class period of the day and drove his car out of the parking lot. His plan was to change the events of the fight, thereby saving Russ Smallock's life and erasing the manslaughter charge pinned on him. He drove down Hegel Road away from Goodrich High School and turned onto M-15 before stopping at a gas station that doubled as a Subway restaurant. He entered to get something quick to eat, but when he exited the building only a few moments later, his car was gone.

He took a couple of quick steps toward the main road, hoping he could catch the car thief driving away. He glanced to the right before looking to his left precisely as Russ Smallock and his four buddies rolled into the tiny parking lot and unloaded from their car.

"Skippin' school, Flint?" squawked Smallock.

"Honestly, I haven't been in school in six years. But I came back from the future to save your life."

"Very funny, boy wonder, but the only one whose life needs savin' is yours."

Before he could talk some sense into Russ, he was surrounded and the first foolish goon made a lunge for Cole. Cole quickly sidestepped, grabbed his arm, and wrenched it behind the muscle-bound senior, hyperextending it and cracking it at the elbow. The punk let out a scream of pain while Cole twirled and kicked directly into the knee of the next thug, dislocating his kneecap and tearing ligaments.

As both boys lay on the ground in pain, Cole backed off with his fists raised. "I don't mind maiming Heckle and Jeckle as a warning, but the rest of you need to leave now before the local hospital runs out of beds in the emergency room."

"We've had enough of you interfering in our business, Flint. It's time you paid the consequences."

"Smallock, you're even stupider than I thought. I'm giving you a chance." As he spoke, Smallock slid some brass knuckles over his hand. Another foolish buddy gripped a baseball bat. The third remaining future victim wielded a knife. Out of the corner of his eye, Cole noticed a metal garbage can, and he quickly grabbed the lid.

The bully with the baseball bat swung it while Cole lifted the lid to block the blow.

Ponngg!

As his foe drew back the bat for a second swing, Cole punched him in the ribs, doubling him over, and then he kicked the kid so brutally in the jaw that he dropped like a rock on the pavement. The derelict with the knife charged, but Cole smashed his wrist with the garbage can lid, and the knife simply dropped from his grip. Cole pummeled him violently with four punches to the ribs, and when he doubled over, Cole smashed his face with his open palm, dropping him to the ground with a broken and bloodied nose.

"I'm giving you a chance, Smallock. You can leave, and you won't get hurt."

Smallock regarded his friends either unconscious or writhing on the ground before running to his car. As he raced away, another vehicle—Cole's missing car—sped into the parking lot and plowed into Smallock. Russ's body crumpled, his head shattering the windshield of the speeding vehicle which didn't stop moving until it crashed into a gas pump. Gas began spilling onto the pavement.

Cole watched in horror as Russ Smallock died again, this time by his own vehicle. He glanced into the interior of the car as a Middle-Eastern-looking man with a full gray beard and long gray hair mouthed what appeared to be the words "I'm sorry." Cole rushed to the car, but when he reached the door, the man was gone. He'd vanished. Knowing that Russ had died anyway and he would be blamed again, Cole followed suit and time traveled to his next stop. As he reunited with his motorcycle three years into the future, the gas pump exploded, engulfing the car and Russ Smallock in flames.

● ● ● ● ● 🌑 ● ● ● ● ●

Three Years Before the Discovery

Cole climbed the steps to the Genesee County Courthouse. Across the street was the county lock-up where he'd spent three full years of his life from the ages of eighteen to twenty-one. Still shaken from the knowledge that he was unable to change the past, he found the records office and strolled casually inside, wearing fake glasses and a backward Detroit Tigers baseball hat he'd stored under his bike seat. He stood silently at a counter, waiting.

"May I help you?" a lady finally asked.

Cole knew he'd left Hannah alone, and he shouldn't be wasting time. He composed himself so he could finish his list of activities. "Yes, ma'am. I've been trying to locate a family member of mine that I haven't seen in five or six years. I was wondering if he'd ever been incarcerated at the county jail."

"Could you tell me his name?"

"It's Cole Flint...from Goodrich, Michigan."

"One moment please." She left and went to a computer to enter the name. After a few minutes, she renewed their conversation. "We have no record of a Cole Flint."

"Okay. Could you try Dirk Pitt?"

"Another family member?" the lady asked skeptically.

"He'd be a 'friend' who told me he was in prison with Cole," he lied.

She left, clicked a few more keys and returned. "Nope. No one by that name either."

"Will you try one more? Myron Bolitar."

She rolled her eyes and tried again before sidling up to the counter one last time. "That would be oh for three. Should I try Lincoln Rhyme?"

"The book character? Are you serious? No, thank you. But you could try Alex Cross if you'd like." He winked at the lady and watched her blush from the gesture. "I guess I'll have to follow other leads," he said. With that, he walked away and headed back for his motorcycle which he had parked temporarily along Saginaw Street. When he got back to his bike, Perisa was there.

"You're not the easiest person to find, Cole. Are you having a productive day?"

"We have to stop meeting like this," Cole responded. "Are you a time traveler too?"

"I'm simply the one assigned to keep an eye on you. You, on the other hand, are supposed to be keeping an eye on Hannah. She's already had one attempt made on her life while you've been out and about, and another will happen soon."

"Really?" he questioned. "I figured I could leave and return right when I left."

"That would be a good strategy if time stood still or she somehow managed to stay uncaptured and alive while you were gone. What have you been doing?"

"Well...first of all, I watched the news. Some news lady—Lauren something—announced my name...and Hannah's. She says Hannah's family is in Jordanian custody, but no one is speaking about it."

"You'll have to get them out."

"Yeah, sure. But I decided to start dealing with my future before I got around to *your* work."

"What have you accomplished?" Perisa asked.

"I changed my name, for one. Actually, I've already changed it three times—twice when I was eighteen and again when I was twenty-one. It's a lot harder to do than I thought. I've been popping in and out of time with abandon. I was Dirk Pitt when Russ Smallock died because I changed my name legally three weeks before the incident. Then I changed it two more times before I went back and tried to avoid the fight completely. I thought it would work, except we all ended up fighting anyway, and Smallock still ended up dying. I guess I couldn't stop it. Today happens to be my release day from prison. I just checked and no Cole Flint ever went to prison, and neither did Pitt or Myron Bolitar, my next name. Apparently, you actually managed to change my past, lady, but I'm trying to change my future. I don't want to be a fugitive my whole life. Right now, I'm Spenser N. Hawk."

"That's nice, Spenser. Before long, you'll be named after every suspense novel action hero in the world.

"My mom liked those guys."

"I'm sure she did, and I admire her taste in literature, but as much fun as it appears you're having, there are some things you *need* to do."

"Who *are* you?"

"I'm a friend…someone who watches over you, and I've brought you some help."

He hadn't noticed anything in her hands before, but suddenly, she had photographs. "I brought you a few things," she expressed as she gave him the pictures. Cole started sorting through them. "That first one is Hannah's home in Missouri. The second one is the Jordanian Special Operations Command Center, often referred to as SOCOM. Hannah's family is being held prisoner inside. Now you can teleport there. SOCOM soldiers are famously well-trained, and four of them are closing in on Hannah in the woods right now. The third picture is of an Alpine valley in the Swiss Alps where you need to take Hannah. Rescue her and take her back four years in time. You'll be provided for during the short time you're there."

"Why there?"

"Because it's where she is destined to go. And take these apples with you," she said as she supplied him with two full, large plastic bags that materialized out of thin air.

"Seriously?" he replied as he strung them over the back of the motorcycle.

"Nice choice of rides, by the way," she complimented.

"Perfect for carrying apples."

"*This* photo is of a house in Montana that Hannah's family needs to take residence of…that is if you get them out of Jordan and you somehow manage to stop four special ops soldiers in the Smokys so you can get Hannah to Switzerland."

"Why don't I simply teleport in and teleport out, safe and sound?"

"The answer to that is simple…because the four highly-trained soldiers will shoot you dead if you pop in out of nowhere. You can't just escape them…you'll have to stop them. Plus," she paused, "from what I last knew, she doesn't have the staff—it's in the cave, and she's not." Somehow, once again, Perisa's hands were full. She furnished Cole with a bow and a quiver of arrows. "It would be best if you arrived silently and took them by surprise." She passed him another picture and smiled. "This is where you'll find one of them."

●●●●●◉●●●●●

TWELVE

Israeli President Shalom sat in his office, watching a videotape of Prime Minister Edelstein and his minister of defense, Ibrahim Swartz. Shalom had secretly recorded the meeting, as he had done many times in the past.

Edelstein stopped his own recording that he had shown to his minister of defense. Swartz spoke first. "The United States will never allow King Adnan to get away with the illegal arrest of three American citizens."

"Do you think I brought you here so we could discuss the King's arrests?" A legion of Hoaxal's minions rooted themselves throughout the meeting room, intending once again to influence the thinking of the Israeli prime minister.

"Well, it's going to bring more negative attention to the Middle East. Military action could take place if Adnan doesn't release his American prisoners. I assumed you had me here to discuss our role if the United States seeks our involvement."

"Ibrahim, I don't care about that family. That's the problem of the President of the United States."

"So...why *am* I here then?"

"Because I want you to find the Staff of Moses and take possession of it before Jordan's king gets it." The demonic emissaries of Hoaxal continued to note the conversation and whisper lies to Israel's prime minister.

"Run a wild goose chase around the world for a sapphire staff? That's what you're asking of me?"

"No, I'm telling you. That staff is a relic from our nation's past. Moses was our countryman, and his staff belongs to the nation of Israel. We have intelligence channels. Use them...and find Cole Flint. Find Hannah Carpenter. If King Adnan gains possession of the staff, he could become the most-powerful man in the Middle East."

"And if *you* possess it?"

"*I* become the most-powerful man in the Middle East." Demons snickered at the comment. The lies had been planted and were working their desired effect.

As the meeting trailed off to small talk and Swartz's uncomfortable exit, Elias Shalom sadly shook his head in concern. The most-influential man in Israel was directing the search of Moses's staff, knowing full well, he would be vying for it by way of a competition with the evil King of Jordan.

●●●●● ● ●●●●●

THURSDAY, JUNE 14
Two Days Before the Discovery

Jordan's highly acclaimed and respected SOCOM unit included four, sixteen-person platoons. On hand in the Smoky

Mountains of Tennessee was a four-person element of one of those platoons. An officer and three enlisted men made up the team that hunted for Hannah Carpenter. Each carried an M-14 sniper rifle and holstered the MK23, Mod O .45-caliber handgun with a suppressor and laser-aiming module.

The soldiers spread out and eased into their positions where they each could get a clean shot at Hannah. The officer took several pictures of the girl to send to General Marid. The pictures were somewhat unsettling. There she was splashing around in the water, giggling and playing with a huge grizzly bear. Next to their "play" area was the dead body of a man with most of his head ripped from his shoulders. Hannah was no more than an innocent-looking, teenaged girl. On top of that, there was no staff, so there was no way of knowing that if the team killed the girl, the staff was even present for the taking.

The soldiers wore camouflaged mountain-climbing gear. The single phone headsets they wore over their ears also consisted of a noise-canceling boom mic for oral communication. "Hold your places," whispered the commanding officer into his mic. "Until we see the staff, we stay put." After a pause, he added, "She's just a kid. There's no need to harm her if we can avoid it."

They watched in amazement as Hannah touched and then hugged the bear. "You saved my life...Teddy, you're my hero." As Hannah spoke, she noticed a fish swimming by which gave her an idea. "Stay here a minute, Teddy." She grabbed the rope and quickly climbed into the cave to retrieve her staff. From the mouth of the cave, she tossed the staff into the water, and once again, the river divided. Each of the SOCOM soldiers observed in amazement. Incredulous, the officer managed to discretely shoot a couple more pictures and send them to the general in Jordan. Since they knew where the staff was and the girl was safely up in the cave, all they needed to do was get to the river and take possession of the sapphire rod lying partially in the water.

"Move in," the officer ordered.

The waterfall flowed faster than the day before because of nighttime rain farther up the mountain, so the water level in the pool rose another four or five feet quite quickly. Much to the chagrin of the soldiers, Hannah took a running start at the cave entrance and dove into the water. After swimming to the water's edge, she stepped out next to Teddy who seemed curious about the water wall that had formed. Hannah grabbed the staff and walked across the riverbed until she saw a couple of fish that she scooped out onto the ground. Teddy pounced on them, devouring them ravenously.

While Hannah fished for the bear, the SOCOM team made their way undetected to the river taking four different paths. The officer slid down the river bank and entered the dried out stream bed from the south. One soldier headed all the way to the northernmost part of the river next to the waterfall. The other two soldiers set up about thirty yards apart, hidden at the river's edge with their M-14's trained on the girl. Unknown to Hannah, they were moving in from both directions and had guns aimed to kill if necessary.

After Cole nodded his goodbye to Perisa, he plucked an arrow from the quiver and memorized the picture he'd been given. He started his motorcycle and commenced driving down the street at about ten miles per hour before shifting to neutral and turning off the engine. The bike began to slow while Cole silently rolled down the street. He visualized the picture and jumped to the Smoky Mountains—three years into the future. The camouflaged soldier farthest south on the riverbank, stood with his gun trained on Hannah when suddenly, a tremendous weight hit him in the back and knocked him to the ground. The motorcycle tipped over with barely any noise and fell into the green brush and soft dirt. Because of the noise from the waterfall, the officer on the riverbed didn't hear a thing, but the shooter thirty yards to the north peeked to identify the faint, unusual sound. Cole and the soldier, however, were on the ground behind a tree, and there was nothing to see.

Cole quickly rolled over on the forgiving ground. The SOCOM enlisted man anxiously reached for his knife, but realized his fate as soon as he saw the intensity in his attacker's eyes. Lightning quick but as soundless as a stalking panther, he stabbed the arrow into the soldier's throat. He died within seconds. Cole hastily donned the dead man's communication headset as well as his camouflage jacket. He then rose to his knees next to the tree and began to search for the other three soldiers. Through the headset he heard, "Is everyone in position?"

The remaining two soldiers responded in the affirmative, and Cole copied their short response, managing to not give himself away. Finally, he saw the officer working his way cautiously toward Hannah—out of her view around the bend in the river. Next, he saw a soldier ease into the water that had risen to nearly overflowing while Hannah apparently fished for a huge, brown bear. It appeared that there was a dead body, lying in the river bed in front of the water wall. *What has the world come to?* he thought. Nervously, he continued to scan the river banks. Anxious that he might run out of time, he spotted the fourth soldier hidden behind a tree but aiming his rifle directly at Hannah.

Cole removed another arrow from his quiver and steadily aimed a shot at the focused, still sniper who awaited his commander's orders. He took in a deep breath, letting it out ever so slowly. His passionate eyes keenly concentrated on his target as he gradually released his steady fingers from the bowstring. The arrow flew from the bow and sliced directly into the man's exposed chest and heart.

His gun discharged as he fell dead—two down, two to go— but the gun shot warned the officer and Hannah, who turned in alarm. The officer ducked behind a rock and scanned the riverbank for information, but there was none. "Whose weapon discharged?" he demanded into his mic. Two of his comrades lay dead and didn't reply. The third was underwater and his headset was left behind on the shore before he slid into the pooling river. The brown bear finished up the last fish that lay on the ground and searched for more as Hannah scanned the riverbanks for a shooter. Cole grabbed the .45-caliber handgun from the dead man beside him and flipped on the laser-aiming module. He focused the dot on the heart of the officer in the river just as the third soldier reached out of the water and grabbed Hannah by the leg.

What happened next was as much shocking as gratifying. When the soldier grabbed Hannah's leg, she gave a short scream but followed it instinctively with a twirl of the staff, hitting him in the elbow with the three-hundred pound force that she wielded. The soldier's arm collapsed as the bone snapped and buckled inwardly. His cry of pain was choked off as the giant bear chomped his powerful jaws on the man's throat, killing him almost instantly.

"Hold it right there!" the officer yelled. "I don't want to shoot you, but I will if I have to! Give me the staff, and I'll be on my way."

"I don't think so, soldier boy," Cole sneered from the top of the river bank. "Put your gun down before I turn that little red dot on your chest into a full-blown hole."

"It won't be that easy," he retorted. "Are you willing to take a chance on that girlfriend of yours? I have her in my sights."

Hannah backed away from the river with the staff in her hands. Teddy gnawed away at the soldier's neck. "That's enough, Teddy. Come!" she ordered. "Put the gun down, Cole."

"Not a chance, Hannah. He's a dead man if he moves a muscle."

"I'll throw him the staff, Cole. He can have it. It's not worth dying for. Put the gun down and let me do what *I* choose to do."

"You heard the girl. All I want is the staff, and I'll leave. No one has to die."

The water began pouring over the banks of the river when Cole put his gun down and raised his hands over his head. He was about to teleport to the soldier and finish him off when Hannah touched the tip of the staff into the river and the wall of water released with a roar. The officer saw the water splashing down as it hurled between the banks. He dove behind a rock, but it was to no avail; the water rampaged around his protection and propelled him, the other dead soldier, and crazy Graham Washburn down the river, careening into rock after rock with staggering force. There was no chance he survived the powerful surge of water, and within seconds, all three bodies were gone for good.

Cole teleported to the other side of the river and aimed his handgun between the eyes of the grizzly. "No!" Hannah yelled. Cole hesitated while the bear eyed him carefully and then lay down on the rock before rolling over and exposing his underside. He looked at Cole carefully, waiting. Hannah began laughing. "I think he wants you to rub his belly!"

●●●●● ◉ ●●●●●

THIRTEEN

· · · · · · · · · ● ● ● ⬤ ● ● ● ● ● · ● · · ·

THURSDAY, JUNE 14
Two Days Before the Discovery

General Jibril-Marid entered Bab As-Salaam, the home of King
Adnan, a dwelling only a short distance northwest of Amman.
A member of the domestic staff ushered the general to the king
inside his study. Marid quietly opened the door but didn't step
into the room when he noticed the king bowed in his prayers
before five black candles.

"Tonight I petition the prince of darkness, the great serpent of
the bottomless pit who is the purveyor of deceit and chaos and the
Lord of the Earth. Hear me, oh potent God of Perdition. Come
forth from the black Abyss, from the ends of the earth, and from the
nighttime sky! Ruler over the great Hoaxal, Azazel, Belial, Samael,
and Set! My Lord and Master, come forth from Hades and greet me
as your servant and friend. Join me as I serve and honor and give

reverence to you. Guide and strengthen me, and if need be, deliver me from my enemies. Prepare me and use me to accomplish thy plans. I implore you, my Lord, to deliver the Staff of Moses to me that I may use it to achieve thy purposes. Amen."

Hoaxal smiled in appreciation of hearing the prayers to himself, his brothers, and his father. The staff would be the King's, and therefore it would be his, and he would be honored by the most-powerful and influential of demons. It was only a matter of time.

King Adnan rose from his knees and blew out the burning candles before recognizing his guest. "Come in, General. I assume that a visit to my home suggests you have important news for me."

"Yes, my King. My SOCOM soldiers located the girl and the staff and have sent photographs." He handed them to Adnan.

Deliberately, he flipped through the pictures as he regarded Hannah and her relic. Finally, he drew in a deep breath, exhaling it gradually. "I have persisted in searching for this girl and the staff, yet I do not understand why she looks exactly the same after all this time."

"I cannot explain, but we shall have the staff soon. My men reported she was alone."

"Not alone. There is that bear that she cares so much about. How is it that the bear finds her but I cannot? How is it that she has eluded me for so long? Where has she been?"

"I don't know. But when the staff is delivered, you shall have its power. She used it to divide the river."

"She disgusts me. She uses it as a toy to play with her precious pet. She has no idea of the power the staff possesses. In my hands, I'll become the most-feared leader in the world. I will have dominion over the entire Middle East and its resources and will soon hold the rest of the world hostage to my demands. Make sure that the soldiers bring the staff to me directly as soon as they return to Jordan," he commanded.

"Yes, sir, I will see to it personally. My men will not fail." As General Marid exited the room, however, he was worried. It had been nearly two hours since the last communication and pictures had arrived, and he had yet to hear a word from his team of soldiers. Something almost certainly had gone wrong.

● ● ● ● ● ⬤ ● ● ● ● ●

THURSDAY, JUNE 14
Two Days Before the Discovery

Cole cautiously rubbed the bear's belly, ready to teleport himself and Hannah away at the first hint of danger, but there was none. When he stopped momentarily, Teddy swung a paw playfully at Cole's arm with the obvious intention of persuading him to rub more.

"Did you put some kind of spell on him with the staff? This is a ferocious grizzly bear, isn't it?"

"No, I didn't. I think he knows us."

"How could that be? It's my first encounter with a bear. I swear it. You?"

"Me too, but he knows me. I'm pretty good with animals, and this one is acting like a pet."

"Well, I can't just stand here rubbing his belly. You…*we*… could still be in danger. We have to get away from this place."

"Sure thing, Cole. Just let me get my essentials kit, and we're out of here," she announced sarcastically, her irritation beginning to emerge. "Where were you? Do you realize Teddy here saved my life while you were out jumping around the universe? I thought you were supposed to be protecting me!" Her irritation had changed to anger. "*And,*" she huffed, "between me and Teddy, we stopped *both* of the soldiers from hurting me and getting the staff. You're not doing your job!"

"There were *four* soldiers, and here you are, safe and sound," he said, ignoring her tone. "But maybe you have someone else watching over you too."

"Take me home, Cole. Or take me to Jordan to get my parents. One day roughing it with you is all I can take."

Teddy rolled over and moaned and then waded into the water in search of more fish. Cole ignored Hannah and watched the bear, shaking his head in amazement. He disappeared and reappeared in an instant, but when he popped back into sight, he was sitting on his motorcycle and had one of the bags of apples in his hands. "Figure out what you want to take. I've been instructed to move you," he stated as he started feeding the bear apples. "And you might want to put on some dry clothes."

"You gonna help me up?" When Cole didn't answer, she added, "To the cave?"

"I'm busy feeding your pet. Besides, you don't need my help."

"Jerk!" But Cole was right. She tossed her staff to the ground and climbed the rock wall. She'd proven once again that she was more capable than she'd ever thought. She changed her clothes, pocketed her phone, threw several things to the ground, hesitated a minute, and then managed to find her way back down the mountain wall by the time Teddy had eaten the entire bag of apples.

While Hannah petted and scratched her grizzly, Cole teleported with a smirk into the cave and back. When he returned, he had his own bag packed and stuffed inside the large plastic tub which included the weapons and other gear he considered to be necessary.

Hannah was still irritated. "We've already concluded that you're not doing too well protecting me, and I don't recall a lot of preparation since we've been here, Cole. What makes me need you less than before?"

"You haven't figured that out on your own?"

"Why don't you enlighten me since I'm too stupid to figure it out myself?"

"Okay…and then will you stop yapping and complaining?" She rolled her eyes which Cole took as a yes. "First of all, that staff in your hands is a weapon. Only you are strong enough to use it, and when you needed to, you used your twirling skills and put down one of your attackers. Second, you're coordinated enough and athletic enough to cross the river without falling in and to scale a mountain wall both up and down. Third, you have some sort of power over ferocious, wild animals. Fourth, someone besides me, somewhere, is also watching over you. Fifth, you were smart enough and brave enough to take down one of the world's most-elite soldiers with his gun trained on you. Finally, if you hadn't noticed, you have control over a staff that can perform miracles. Only you. No one else can even lift it. Personally, I think you learned quite a bit about yourself for one day. At least, I for one have seen enough miracles to believe that there actually *is* something special about you. So grab your gear, say goodbye to your teddy bear, and hop on the back of the motorcycle. We're heading for Switzerland."

"I don't want to leave him," she pouted.

"I wasn't told to bring him, but maybe we can find him again someday," Cole said with a hint of compassion. "It really *is* pretty cool to have a pet grizzly bear."

Hannah scratched behind his ears and gave a gentle hug. "Bye, Teddy. I have a feeling we'll see each other again. Thank you for saving my life."

Teddy gave a heartbreaking howl as Hannah picked up the staff and climbed onto the back of the motorcycle. While still standing, Cole glanced at his picture, picked up the storage tub with a single arm, and reached to touch his bike. He and Hannah disappeared from the Smoky Mountains and reappeared in an Alpine valley four years earlier.

●●●●● ● ●●●●●

FOURTEEN

· · · · · · · · · ● ● ● ● ● ● ● ● ● ● ● · · · ·

Followed by an armed security guard, General Marid stormed into the secured holding cell where the Carpenter family was being held. The cell was furnished with three cots, a table and chairs for eating, and a television which was set to broadcast Jordanian news and weather. The walls were a drab gray, and the cement floor was simply adorned with two throw rugs. There was a toilet and sink in the corner, made private by a curtain. It wasn't a prison cell, but it wasn't comfortable living conditions either—certainly not the preferred lodging for their "vacation."

When Marid unlocked the door and made his way into the room, it had been five days since his soldiers had failed to take possession of the staff in Tennessee. It had been three days since the staff was first discovered on Mount Nebo, and it had been twenty-four hours since Hannah Carpenter, the nuisance who was making his life miserable, had reappeared and taken the staff away from his king.

"Take the girl," he announced immediately.

The armed man handcuffed Sarah and thrust his weapon into her back as Richard and Kristina sprang to their feet with voiced protests. Marid had no intention of hurting the girl, but he needed information. He struck Richard in the stomach, doubling him over. Sarah was escorted, crying, out of the room, and the general spun back to her father.

"I've given you time to reconsider your lies. It's time you told the truth. Where is your daughter right now?"

"I don't know."

"Who is Cole Flint?"

"I've never heard of him."

"He's the man who disappeared with your daughter. He's a wanted American criminal…for killing at least three men. Why is your daughter with him?"

"Because he kidnapped her."

"You're taxing my patience, Mr. Carpenter. What was your daughter doing in the Smoky Mountains of Tennessee five days ago?"

"You have her confused with someone else. Five days ago, we were getting the house and yard ready for her graduation open house in Belleville, Missouri."

"You're lying, and you're putting your precious Sarah in danger. What was Hannah doing in Switzerland four years ago?"

"She's never been to Switzerland."

"She was there with her pet bear…just like in the Smoky Mountains."

"Pet bear?" Richard asked incredulously. "What in the world are you talking about?"

"She was also spotted in Montana, nearly five years ago. With the staff...and a bear—the same as the other times we've found her. For the good of your daughters, tell us how she got possession of the Staff of Moses and where she hides herself."

"She wasn't in Tennessee. She's never been to Switzerland or Montana, and her pet is a tiny shih tzu dog named Teddy. I don't know where she is right now, and I've never heard of that murderer you mentioned. She pulled the staff out of the mosaic at the church at the top of Mount Nebo yesterday. You don't have your facts right. What you're saying isn't true. Please don't hurt Sarah. I'd tell you if I knew anything, but nothing you've said makes a bit of sense."

"You're lying."

"It can't be legal for you to keep us here. We've done nothing wrong...and neither has Hannah."

"I'll let you sit here while we spend time with your daughter. Maybe you'll find your memory in the meantime."

"You can't do that!" Both Richard and Kristina reacted at the same time. Richard shot out of his seat and rushed toward the general. As he reached for Marid, the general slid his right arm inside the grasp of the angry father and tugged Richard into a clench, putting his left hand behind Richard's head. Marid slid his fingers up to the notch in the man's throat precisely above his collarbone, pressing in and down while holding his head steady with his left hand. Richard dropped to the ground like a stone, miserably choking and gagging.

"We'll do whatever we have to in order to locate your daughter and gain possession of the staff, Mr. Carpenter. It's King Adnan's destiny to wield the power that the staff holds. Until you tell us what you know and help us find your daughter, your entire family is in danger." With that, the general whirled toward the door and exited the room. The lock clicked loudly, leaving a frightened Kristina to attend to her husband on the floor of their holding cell.

●●●●● ◉ ●●●●●

Four Years Before the Discovery

Cole and Hannah appeared near the door of a vacated cabin in the Lauterbrunnen Valley in the Bernese Alps in Switzerland. They both gawked in wonder. The River Weisse Lutschine weaved its way through the landscaping. Leafy, deciduous trees populated the landscape while coniferous trees dominated the higher-elevated areas, scattering around the limestone precipices. Where they stood, primroses, gentians, daisies, and buttercups added colored splendor. Pure, clean water from melted snow high in the mountains fell from the nearby Staubbach Falls which were less than a kilometer from Bern, the capital city of Switzerland. The U-shaped valley displayed scenic beauty, which included numerous additional waterfalls and several extremely steep mountains rising directly on either side of the basin.

"Wow, this is Switzerland?" commented Hannah. "It's like we're travelers in *The Lord of the Rings*."

"It could be Rivendell," Cole agreed.

"Are we staying in that cabin? Why were you told to take me here? How long are we staying?"

"There you go, asking a million questions again….I was told we'd be provided for, so I imagine this place is ours for the time being. I don't know the answers to the rest of your questions."

Cole surveyed the area and then grabbed the bag of apples and his tub of supplies and carried them directly to the cabin door. Hannah, who had dismounted the bike, followed closely behind. When they reached the entrance, Cole took a gun from the tub and peeked through the front window before knocking on the door. He tried the door handle when there was no response. The door swung open, so the duo stepped in. "Is there anyone here?" Cole called out. "Hello? Is anyone home?"

With gun in hand, he cautiously explored the entire cabin, Hannah nervously at his heels. There was no sign of any occupants—no clothes, wet towels, dirty dishes, garbage, or anything else to indicate that the dwelling was inhabited—but it was stocked with food, toiletries, and other necessities. Hannah set the staff on the floor next to a living room chair and sat down, turning to Cole for direction. "What do we do now?"

"Pick our bedrooms? I don't know, Hannah. I think this is where you'll be safe while I go help your family escape."

"I should come too. If I'm so special, maybe you'll need me somehow."

"That could be, but unless I'm told to bring you, you'll have to stay here. This is where I was told to bring you."

"Who's telling you all this stuff?"

"I don't know. Another time traveler maybe. Or a guardian angel. Or something else I haven't thought of. But regardless, unless I hear otherwise, I assume this is where you'll be safe while I help your family."

After a long hesitation, Hannah questioned, "There were *four*...at the river?"

"Yeah, two on the banks with guns aimed at you."

"You killed them?"

"Yes."

"Have you killed other people?"

"In self-defense...just like you did."

"I know I needed to do it, but I still feel terrible. Is that how *you* feel?"

"Yes." Cole hesitated. "I'm sorry I wasn't there with you, but I went back in time to try to avoid a fight where I killed a moron named Russ Smallock in self-defense. He and four others jumped me. I was just defending myself, but I ended up going to prison for three years because all his friends claimed I started it. I was hoping he wouldn't have to die."

"Did it work?"

There was another long pause. "No."

"What happened?"

"The first time, they were at my car waiting for me. I figured if I never went to the parking lot after school to get the car, there'd be no fight…and if there was no fight, Russ wouldn't die. I took the car before the school day ended, and I parked it outside a Subway restaurant while I went inside, but when I came out, the car was gone. I stepped out into the parking lot, hoping I could see who stole it when Russ and his friends arrived. When they surrounded me, I considered jumping out of there, but who knows what problems it would've caused if they saw it, so I fought again. I dislocated an elbow, wrecked a knee, cracked a jaw, and broke a nose, but I never did anything to hurt Russ. And when it was only the two of us left, I let him go. He took off running… and he was hit by a car…*my* car."

"What?"

"Whoever stole my car killed Smallock with it."

"Did you see who it was?"

"Yeah, I saw him. He looked at me, and I'm positive I saw him mouth the words 'I'm sorry,' but when I ran to the car, he was gone. And once I realized that Russ had died again—and that it was my car that did it—I moved on too."

That now-familiar sadness crept back into Cole's eyes, and this time, it touched Hannah. She reached over and tenderly took his hand. "So there was still a death, and you'll still be blamed."

Cole hesitated as he appeared to study Hannah's hand. "That's the way I see it…except this second time, my name wasn't Cole Flint. I changed it before the fight. I'm hoping that was a good strategy because if it was, you and your family can try it too and maybe live out your life a little more anonymously than you currently are. Your whole family is all over the news. Everyone in the world knows you have the staff."

"Well, until we figure out what we're supposed to do, at least we have a safe place that no one else knows about."

Cole drew his hand from Hannah's grasp and gave a smile to let her know he appreciated the gesture. "I'm not sure we're as alone as you think we are."

"Why not?"

"Obviously you didn't notice the tracks outside."

• • • • • ● • • • • •

FIFTEEN

· · · · · · · · · ● ● ● ● ● ● ● ● ● · · · ·

Cassiel and Uriel hid themselves inconspicuously in a corner of a conference room in the Raghadan Palace in Amman, Jordan. Excessive demonic activity around the palace had drawn the angels furtively inside. Unidentifiable, wispy shadows glided across the carpeted room as demons settled into dark corners and dim ceiling recesses. An ominous, oppressive feeling infested the room as the six invited members of the council of ministers seated themselves around a table in the unusually humid meeting room, awkwardly awaiting the arrival of Egyptian President Mahmoud Massri and Turkish Prime Minister Tali Demir. A foul fragrance of sulfur added to the unpleasant atmosphere.

When President Massri and Prime Minister Demir were escorted into the room, Jordanian King Adnan smiled, and the powerful demon, Hoaxal, gestured to four demons to settle in beside the men as they slid uneasily into chairs at the conference table.

The king welcomed his guests in Arabic. "*Marhaba*, and welcome to my palace, Mr. President and Mr. Prime Minister. I expect that you have been made at home by my staff?"

With uncomfortable expressions on the faces of the men, they nodded their heads in affirmation, noting the obvious nervousness of the Jordanian council members which included the minister of state for prime-ministerial affairs and the ministers of communications, defense, energy and mineral resources, foreign affairs, and environmental affairs.

"I trust you have familiarized yourselves with the documents that were faxed to your offices several days ago and are here to sign the treaties." Akmal-Adnan's eyes seemed inhuman as Hoaxal communicated through the body of the King. His tone was one of disdainful arrogance, causing the air of hostility in the room to increase even more. The demons sidled up closer to the Turkish and Egyptian political leaders, whispering encouragement to sign the documents.

The minister of foreign affairs mustered up the courage to speak up. "Sir, you've invited us here to witness and sign the documents. What is their purpose?"

The king stared daggers. An air of extreme malevolence palpitated, but Jordanian Prime Minister Ghazi-Hazim quickly interceded with the answer as fear gripped the man's heart. "We expect our honored guests to add their signatures to a Peace Information and Aid Treaty. We're agreeing not to attack each other and to share information and aid. We will also sign a Mutual Aggression and Defense Pact agreeing we'll all defend and attack together."

"Defend ourselves against whom? Attack whom? Is there something going on that we are unaware of?" Sweat dripped off the minister's forehead.

The slinking demons continued whispering lies of encouragement in the ears of the foreign guests.

"There is *always* instability in the Middle East, so we're aligning ourselves with our allies. Israel will be next, and if they do not agree to our terms voluntarily, we will force their subservience," Hazim answered.

The king interjected. "When I gain possession of the Staff of Moses, they will have no choice but to pledge their allegiance to me. Until then, you all shall see that I am serious about uniting the entire Middle East under my leadership. I shall rule the Middle East, and once I'm in control of the oil reserves, I shall begin enlarging my kingdom even further."

"I beg your pardon, Your Majesty," interrupted the minister of defense, though he had never before referred to the king with such reverence. His voice shook. "Have you located the staff? According to American Fox News, it is in the possession of a young lady or her kidnapper. Have you located them? They also claim that you're holding the girl's family hostage."

The King's entire countenance seemed to change as he exploded in anger. His face appeared to change shape before returning to normalcy. Eyes in the King's audience widened in shock as the king growled in a terrifying, demonic voice, "She has avoided my grasp for years! I will not stop until she is found…and that kidnapper and the reporter will soon be dead! The family too…if they continue to be uncooperative. I will not be hindered! I *will* possess the Staff of Moses for my own glory!"

President Massri of Egypt spoke next as the temperature seemed to rise in the room. "I intend to sign these documents." He lowered his eyes and held his shaking hands in his lap. "I pledge my loyalty to you, King Adnan," he said as the two devious demons continued to whisper in his ears.

"I, too, pledge my loyalty," Prime Minister Demir squawked. "It's time for an alliance in this part of the world. King Adnan, my people will defend you as needed, and we shall fight alongside your people as you see fit." Deceptive, demonic words continued to be whispered, manipulating the prime minister's emotions.

As the documents were being signed, Cassiel whispered to Uriel, and the two principalities vanished from the room having learned what they needed to know. Cassiel's next stop was Israel while Uriel headed four years in the past to the Swiss Alps in the Lauterbrunnen Valley.

●●●●● ● ●●●●●

Four Years Before the Discovery

Cole grabbed the second of the two bags of apples that Perisa had given him and handed it to Hannah.

"Why are you giving me these?"

"It's a hunch I have, but the whole world has gone topsy-turvy, so I wouldn't be surprised if you find a friend outside. Let's go see."

"Teddy?" She grabbed the apples and threw open the door, rushing outside, followed closely by Cole with the gun back in his hand. As Hannah glanced around for her pet bear, she noticed Cole's gun. "Why do you have that?"

"Remember how I'm supposed to protect you? Well, if there's a bear, it might not be Teddy, and if it's Teddy, he might not be quite as friendly this time. We're four years back in time."

"You shoot my bear and I won't be holding your hand again anytime soon," she retorted.

Cole smiled but continued to shadow Hannah. A grouping of trees stood about thirty yards behind the cabin, and one of several sets of tracks seemed to lead directly to it. A river flowed briskly beyond the trees, so it made sense that the bear would be close. Both of them stopped to listen, hesitating out of caution and curiosity. There was no noise at all.

"Maybe he's sleeping…or he's not here anymore," suggested Cole. "Or maybe we're being totally stupid and the bear tracks don't belong to our friendly bear."

Without warning, there came a half roar/half whine from behind. Hannah screamed and ran impulsively toward the trees, but Cole wheeled around and spotted a brown bear trotting right at him. He raised his gun out of instinct, but Hannah, who had stopped, shrieked, "*Nooo*!" When the bear got to within tackling range, he leapt, but Cole vanished into thin air. The bear landed in a cloud of dust as Cole reappeared next to Hannah. The determined grizzly stood right back up and loped his way toward the couple once again. He wasn't growling, nor did he appear angry, but he was large and seemingly determined to hurdle upon them both. Cole grabbed Hannah's hand and they both disappeared as the bear leapt a second time, coming up empty again.

"Teddy…stop!" demanded Hannah. The furry bear turned and whined. "How could something so gigantic and scary be so cute?" she wondered aloud. Teddy, seemingly determined to provide an answer to the rhetorical question, lay down and rolled onto his back with his front paws waving—pawing—at the air. "But cute he is." She ran up, dropping the apples before jumping on the grizzly and playfully wrestling the beast. Cole came alongside and gave the creature a few scratches and pats of his own. He was smaller, but it was definitely Teddy, apparently four years younger. Maybe he wasn't full-grown yet. It was like a reunion except it was four years *before* the trio had actually met in the mountains of Tennessee—at least as far as he knew. Hannah started feeding the apples to her pet and eventually led him back to their cabin.

"You're going to let him stay inside, aren't you?" Cole asked incredulously.

"The last time you were gallivanting around time and space and left me alone, he saved my life. I think I want to keep him handy, if you don't mind. Besides, he knows us. We can't lock him out of the cabin; that wouldn't be nice."

"How does he know us?"

"Maybe he traveled with us when we left. I don't know... maybe he's a time-traveling bear and he followed our time-warp signature or something."

"Our what? You don't believe that, do you? Besides, Captain Kirk, he was in Switzerland before we were. And if he knew us in Tennessee because of here, how does he already know us here?"

"I don't know...but I like having a pet bear." Hannah noticed the scowl on Cole's face. "What's wrong?"

"Don't you think it's about time we learned some answers to our questions? What are we supposed to do with that staff? How did a special ops squad find us five days before you grabbed it? Why me? Why you? Why Teddy Bear over there?" he asked as Teddy rummaged through a closet and tore open a bag of potatoes. "And what if we need those potatoes to eat?"

Hannah smiled at Cole's attempt at humor. "We'll figure it out... and while we do, maybe you can get my family out of Jordan."

Cole's sour demeanor immediately improved. "Now *that's* a good idea."

●●●●● ● ●●●●●

WEDNESDAY, JUNE 20
Four Days After the Discovery

Once the treaties were signed and the political leaders from Egypt and Turkey as well as the witnessing cabinet ministers had exited the Raghadan Palace, King Adnan sent for General Marid. They met in the king's plush office, and after a bowed greeting, the general sat in a chair opposite the king's desk.

"What have you learned from Richard Carpenter, Jibril?"

"My apologies, Akmal, but so far he has admitted nothing. He's sticking with his story that his daughter never possessed the staff before our encounter on Mount Nebo."

"How about the little sister? Surely the child hasn't been able to keep a secret."

"She's scared to death, yet she doesn't appear to know a thing. You've demanded that I not harm them, but it seems necessary at this point to motivate Mr. Carpenter in a different way. Of course he's lying. He must know something."

"Separate them all. Lead Mr. Carpenter to believe his wife and daughter are in danger. Raise the heat and limit his food and water. Pipe in some annoying sound. We'll torture him mentally for a while and see if he changes his tune. I also have something else I need you to take care of."

"As you wish. What else may I do for you?"

"Lauren Molina, the American reporter that has embarrassed me. I need her taken care of…permanently."

"Is she back in Jordan?"

"No. I've learned that she's investigating the man on the motorcycle, Cole Flint. I believe she's trying to find him. Have her followed and kill her. If she leads you to Flint, take him alive because he'll know where the staff is. But because the reporter continues to vilify me, I want her eliminated as soon as possible. I've had enough publicity." The king hesitated. "Oddly, Jibril, according to the reporter, Flint is a fugitive for three killings, yet there was no such man in the supposed fight in Florida of the United States, and the story from the state of Michigan is not accurate. There is no record of a Cole Flint since 2006. Something is fishy, and I'm wondering if the reporter is giving misinformation to protect the man we saw on the mountain."

"She was on the mountain. Maybe she's an accomplice. When she's located, I could interrogate her before we silence her permanently."

"Just do away with the nuisance...the sooner the better. I'm getting impatient."

●●●●●●●●●●●

SIXTEEN

Elizabeth Desmond, the Fox News producer, had given Lauren a file on Cole Flint which made no sense at all. Lauren had made a live report based on facts procured and verified by Elizabeth and her staff, but it appeared she had made a false report.

There had been no fight in the Goodrich High School parking lot. Four boys had been injured and Russ Smallock had died just as she had reported, but the fight occurred off campus and Russ hadn't died when he hit his head after a fall. A car struck him and smashed him into a gas pump which exploded. The car belonged to Carter Flint, Cole's father, and was the car that Cole drove to school. How Cole had beat up four boys and then brutally committed vehicular homicide against Smallock was difficult to figure, but that's what the four friends claimed. She obtained the information easily from local newspaper stories. *How had Liz's staff missed that?* thought Lauren.

Because of the faulty information, Lauren checked out the registration again for the motorcycle that she observed on Mount Nebo. It wasn't registered to Cole Flint as her previous information stated; it was registered instead to Dirk Pitt.

Lauren did a quick Internet search for the news story regarding the fight Cole had outside the training gym in Port St. Lucie, Florida. The fighter who killed the bouncers outside the gym was named Spenser Hawk. Hawk had signed a register for the fight and signed a payment voucher. The bouncers who claimed he'd murdered their friends, called him Hawk, and the motorcycle outside the building, the motorcycle that previously had no registration or insurance, was oddly and unexpectedly registered to a Myron Bolitar. After some digging and a few favors, she managed to get a photograph from the cage fight, and sure enough, it was Cole. The mystery was getting stranger and stranger.

Lauren steered her rental car into the driveway of one Carter Flint before exiting the vehicle and stepping onto the front porch of a vastly undermaintained home in Goodrich, Michigan. She rang the doorbell and waited patiently for an answer. As she prepared to push the button again, the door swung open and a disheveled man growled, "Yeah, what do you want?"

"Are you Carter Flint?"

"Could be. Who're you?"

"My name's Lauren Molina. I'm a news reporter for Fox News. I'd like to talk to you about your son, Cole."

"Ain't *my* son. I seen you on the news, now that you mention it."

"May I come in, sir? I have some questions I need to ask you."

"You got some hidden cameraman or somethin'?" he asked as he craned his neck outside the door, surveying for the unseen photographer.

"No cameras. May I come in?"

"Yeah, sure. Why not? Hope you don't expect any hospitality 'cause I ain't got nothin' to offer you. Stinkin' auto industry let me go more'n four years ago. Now I have to rely on free health care, welfare, unemployment, food stamps…you know…whatever I kin git. Ain't got no extras to be just givin' away to strangers."

"Have you thought about finding another job, Mr. Flint?"

"Heck no! I'm a victim…so now the government—sure enough—has a responsibility to take care of me. I'm an American, and I'm entitled to health care, food, housing…you name it. I paid taxes for years, and now I'm receivin' the benefits of my past generosity."

"Don't you think you should take some personal responsibility for your future?"

"Shoot, no! Now, how kin I help you?"

Wow. The loser actually believes he's living the American dream, thought Lauren. Merely being in the man's presence already made Lauren feel grimy. "I was under the impression that Cole Flint is your adopted son, but you just said he wasn't. Can you explain?"

"Well, yeah, me and the wife adopted him, but I long since disinherited the punk. I don't make no claim to him as my son."

"Is there a reason?"

"Two reasons. First, Ellie—that was my wife's name—she loved him more'n she loved me. That ain't right. And B, he blamed me for her death. And third, the last time I gave him the back of my hand—which I had every right to do seein' how I was his legal father—he threatened to hurt me bad if I ever touched him again. That there is two really good reasons to forego any future responsibility for him."

Lauren was awed by his logic…and counting abilities. "*Were* you responsible for your wife's death?"

"Course not! She was killed by a irresponsible driver. Smashed right into the side of my car."

"Why did Cole blame you?"

"'Cause the accident report said I ran a red light. That was a lie. I'm a good driver. Always have been."

"When was the last time you heard from Cole?"

"I don't know. Week or so before he ran that kid over with my car. Didn't much pay attention to the punk."

"I thought he got in a fight in the school parking lot."

"Lady, he plowed the kid right into a gas pump which blew up my car. Insurance didn't pay for it, so I ended up makin' payments on a car that was sittin' in a salvage yard burned like a piece o' toast. And then he never came home again. Never heard a word from him again, which was just fine by me."

"That's sad, Mr. Flint."

"You better believe it. The car didn't have collision insurance, so I lost my shirt."

Lauren's mouth fell open. Carter Flint was a piece of work. "What was Cole like?"

"Perfect, of course. That's what his mother would say. Responsible...determined...watched out for people in need. Athletic... smart...strong. But he also didn't think I was good enough for his mother, and when he saw me slap her once, he took to learnin' how to fight, and the boy scared me."

"Do you think it was okay to hit your wife, Mr. Flint? I, for one, can see why he might be perturbed."

"No, I don't. I only slapped her that one time, I swear it, and it was a mistake I regret. I'd slapped the kid around a few times, but everything changed when he saw me slap his mother. I lost his respect; I admit it. And when his old lady passed, he didn't want nothin' to do with me...which was fine 'cause, like I said, the kid scared me."

"Scared you?"

"You ever see his eyes? No, I s'pose not. There was a intensity in those eyes like fire. The intensity made him a great football player…and scarier than anyone I ever seen. The kid could fight like no other. Scuse me for a minute, lady." Carter got out of his chair, rummaged through a drawer, and found a picture that he brought back and handed to Lauren. "That's him headin' to the sideline during a football game. The team was behind by a coupla scores and Cole rocked a running back so hard the kid broke four ribs. *Four*. No kidding. That's him when he came off the field. Check out those eyes."

His eyes made the hair stand up on the back of Lauren's neck. She smiled. The last time she'd had that feeling was when she missed a deadline and her producer was fit to be tied. "May I keep this?"

"Sure…I got no need for it."

Lauren slid it into her file folder and paused a second before asking, "Did Cole know he was adopted?"

"Far as I know, he didn't. Ellie made me promise to never say, and a man ain't nothin' if he don't keep his word."

"At least you have one good quality, Mr. Flint. I can't much say I'm too impressed with anything else about you, but I thank you for your time. I'll help myself out if you don't mind." With that, Lauren left Cole's childhood home with a fresh perspective of Cole and a strong desire to shower and rid herself of the filth of Carter Flint.

●●●●● ● ●●●●●

Four Years Before the Discovery

After a full bag of apples and a full bag of potatoes, Teddy seemed to have his hunger satisfied, so he initiated a curious investigation of the cabin. Cole took a peek inside the refrigerator and found some eggs, cheese, ham, and onions which he used to make omelets. There was juice to drink and bread and butter for toast. Hannah set the table where they sat down to eat.

After several quiet bites, Hannah said, "This is delicious. I never pegged you as the cooking type."

"Thanks. My mom used to make omelets a lot. I learned from her." Cole responded without making any eye contact. Hannah could see she'd managed to hit on a touchy subject, so she didn't ask a couple of gnawing questions that popped into her head. Instead, she took a drink of juice and a bite of toast and continued to eat silently, wondering what the future held.

Through the kitchen window was a view of the valley from the back side of the cabin where they had located Teddy. There was a rocky waterfall which was the source of the river they had seen beyond the trees. It was stunning, winding through lush, green trees and splashing against exquisitely sculpted rocks. The frothy water cascaded down several short drops while the trees climbed up the mountainous elevation. It seemed like a great place to explore and relax, and Hannah was daydreaming about a future journey up the Alps when Cole broke the silence.

"What in the world is that horrible stench?" He shoveled his last bite of omelet into his mouth and stood up from the table. Hannah wiffed the awful smell too and pressed the sleeve of her arm against her face protecting her olfactory nerves from rancid overload. Cole made his way into the living room. "*Teddy!* Oh, man! This is disgusting!"

"What is it? What did he do?" she asked as she followed Cole into the other room.

"Your pet teddy bear just crapped a massive pile on the floor in here." And massive it was—about a foot in diameter, filled with roots and elderberries piling up several inches high on the hardwood floor.

"Bad bear!" Hannah scolded. "You know better than that, Teddy! You don't poop inside!"

"Now, how would he know that, Hannah?" Cole wondered as he lifted his shirt and held it over his mouth and nose.

Hannah stared at his rippling abs a second before replying. "I don't know. If he's my pet, I must have taught him somewhere in time, don't you think? He seems pretty domesticated to me. You get outside right now, Teddy! Bad bear!" Teddy's head seemed to slump down further below his shoulder hump. He slinked right over to the door where Hannah pointed and waited for her to open it before lumbering outside and lying down, planting himself right on the doorstep. "Oh my gosh, Cole! I'll open some windows while you clean that up."

"*Me*? Are you kidding? I'll need a crane! *You* should clean it up. Maybe you can use that staff to make it disappear."

"Sure, and while I perform my little miracle, I should send it to the King of Jordan. It'd be like a plague, warning him to let my family go or else more 'crap is gonna hit the fan.' Use a shovel or something. You'll be my hero if you do this for me. Holy cow, I can't breathe!" she exclaimed as she finally got a window to slide open and hung her head outside, gasping for sweet-smelling air.

Still holding his shirt over his nose and mouth, Cole moved to what appeared to be a pantry and opened the door. Unbelievably, there actually *was* a shovel inside along with a broom and a mop and pail. He grabbed it and shoveled up about half the pile in one scoop, holding his breath the entire time. "Get the door, Hannah...please, I'm begging you."

Hannah had found a can of air freshener under the sink and sprayed a never-ending stream in the air. When she got to Cole, she started spraying his shovelful of bear poop. "The door...before I suffocate!" Cole begged while turning red from lack of oxygen. When Hannah yanked the door open, there was Teddy, blocking the doorway. "Get out of the way, you big, stupid lug!" he gasped, his oxygen reserves nearly depleted, but the bear simply lay there in his chosen time-out area, apparently discouraged from the yelling.

In near desperation, Cole reeled around and rushed headlong for the open window. When he reached it, he tossed the excrement—shovel and all—right out the window and hung his head outside, sucking in long-overdue breaths of fresh air.

Hannah dove onto Cole's back, herself escaping the fetid air of the cabin. "That was brilliant," she said as she lay there on top of him, spraying air-freshener past his right ear in a trajectory toward the pile of poop on the ground, a mere four feet away from their heads. "Now the shovel's out there and half the pile of death fragrance is still inside."

She had Cole pinned on his stomach on the windowsill. "Get off me and open the rest of the windows. I'll take care of it now that I'm breathing again...and after I smack that bear upside the head."

Hannah pushed herself off her human mattress and Cole climbed the rest of the way back into the cabin. He marched straight for the door, opened it, climbed over the pouting bear, and smacked him right upside the head, exactly as he'd said. "Stupid bear," he muttered as Hannah's pet let out a whiney groan.

Cole marched all the way around the cabin, emptied the remnants of dung that still resided on the shovel, and walked back around the house to the front door, smacking a still-prostrate Teddy a second time before re-entering the house. A second shovelful picked up nearly all of the remaining pile which Cole once again heaved outside through the window, the shovel landing on the dusty earth with a thud, before he headed back out the door and climbed back over the miserable grizzly.

Once he made the trek around the cabin again, he dug a hole nearly three feet deep, thinking anything shallower couldn't possibly contain the rank smell. He then buried all evidence of the scattered pile. The sun had begun to set by the time he finished and returned to the dispirited bear. He bent down and glared into Teddy's eyes. The grizzly lifted his head and licked the man right across the face, leaving a stream of slobber that caused Cole to smile as he wiped the drool with his shirt sleeve. "Come on," he said as he opened the door. "Come on inside. I forgive you."

Teddy climbed to his feet and placed a paw on Cole's back as if to say "I'm sorry." Together, they walked through the doorway, and there was Hannah, rubber gloves intact, wringing out a mop in a bucket, a clothespin dangling from her nose. Cole burst out laughing while Teddy lumbered over to Hannah and put his head on her shoulder.

With tears in her eyes, Hannah removed the clothespin, grabbed his cheeks in both of her hands, and cried, "I love you, you dumb bear, but don't you ever do that again; do you hear me?" Then she hugged him around his neck, a tear trailing down her cheek. She looked at Cole. "In the middle of all this mess we've been placed in, we've been given a gift. You see that, don't you? I think someone's watching over us."

"I'm gonna have to agree with you…and we've been given another gift too."

"What's that?"

"Come on outside and see."

The teenager, seeming a little taller and more confident than any time Cole had seen her before, walked with her pet to the door, and as they opened it, she gasped. There over the mountains to the west was the most-stunning sunset she'd ever seen.

The majority of the mountains were blue shadows, a hue Hannah had never seen before, but the mountain peaks were bathed in gilded sunlight, like golden lava running down the mountainsides. The few scattered clouds were just as golden, impersonating sprays of fire in the heavens. As the couple sat in quiet awe, breathing in the crisp, dusky air, the circular globe of sunshine gradually dipped below the highest peak, rays of sunlight darting down the steep, craggy mountains until the orb disappeared, leaving the gold-plated sky to temporarily glow.

Before the few breathtaking moments had ended, somehow Teddy had lain on the porch with his head in Hannah's lap, and Cole had slipped his arm around her waist and placed his hand on the giant animal to her side. Hannah put her head on Cole's shoulder. "I've never seen anything more breathtaking than that."

"And I've never smelled anything more breathtaking than that bear crap." They both started laughing—a hearty, cleansing laugh that lasted several minutes before they all rose and headed inside.

●●●●● ● ●●●●●

SEVENTEEN

· · · · · · · · ● ● ● ● ● ● ● ● ● ● · · · ·

After using her resources to find the hospital where Cole Flint was born, Elizabeth threw away her cup of coffee. She blamed it for the shakiness of her nerves. She withdrew a bottle from her desk drawer and had a stiff drink of alcohol instead, hoping it would help her relax. After she composed herself, she next went about procuring a copy of the journal from Cole Flint's motorcycle. She reached the sheriff in Port St. Lucie's police department, but he adamantly demanded that the bike belonged to someone by the name of Myron Bolitar—not Cole Flint—and that the cage fighter/parking lot brawler was named Spenser Hawk. The sheriff was just as sure that there was nothing of Hawk's personal effects on the motorcycle. The same man who only two days before had told her about a journal now said there was no such thing.

It was as if the information she had gathered had inexplicably changed. As she pondered what in the world was going on, her phone rang. It was Lauren.

"Hello, Lauren."

"Hi, Liz. Do you have a minute?"

"All the time in the world for you, sweetheart. What have you found?"

"Well, mostly I've found that pretty much all of what we claimed on the air about Flint is wrong. The location of the high school fight, how Russ Smallock died, who purchased the motorcycles, who fought in the Florida fight—all of it is different than we reported."

"I would say that's impossible—you know how thoroughly we check out our facts before we report them—but the sheriff in Port St. Lucie seems to be of the same opinion as you. Do you happen to have an explanation?"

"Well, either the facts you first discovered were somehow wrong, or somehow they've been changed. I'm leaning toward explanation number two. First of all, Flint's dad—he's a piece of work—maintains that the fight was at a gas station, and he hasn't heard from his son since it happened. And, by the way, listen to this. Cole's father was responsible for his wife's death, and the dad physically abused Cole."

"Oh, no!" Elizabeth seemed genuinely disturbed by the news.

"Listen, Liz. The guy who fought in Florida was named Spenser Hawk—not Cole Flint—but I have a picture and Spenser was *definitely* the Cole we reported on. The motorcycle that used to have no registration evidently now belongs to someone named Myron Bolitar. The guy who bought the Kawasaki Ninja that I videotaped on Mount Nebo seemingly was Dirk Pitt. I did Internet searches on each of those names, and guess what? They all belong to characters in suspense novels...well, Spenser and Hawk are *two* characters from the same Robert B. Parker series. So I wondered if maybe Cole changed his name several times. I went to the city hall in Flint, Michigan, after talking to Cole's pathetic adoptive father, and sure enough, Cole changed his name three weeks before the high school fight to Dirk Pitt. After the fight, he must have bought the motorcycle in Lansing using that name. Three days after the fight, Myron Bolitar came into existence. Three years later, at the same location, Spenser N. Hawk came to be. Can you see if there are any records regarding those three names, so I can track down an address or something?"

"My pleasure. And while you're investigating, go to Hurley Hospital in Flint or the city hall and find his birth records—October 19, 1988. See what you can find out about an abandoned baby boy, born with the name of Cole. I want you to confirm that our Cole was born there at about 8:30 p.m. Maybe someone will remember something."

"Will do. Do you want me to head to Florida next?"

"I'm going to check into the information that you just gave me, and I'll let you know what to do when you call with whatever you find out at the hospital."

"All right. I'll call again when I know something."

After she hung up, Elizabeth poured herself another drink. She was getting strange answers, but at least she had some leads to follow.

• • • • • ● • • • • •

Four Years Before the Discovery

With all the windows open and the sun behind the mountains, it cooled off quickly in the cabin. While Hannah shut the windows, Cole started a fire. Hannah grabbed a blanket and sat down on the comfortable living-room couch, and Teddy found a large place on the floor to lie at her feet. Cole heated up a couple mugs of hot chocolate and sat down with Hannah. She threw the blanket over Cole too before sipping from her cup.

"Thank you. Are you always so chivalrous?" she asked.

"Maybe. Unless it doesn't mean what I think it means. Does it mean valiant and magnanimous?"

"Maybe. Unless those words don't mean what I think they mean. Do they mean well-mannered and considerate?"

"Yes, I believe they do."

"Then thank you again for being chivalrous."

"You're welcome."

"Are you going to Jordan in the morning to try and free my family?"

Cole displayed the pictures that Perisa had given him. "This one is the SOCOM compound in Jordan. It's where your family is. I'm pretty sure they'll be willing to escort me into the facility, but I don't know where your family is. I'm gonna have to wing it when I get there, so I can't make any promises."

"I understand. Are you sure I'm not supposed to go with you?"

"Yeah…you need to stay safe. This must be the place for that. Teddy can protect you while I'm gone."

When he heard his name, the grizzly lazily lifted his head but quickly put it down again and immediately dozed back to sleep.

"Cole?"

"Yeah?"

"Why did you look so sad when you mentioned your mother?"

He studied Hannah's light-blue eyes and paused as if to decide whether to risk sharing his personal life. "My dad was a complete loser, but my mom was a saint. Dad would smack me around occasionally when the mood was right, and I put up with it for a while. But one day he slapped my mother. I was twelve. It was then that I learned how to fight. I decided if he ever struck my mom again, it would be the last thing he ever did. He never hit her again that I know of, but when I was thirteen, he ran a red light and the car that collided with ours killed my mom."

"I'm so sorry."

"Though Dad was ticketed, the other driver wasn't hurt and there weren't any charges pressed against him. He swore it wasn't his fault and never took personal responsibility, but I could tell he knew it was his fault. He wouldn't have anything else to do with me, and one time when I challenged him about the accident, he hit me again. I threatened him with a baseball bat and told him if he ever touched me again, I'd kill him. I'm not proud of that, but I'm pretty sure I meant it when I said it. He was never a father to me again. Seemed like he was ashamed of himself and afraid of me, so I raised myself through junior high and high school…then spent three years in prison with no one to care about me at all."

"Was prison terrible?"

"Yeah, it was terrible. I did a lot of reading…worked out a lot. It was minimum security and really wasn't too dangerous if that's what you're thinking. I had a couple of incidents early on, but people learned not to mess with me. I've been out three years and pretty much a loner the whole time."

"Do you miss your mom a lot?"

"Do you miss yours?"

"Yeah, I do."

"Me too. Family's supposed to be a good word…you know…something to be proud of and look forward to. I don't have a family."

"Well, when you get my family out of Jordan, I'll share them with you." She said that in such a sweet voice that Cole was touched.

"You mean that, don't you?" He set his unfinished mug on the floor and gave Hannah a light hug. "Thanks."

Hannah beamed contentedly as Cole reached his hand down to retrieve his hot cocoa, but what he grabbed instead was a big, hairy bear head. Teddy had his mouth entirely around the mug and his tongue was frantically licking the warm liquid from the container. Hot chocolate dripped out of his mouth onto the floor as he snapped his jaws shut, breaking the glass in pieces. He yelped in pain, and Cole was forced into the new, unfortunate experience of prying the pieces from his bloody jaws.

"Obviously, this dumb bear is going to give us one adventure after another."

●●●●● ● ●●●●●

WEDNESDAY, JUNE 20
Four Days After the Discovery

General Marid slowly opened the door to Richard Carpenter's room. Kristina had been out of the room for several hours and Richard had done nothing but worry—and occasionally pray—ever since she had been taken away like Sarah. Brief, steady and annoying, high-pitched buzzing sounds burst over and over again. The room was stifling, yet the sink's water faucet was no longer working. Richard was hot, hungry, thirsty, anxious, and mentally exasperated when the general emerged drinking a bottle of water and tossing some nuts in his mouth. He also had a whip in his right hand and a pleasant smile on his face.

"Your wife and daughter were quite a bit easier to break than you, my friend," he lied.

"I'm not your friend, and you had better not've hurt them."

"I didn't, Mr. Carpenter. I told them I would be hurting *you*. I told them to tell me about Hannah and the staff, and if you didn't tell the same story, I would whip you until you told what you know."

"I've already told you everything I know."

"Well, there you go again, being strong and brave. Very admirable…but also very stupid. Let's see. Hannah had the staff in Montana five years ago. She nearly killed my king while protecting that bear of hers. She spent some time in Switzerland four years ago. Here's a picture of her while she was spotted mountain climbing with the bear in the Lauterbrunnen Valley. Six days ago, she took out a whole four-person element of one of my best-trained SOCOM units in the Smoky Mountains of Tennessee. Here's a picture of her playing with that same bear."

Richard's jaw dropped at the sight of the pictures.

"Then we saw her again with you four days later on Mount Nebo, retrieving that sapphire staff that she seems to think belongs to her. Well, it *doesn't!*" Finally some emotion was released and the calm, cool exterior was thrown off, replaced by an infuriated glare. "Your family has confirmed that these facts are true, Mr. Carpenter! Now, who is Cole Flint, and how do we find your daughter?"

Richard's physical and mental strength were nearly drained, but he eyed the pictures again and said, "You're lying. Sarah and Kristina know nothing of this. They didn't confirm it because it's impossible." He pointed at a picture. "Four years ago, when you say this picture was taken…Hannah would have been fourteen years old. She's not fourteen in this picture. You've doctored some photographs or something. Hannah was kidnapped in front of my very eyes. For the last five years when you say she's been touring the world with the Staff of Moses and a huge brown bear, she has been with me and my family in Missouri until we left together for a trip we won to the Holy Land. You can continue to torture me if you choose and whip me if you desire, but I can't tell you something that is impossible and that you're making up. And I'm certain my wife and daughter didn't tell you anything because just like me, they have no knowledge of anything you're talking about except that my daughter walked out of that church with the staff in her hand, and she was kidnapped by some man on a motorcycle."

The infuriated general fumed, his face red and a vein nearly bursting in his forehead. He felt a strong desire to wrap his whip around the prisoner's neck and squeeze the life out of him, but Richard was right. His family hadn't told Marid anything. They were as clueless as Richard concerning Hannah's adventures over the last five years.

The general realized that killing the man would just lead to an international incident. He didn't get to the position of leadership and authority that he currently possessed through a lack of self-control, so he took a few breaths and refrained from the murder that was so appealing. "Your family will be returned to you, Mr. Carpenter. Your daughter is apparently leading a dual life of which you are inexplicably unaware. We will continue to hold you so when we locate her, we can trade you for the staff. Make yourself comfortable because you won't be going anywhere."

He closed and relocked the door and almost immediately the torturous sound and the stifling heat subsided, and the water in the sink suddenly worked again. Richard washed his face and drank his fill before collapsing onto his cot. Once he exited the room, General Marid made a phone call and gave the order to find and kill Lauren Molina. If he couldn't be successful with the king's first demand, he was surely going to be successful with the second.

●●●●● ● ●●●●●

EIGHTEEN

· · · · · · · ●●●●●● ● ●●●●●● · · · ·

Elizabeth couldn't understand how the information her staff had gathered about Cole Flint had been completely false. Over the past six years, they could find no evidence of Cole's life or activities, but apparently two days later, he didn't even exist *at all* during those six years. In addition, facts found at the time of the Port St. Lucie fight had totally disappeared or changed, including the identity of Cole himself. According to Lauren, Cole had changed his identity in 2006 two different times and again in 2009, so Elizabeth couldn't figure out why the original police report said the fighter in Florida was Cole Flint. Two days later, however, the police said the fighter was Spenser Hawk. She was also having trouble sorting out the fact that Cole's two different motorcycles suddenly belonged to Myron Bolitar and Dirk Pitt. It was as if Cole's entire, mysterious last six years had disappeared entirely in the past two days, replaced by identities that didn't used to exist. "Or did they?" she wondered out loud. "What is going on?"

"Liz? Lauren is on line two," announced Elizabeth's administrative assistant.

"Thank you. I'll take the call." She picked up the phone. "Hi, Lauren. Do you have some information?"

"I have birth information, Liz. There was a baby born at Hurley Hospital in Flint, Michigan, on October 19, 1988, at 8:30 p.m.—exactly as you said. According to records at city hall, after the baby was born, the mother mysteriously disappeared, but before she did, she named the child Cole. Protective services arrived after a few days when the mother never came back, and they took the baby to a foster home."

"The Flints?"

"No, not right away. The baby went to the home of Shanice Brown but only for a few days before Cole was placed with Carter and Ellie Flint. Carter and Ellie had three other foster children but gave them all up and adopted Cole within six months. They never took in another foster child."

"Did you talk with anyone in the hospital?"

"No, but I'm working on that. I have a lead about a nurse from labor and delivery. I also plan to speak with Shanice Brown." There was a pause. "Tell me again why I'm doing this investigation, Liz? You may be right that the key to this story is Cole—or whoever he is—but there seems to be a pressing story in the Middle East and a girl with one of the most-important relics in history. Why is he more important than her?"

Elizabeth hesitated, not knowing if she should say what was on her mind. "I worked my tail off to get into this position as producer at Fox where I had the resources to do what we're doing right now. My instincts tell me to pursue Cole Flint—or whatever his name is. Trust me on this one, Lauren."

"Okay. I'll keep at it if you think it's best."

•••••●•••••

THURSDAY, JUNE 21
Five Days After the Discovery

Mr. President, you'll be on in five…four…three…two…one… you're live."

President Stonehouse faced the camera. The staged press conference was a solo affair with only Martin Sanderson, a well-known anchorman from CNN Headline News, in attendance. The president intended to speak his words from his desk in the Oval Office and then allow Sanderson an opportunity to ask a few pre-rehearsed questions. CNN hoped that their solo, personal interview would generate ratings that would offset the record-setting following of Fox News since Lauren Molina reported on the activities on Mount Nebo on Tuesday, only two days before.

"On Tuesday, June the nineteenth, we were presented with video evidence of several unusual events in front of the Byzantine Memorial Church of Moses on Mount Nebo in the nation of Jordan," the president began. "On that video, we saw a girl, Hannah Carpenter, standing with what is believed to be the biblical Staff of Moses. Within seconds, we saw her whisked away on a motorcycle, and then we saw the King of Jordan, King Akmal-Adnan, and his security force and soldiers handcuff and take the remaining members of the Carpenter family away like common criminals.

"For the past two days, the government of the United States has been attempting to procure information from the Jordanian government in regard to the illegal arrests and detainment of three of our country's citizens. The government of Jordan has steadfastly denied that the family is being held in their custody. The officials have admitted to the initial detainment for purposes of questioning in regard to the motorcycle driver and to Hannah Carpenter, but they claim the family was released.

"Thus far, we have been unable to either locate the family or find evidence of their release. At this point, we are working under the assumption that the family is still under Jordanian custody. I speak to you today to express my deepest sympathy to the families and friends of those involved in this incident as well as to express my determination to locate the Carpenter family and bring them home. We are continuing to gather information, and we will not rest until the Carpenter family is safely home on U.S. soil."

The president smiled into the camera, showing confidence before he nodded toward Martin Sanderson, awaiting the newsman's scripted questions.

A second camera focused on the reporter. "Mr. President, thank you for allowing me access to this press conference. I'm sure I speak for all Americans when I say we are very disturbed by the actions of the King of Jordan. May I begin by asking you why the family was arrested in the first place?"

"We were told that the initial conclusion of King Adnan was that Hannah Carpenter and an accomplice, the man on the motorcycle, had stolen the staff which the king claims belongs to him since it was discovered on Jordanian property. After the family was questioned, it was determined that the girl was most likely kidnapped and that the family had no knowledge of any wrongdoing."

"How did Hannah Carpenter gain possession of the staff, sir? Was that ever determined?"

"As had been reported since the discovery of the staff on Saturday, June sixteenth, it was solidly stuck in the rock floor of the church at the top of the mountain. How it got there, no one knows, and why Miss Carpenter was able to gain possession of it when no one else could is a question for which we have yet to discover an answer."

"Do you believe that Hannah was kidnapped?"

"It appears so, but to our knowledge, no one found the driver or the girl inside the church nor anywhere on the mountain or in its vicinity. We really can only speculate as to the rider's intentions."

"You continue to avoid calling the motorcyclist by name. What do you know of Cole Flint?"

The president shifted in his seat uncomfortably and cleared his throat before answering. "It appears, Martin, that news reports were premature in identifying the rider. The Cole Flint that was named and the reports of his run-ins with the law seem to be inaccurate."

"How so?"

"Well, the owner of the motorcycle was Dirk Pitt. Cole Flint disappeared after a high school fight six years ago, but he wasn't the owner of the motorcycle on Mount Nebo…and he wasn't the man named in the incident in Port St. Lucie three days ago. That was a man named Spenser Hawk. Unfortunately, we know very little about Cole Flint, and we are going on the premise that the motorcycle rider was someone else entirely."

"Have you uncovered any information as to Hannah's or the driver's whereabouts?"

"None whatsoever, I'm sorry to admit."

"What is your opinion of what seemed to be a motorcycle materializing and then disappearing into thin air?"

The president smiled as if the question was humorous. "Obviously, that isn't what happened. It can easily be explained by the poor video quality of a phone camera from a long distance inside a news van behind rain-spattered windows during a torrential rainstorm. It was an optical illusion. The rider rode up unexpectedly and drove right through the church which happens to be an open building that is simply an architectural excavation. The rider, Dirk Pitt, or whoever drove his motorcycle, planned his escape quite thoroughly."

"One last question, Mr. President. What are you planning to do to liberate the Carpenter family from Jordanian detention?"

"Martin, we cannot say for sure that the family is being detained, but we are doing everything in our power to find out the truth. If they are being held against their will, we intend to free them. I cannot be more specific than that."

"Thank you for your time and frankness, Mr. President. I believe I speak on behalf of the citizens of the United States when I say we're all mystified and troubled by these circumstances, and we hope for a speedy resolution to the situation. Thank you once again."

With that, the cameras were shut off, and the interview ended. The talking heads of all the news stations were left to discuss and speculate as to what would happen next.

• • • • ● ● • • • •

NINETEEN

Four Years Before the Discovery

After heading to bed early and getting a good night's sleep, Hannah and Cole both woke before the sun came up. They chewed toasted Pop Tarts and sipped more hot chocolate as the sun rose over the mountains in another extraordinary display of beauty. From their back window, their view was somewhat obscured by trees, but the dazzling light seemed to envelop the plant life, surrounding the greenery with a diffused glory and radiance.

"Wow! Seeing that almost makes me forget how screwed up my life currently happens to be. It's like light is penetrating and deflecting off the leaves at the same time. It's just like you."

"What?" Cole asked, completely lost in the analogy.

"You penetrate time when you time travel—sort of like that light that somehow radiates through the trees up there on the mountain—but you're also able to deflect like the sunlight off the leaves when you jump from one place to another. You're like sunlight in the mountains."

"If you would've simply said I was 'bright' and 'hot,' the sunlight analogy would've made sense right away," he teased.

Hannah giggled at his comment. "Teddy's outside. I didn't want to take a chance on another accident," she laughed. "I emptied the entire can of air-freshener."

"I'll have to get some more, just in case." Cole laughed too, thinking about the bear waste he'd buried deep into the ground the evening before. Finally, his laughter calmed and he became quite serious.

"What are you thinking?" Hannah asked.

"I guess it's time for me to try to get your parents." He frowned again.

"So what's wrong?"

"What if something happens to me? You'll be stuck in Switzerland four years into your past with nothing except a huge, stinky grizzly bear. And who knows what would come of your parents."

"Seriously, Cole, why are you even thinking that? Just jump in and jump out and bring them home."

"I can only get to the entrance to SOCOM, and it's there that specially trained soldiers will unquestionably arrest me. I'm a little anxious about that if you know what I mean."

Hannah didn't know what to say, so she changed the subject. "I had a dream about you before we left Missouri and flew to Jordan. Well…it wasn't entirely about you. I had the sapphire staff in my hand, and you appeared right out of nowhere exactly like how it really happened."

"Are you thinking that's somehow kind of meaningful? I mean…have you figured out the significance all of a sudden?"

"When I saw that staff in the church, I knew I was supposed to pull it out of that rock…probably because I'd seen it before in the dream….I don't know…maybe because it was like it was calling out to me too. It *seemed* like it was meant just for me. Anyway, after I pulled it out of the ground and you appeared, I knew you were meant to be in my life too. It's why I broke down and cried. It's why I believed you. You didn't kidnap me; you saved me. But it also means that I have to climb that mountain back there."

Cole raised his eyebrows in confusion, wrinkling his forehead. "I honestly don't see what one thing has to do with the other."

"I had a dream last night where I was sitting on a rock ledge way up in that mountain," she described, pointing to where the sunlight had mesmerized her only moments earlier. "I'm pretty sure I need to go there."

"Okay. Maybe you'll find some prophecy on a rock with clues to our destiny. Seriously, maybe that legendary staff you possess is the key that unlocks some secret treasure trove or gateway or something."

"Yeah, and maybe I'll find dwarves with pickaxes, mining for treasure, and there'll be elves with pointy ears who can lead me to the land of eternal life."

Cole shrugged his shoulders. "You never know. The only thing we do know is that we don't know anything. You might not find a hobbit or a wizard up there, but maybe you'll figure something out."

"Cole?"

"Yeah?"

"If you can't get them out safely, come back to me. If they have you in handcuffs, I'll get Teddy to gnaw them off."

Cole didn't know if he should be touched or if he should laugh. He chose to laugh. It was something that he'd already done several times with Hannah, and it was something he hadn't done much since his mother had died. It felt good, but it made him think of his mother, so instead of letting Hannah see the sadness creep back into his eyes, he said, "I'll go find Teddy. He's going with you. And I assume you'll be taking the staff too…for protection."

Hannah nodded as Cole swung around and headed for the door. "I'll be back soon…unless that dumb bear is causing trouble again. Cross your fingers."

•••••⬤•••••

Four Years Before the Discovery

When Cole walked out of the cabin, he spotted a trail and decided to investigate before he headed back to the river behind the dwelling. Shortly into his walk, he saw a sign which said, "Cable cars to Mürren…Three miles." There wasn't much ahead except the trail, so he turned and headed around to the back of the cabin and then on to the river when he didn't see Teddy. His mind was on Hannah—which he found strange because he knew he was about to rush headlong into danger, but he found her to be so simply fascinating that he wasn't thinking about himself. Hannah was different than all the girls that threw themselves at him when he won a fighting exhibition or rode up on his motorcycle. They were one-dimensional strangers—people cut-outs—and they didn't care to know anything about what made up the real Cole Flint. Hannah was humble and brave. She had a good sense of humor. Over and over, she had surprised him with her strength, courage, poise, selflessness, and genuine, caring heart. She had been chosen—he was sure of it—because of those qualities…and, well, her ability to tame wild grizzlies in an instant.

Hannah somehow drew out of him the compassion and gentleness that his mother had nurtured and his father and prison had helped him forget. He discovered that he was grateful and relieved to see that he wasn't utterly bitter and permanently sorrowful and unhappy. She showed him he could have hope for a brighter future.

After entering a dark, tight grouping of trees, he could see the river ahead, but Teddy wasn't at the river; he was lying on his back on the shaded ground where no one else could see him. Petting his belly was a tall, thin man with an easy smile and a twinkle in his eyes. Cole drew his gun, cocked it, and pointed it at the stranger.

"Get away from my bear."

"Easy, Cole. I'm not here to hurt him...or anyone else. I'm here to give you a message and to let you know I'll be keeping an eye on Hannah while you time travel back to the present."

"Who are you?"

"I'm a friend whose job it is to keep an eye on Hannah."

"Well, I don't know you, and therefore, you're not my friend, and I don't trust you. Back away and go back to wherever you came from...and stay away from Hannah."

"She's really quite a nice girl, isn't she? I especially like how Teddy here adores her so much. I think humans could learn a lot about relationships and devotion from animals."

Cole was unimpressed by the man's suave, lackadaisical personality, so he kept the gun leveled at his brain. "You don't seem too stressed out about this gun of mine, but I imagine maybe a hole through your leg or shoulder would get your attention. How do you know Teddy, by the way?"

"I'm kind of Teddy's keeper too," he answered just as unassumingly as before. "I watch over both Hannah and her bear and make sure they connect...you know?" Uriel laughed, but Cole held the gun steady...unsmiling. "Cole? You're familiar with a cute lady...fiery personality? Lady who seems to pop up wherever you are?"

"Yeah? So?"

"I'm to Hannah—and Teddy here—what she is to you. But right now she's following around a reporter named Lauren Molina, and I have an appointment with Hannah, so I figured I'd bring you a message from her."

Cole continued to aim his gun at Uriel, still with no hint of relaxation. "Hannah didn't tell me anything about this appointment you have. We'll have to check her calendar and get back to you. Get away from the bear and move along before I shoot you right between the eyes."

Uriel raised his eyebrows and gave a half smile. "I guess you don't believe me, so I'll show you." In a flash, he disappeared. As calm as could be, Cole time traveled about one minute into the past with the gun still pointed at Uriel. "I don't know where you're planning to go in about one minute, but if you don't start explaining, I'm gonna put a bullet in your forehead like I said I would... about forty-five seconds from now." Cole shrugged his shoulders at the absurdity of his last comment.

Uriel disappeared again and Cole zipped back in time another minute, and there they were again in the exact circumstances. "We can keep playing this game, or I can simply shoot you dead when I get tired of it, but I'd rather hear your story than scare my bear."

"Okay," he acknowledged patiently. "I surrender.... My name's Uriel, and I'm an angel...and so is Perisa. We're principalities, which means our assignments deal mostly with political, military, and economic issues. This isn't our plane of existence, so though we can manipulate things to some degree here on earth, sometimes we need help. Our latest mission...well, we need help... and the two of you are proving to be the right people for the job."

"Perisa's the babe that keeps following me around?"

"Yep. She's nice-looking for an old-timer, isn't she?"

Cole shrugged his shoulders again because he didn't really care about her appearance. He was just making an observation. "So what's this 'job' we're doing?"

"That, I'm afraid, I can't exactly tell you."

"And I suppose if I put a bullet in your head, I won't learn anything that you're hiding, so we're kind of at an impasse."

"That we are. Hey, I'd tell you if I could, but that's not how we do things. We steer and sometimes manipulate, but we don't have a master blueprint to go by. We're not in control of things—that's for a higher power—but we've been allowed to right some wrongs that occur, and occasionally, when it's not the right time for them to occur, we prevent some things from happening. If you'll put that gun down and trust me a minute, I can aim you in the proper direction right now, and *you* can be responsible for the choices you make."

"Which are…?"

"Right now, Perisa told me to send you to 3910 Calumet Street, Flint, Michigan. Ms. Molina is about to be murdered, courtesy of King Adnan of Jordan…unless, of course, you're able to stop it from happening."

"So I'm supposed to rush to stop the murder of the lady that announced to the world who we are, or I can stay and protect someone I care about? That's a super easy choice, dude. Pop out your cutesy angel wings and fly away before my weapon accidentally discharges."

"I brought Teddy to Hannah's rescue in the Smoky Mountains. I'll continue to keep an eye on her while she climbs this mountain. There're still a few things she needs to learn. I'll be helping her. Here's a picture of the inside of the house Lauren's in. Take your motorcycle. You would be best-served to help her before you head to Jordan to help Hannah's parents."

"Inside the house? You want me to teleport my motorcycle into the house?"

"Trust me; it'll be the best way out."

"And what do I do with Hannah's family if I get them out?"

"Do you have the picture of the ranch in Montana?"

Cole nodded.

"Take them there…five years in the past."

"Why?"

"Things have been set in motion, Cole. That's our job. Your job is to make sure they don't spin out of control. For events to go as planned, the family has to unite in Montana."

●●●●● ● ●●●●●

THURSDAY, JUNE 21
Five Days After the Discovery

Unknown to Lauren, she was being followed as she used her GPS to find the home of Shanice Brown. She drove down Court Street past Mott Community College before turning onto South Franklin Avenue. One block down, she took a right onto a side street and parked in Shanice Brown's driveway. Lauren's tail parked along the street slightly down from Franklin and covertly watched.

It wasn't a terrible neighborhood, but it was in downtown Flint, one of the most-violent cities in America. The Jordanian sharpshooter's instructions were quite specific: "Kill Lauren Molina." In Flint, it would be just another of the multiple monthly murders the police department would never solve. The hired killer, Saeed Momani, sat patiently in the passenger seat of a rental car, his driver playing a video game on his cell phone as the newswoman climbed out of her vehicle and made her way to the front porch where she knocked on the door.

The door opened and Lauren introduced herself. "Ms. Brown? My name is Lauren Molina from Fox News. As I mentioned on the phone, I'm here to talk about Cole Flint."

"Yes, yes...of course. Y'all come in out of the heat, Miss Molina. Excuse the mess, honey. My daughter jus' came by to pick up my grandbabies, an' I don't have the mess picked up yet. I love those babies, but they kin shore 'nuff make a mess. Kin I git you a glass of lemonade, honey? Come in...come in and make yourself comfortable."

"Please...call me Lauren, Ms. Brown, and thank you for allowing me to see you on such short notice. I don't plan to take up much of your time, but lemonade sounds wonderful. Thank you."

She left and returned in barely more than a minute with two glasses of lemonade in tall, clear glasses filled with ice. After handing Lauren her drink, she sat on a couch across from the chair Lauren had chosen. A large fan blew humid air across the sticky room, but Lauren was happy to be sitting and sipping the cool beverage. The small home was proudly decorated with dozens of family pictures. A lacy sheer, blown by the fan, brushed on Lauren's arm as she took a gulp of her drink.

"Are all these pictures of your family?" Lauren asked.

"I had three children of my own, and now I have eight grand-babies, but most of these here pictures are of foster children I cared for. Took pictures of each and every one that came through my door, and I still pray for them all. Do you believe in the power of prayer, Lauren?"

"I don't know, Ms. Brown. Sure, I pray, but my prayers never make it past the ceiling. Maybe I don't do it right."

"Well, if you don't have faith, you ain't doin' it right, young lady. What was the last thing you prayed for?" she asked as she surveyed her wall of pictures.

Lauren let out a half-embarrassed giggle. "Well, to be honest, I've been wandering around Flint all day, and I prayed for safety."

"It's a wise thing to pray for, but you don't think the Lord is listenin', do ya?"

"I don't know...He might be. I'm still safe." She smiled weakly.

"Well, Miss Lauren, I started prayin' for your safety the moment you called. The Lord laid heavy on my heart the desire to pray for you," she explained as she removed a picture from the wall and handed it over to Lauren. "When you pray in faith, the Lord kin do miracles."

Lauren studied the photo of a newborn baby boy, a blue knit hat on his head, happy brown eyes with flecks of emerald, and an actual smile on his face. "Well, I don't need a miracle, Ms. Brown, but I *do* want to know what you know about Cole Flint. This is him, isn't it?"

"That's Baby Cole, as I call him. The pleasantest, happiest baby I ever did see, and believe me, I seen lots of babies. That one was special. I'm still prayin' for that boy. It'll be nice to give him a full name." Shanice sidled up to her front picture window and peered outside from behind a curtain. A silver Infinity with two men cruised slowly past the house. "Miss Lauren, I raised plenty of troubled children for extended periods of time, but what I did most was take in temporary children 'til the agency could find a family. Three days I had Baby Cole—long enough to fall head over heels in love with that child, but they placed him with some white folks in a better neighborhood, I assume. I only got to keep the little black boys or the ones who was saved outta hell to spare their lives. Baby Cole was placed somewhere else in record time. I been prayin' for that boy ever since. Sometimes I wonder if I'll ever see him again."

Shanice's phone rang. "Excuse me, honey," she said. "Hello, Reverend....Yes, I did. I put the neighborhood watch on notice because I had one of those feelings I have...."

There was a pause as she listened, throwing in an "uh huh" and "umm hmm" and "I see" every once in a while as she continued to sneak peeks out her front window.

"Well, the young white woman is callin' on me, Reverend. She's my guest, but the silver Infinity that's turnin' around at the end of the street...you best be watchin'. Could be we're about tuh have some trouble....Thank you, but I'll be fine. The Lord's about to send a miracle; I kin jus' feel it."

As she ended her call, out of thin air, a motorcycle with a rider in a sleeveless red T-shirt sat in the middle of her living room. Lauren, who had been nervously listening to Shanice's conversation, screamed and yanked out her pepper spray. Before she could aim it at the intruder, however, Cole disappeared from the motorcycle and reappeared next to the reporter, yanking the canister from her right hand. In her left hand was a baby picture that he'd seen his whole life in a photo album his mother had kept. Shanice Brown peeked through her window before she remarked, "You must be the miracle I was expectin'."

"I do make a grand entrance."

"You shor 'nuff do." She stared into his eyes for a few seconds before saying, "I know them eyes of yours. Lord have mercy! All we did was speak your name and the Lord sent my miracle by way of my Baby Cole. It's you, ain't it?"

"Well, I'm not exactly a baby—though I do have soft skin."

"You was born on October 19, 1988, at Hurley Hospital, and your momma named you Cole 'fore she disappeared."

"What? My mother never disappeared. She lived until I was thirteen years old, and she died in a car accident."

"You're Cole Flint?" Lauren finally verbalized, after a moment of shock. "How did you do that?" she asked, still amazed by his miraculous appearance.

Cole totally ignored her and focused his attention on Shanice. "What're you talking about?"

"After your mama abandoned you in the hospital, you was deposited into my care by protective services when you was just three days old. Three days later, you was placed with a permanent foster family. Did they adopt you? You was the best baby I ever did see."

Cole stared at the woman while shaking his head no, but Lauren interrupted again. "I've been investigating you. I want to tell your story."

He glanced at the reporter barely long enough to give her a definitive "*No*" before turning back to Shanice. "You're mistaken."

"Maybe. Maybe not. But I don't 'spect you're here for a history lesson. You're here for Lauren, ain't you?" When Cole simply nodded, she spoke to Lauren. "Keep the picture, honey. I made copies when I took that one. I have another." She refocused her attention on her miracle. "Cole?"

"Yes, ma'am?"

"There's a man just climbed out a silver car that's 'bout to step onto my porch, and I think he's after Lauren. It's about time you do what you came to do."

"I didn't understand why I was told to bring my bike, but I think now it's so I can keep you safe too, ma'am. I have a plan. Hop on the back, Lauren. We're going for a ride." He handed her a helmet to put on.

She stuffed the picture in her bag and climbed on without asking a single question—something quite out of the ordinary for a reporter. Cole climbed on, put on his own helmet, and started the bike. He regarded Shanice once again and nodded in respect, receiving a lovely smile from the woman who had been praying for him his entire life. He revved his bike as the Jordanian hitman took out his gun and stepped onto the porch. He popped his front wheel into the air and drove straight through the front door.

He managed to dematerialize as he passed through the door and rematerialize on the front porch, the wheel slamming into the unsuspecting murderer, driving him off the porch and onto his back where the motorcycle landed forcefully on his chest, breaking several ribs and driving his head into the sidewalk. Cole quickly veered to his left and sped down the street as the man driving the silver Infinity floored his sports coupe and gave chase after the riders. Only then did the neighborhood crime watch patrol surround the badly injured man and kick his handgun away while an approaching siren sounded in the distance.

•••••●•••••

TWENTY

· · · · · · ● ● ● ◉ ● ● ● ● ● · · ·

CHAPTER 20
Four Years Before the Discovery

When Cole went to find Teddy, Hannah searched the cabin for things to take on her hike. She grabbed her backpack and filled it with bug spray, a hat, a couple water bottles, and a few snacks she found in the pantry. Another bag of apples that wasn't there the day before lay in a cupboard, so she grabbed it to feed to her bear and found beside it some hiking boots that fit perfectly. She outfitted herself in the boots, grabbed her staff, and stepped outside as Teddy wandered back to the cabin. She noticed that Cole's motorcycle was gone and was disappointed he hadn't said goodbye. Throughout the entire chaotic ordeal of the past few days, he was the one thing that was constant, and she immediately missed him and began worrying about him. She wondered if he'd be bringing her family back with him or if she'd ever see him again. The more questions that surfaced, the more she knew she had to wear off some nervous energy. "Let's go, Teddy." Whatever it was that the two of them were expected to do, she'd come to realize that she was going to have to wait patiently to find out. Cole seemed to be getting more direction than she was getting.

Hannah grabbed an apple out of the bag and tossed it to the grizzly. Teddy snagged it out of the air and chomped a couple of times before swallowing. He followed along as Hannah headed for the mountains using her staff as a walking stick. Every once in a while, when she needed a short break, she would jump on the bear, wrestling with him and laughing out loud. "I love you, Teddy! Who would have ever imagined me hiking in the Alps with a pet grizzly?" About an hour and a half and one empty water bottle later, they had zigzagged halfway up the mountain where Hannah stopped to rest on a sizeable ledge.

After lugging the gradually-emptying apple bag the entire hike, she was happy to toss Teddy his final apple, but Teddy's attention was immediately attracted to hundreds of thousands of moths he found sheltering from the intense mountain sunlight in the dark, rocky crevices. Teddy seemed to instinctively know that the moths of the army cutworm were an edible delicacy, and he began pawing at them, consuming them by the hundreds. "Ewww, Teddy!" Hannah scrunched her nose. "While you're gorging on gross bugs, you oversized glutton, you're missing an amazing view!" she joked as she raised her second bottle of water to her lips.

"You should see it from the top," said Uriel who sat about five feet away on the same rock ledge.

"Aahh!" Alarmed, Hannah dropped the bottle. She immediately jumped to her feet and raised her staff for protection. Teddy stopped eating moths and repositioned himself on the rock beside Uriel as if to block her from striking the angel.

Uriel patted him on the head. "Hi again, Teddy." Then he refocused his attention on Hannah. "It's okay. I'm a friend…here to talk to you about your future."

Hannah stared at him for a minute. "I've seen you before." After a few seconds of thinking, she remembered. "You're the Federal Express man who delivered the plane tickets—four years from now—aren't you? Odd seeing you again…up here…before I meet you in the future," she commented as if it weren't so odd. Teddy started licking the rock where Hannah's bottle had dropped and splashed some water before it fell over the edge. "Awww, he's thirsty, but now I'm out of water."

"You're completely capable of giving him a drink."

"I don't mean to be rude, but I just told you I'm out of water, Mr. Federal Express, so I can't."

"Use your staff."

"Why? Is there water in it?"

Uriel laughed. "No, but there's power in it to get water from this rock."

"Huh?"

He laughed again. "Tap it on this mountain ledge," he suggested, pointing to the surface he sat upon. "Moses got water from a rock. Surely you can do it too."

Hannah grinned at the strange man who somehow made her feel safe and comfortable. Maybe it was his smile.

"What's your name?"

"Uriel."

"Are you a time traveler too?"

"Ummm…sort of. I'm different than Cole, if that's what you're getting at."

"How does he do the things he can do?"

"You mean like beat people up? And ignore danger?"

"No, like jump and time travel and stuff."

"It's a gift. Just as the staff is a gift to you."

"Did he send you to me to keep an eye on me?"

"No. Actually, I sent *him* on an errand so I could have some time to talk with you alone. Get some water from the rock—the staff has the power to do it—and then we can talk."

She stood and tapped its end on the rock surface and water flowed out of it like a wide, giant water fountain. It streamed up into the air and curved as gravity pulled it down the mountainside like a diminutive waterfall. A cool mist washed over her as a breeze blew the scent of pine trees across the valley. "That's awesome!" she said. Teddy stuck his face in the water, his giant belly contracting with each great gulp. Hannah grabbed the empty bottle she had stored in her backpack and filled it before taking a drink herself. "Ahh, it's good. Do you want some?" she asked.

"No, thank you. I was wondering if you've found it to be inconvenient to carry that staff around?" he asked, focusing kindly on her curious, excited eyes.

"No, of course not," she replied sarcastically. "I enjoy having a six-foot-long piece of jewelry to lug around all day. Plus, I just *love* all the attention I'm getting."

"What do you suggest be done to change that?"

"Um, give it back maybe? I could trade it for my family."

"No…I don't think the people who want it are particularly good candidates to take possession of it. You, on the other hand, have a good heart, Hannah, so I think you should keep it. So, how about we make it a little easier to live with?"

"It's not like I can hang it around my neck like a piece of jewelry…and it doesn't exactly fit in my pocket. I hate to tell ya, but it's kinda too big to hide."

"It could be a piece of jewelry if you wanted it to be." He smiled that friendly smile that always seemed to grace his appearance. "Do you possibly have an open mind to reach a solution?"

"You're kidding, right?" she asked as she took another sip of water. "I'm hanging with a guy who teleports and time travels....I have a pet bear for some unknown reason....I'm carrying around the Staff of Moses which I've used to divide a river and get water from a rock...and I'm currently on a mountain ledge in Switzerland talking to some dude named Uriel who I first met four years from now. My mind's so open my head hurts."

"Well, as has been quoted an occasion or two throughout time, faith can move mountains."

"I kind of took that saying as hyperbole. I can't actually move a mountain...can I?"

"Well, not literally, but what's to keep you from believing so strongly in something that you would be able to accomplish feats you never believed you could do before?"

"How am I to have some special kind of faith when I don't even know what I'm supposed to be doing?"

"You're not *supposed* to be doing anything at all—well, other than keeping the staff from the bad guys."

"I should hide it then?"

"Hidden, it wouldn't be available if you needed it. Any other ideas?"

"Turn it invisible?"

"You're starting to think outside the box, but you'd still have to carry it, and how would you find it if you set it down?" he asked with another big smile on his face.

Hannah rolled her eyes. "I could shrink it down."

"How would you go about doing that?"

"Faith?"

He handed her a necklace with a bell-shaped cap on the end. "This is a gift. Insert the staff into the cap, and you can simply hang it around your neck—until you need it, that is."

"Just shrink it?"

"The staff is yours, Hannah. How do you want to carry it around?"

Hannah held the staff to the cap and immediately it dangled from the necklace, a thin, sapphire stone of about an inch and a half. She reached behind her head and clasped the chain, letting it dangle from her neck. "It worked! Thank you, Uriel."

"You're welcome. Apparently you have faith…so it's time we consider what it is that you fear."

"Is that a question?"

He nodded.

Hannah hesitated because she wasn't sure. "I don't know." She hesitated as she used her fingertips to toy with the shrunken sapphire. "I guess I fear disappointing my parents…failure, probably…the unknown? I really don't know."

"Why did you remove the staff from the rock floor?"

"I was selected for some reason, I guess. It chose me, so I pulled it out."

"No, that's not true. *You* made a choice to pull it out. *You* chose *it*. Don't you see that? And once you chose to possess it, you made a permanent commitment to it. Don't you see? You've been molded and shaped into the person you are, specifically for this moment. There once was a Jewish queen in Persia who was asked to risk her life for her people. Her uncle suggested that maybe she had been put in her position at exactly that moment in time so she could save her people. Maybe you were allowed to possess the staff, not for yourself, but for the benefit of others."

"Maybe that's true, Uriel, but how do I know? How do I know what to do or when to do it?"

"Well, we're back to faith. You need to trust that when you're ready, you'll be able to do whatever it is that needs to be done. But you can't be afraid to make that commitment. Courage isn't the absence of fear, Hannah. Instead, it's the conscious choice that there is something more important to you than fear. All you need is to have faith that you'll know when it's time to play your role."

"You've given me some things to think about."

"And here, Hannah," he added as he reached out to give her a small stuffed teddy bear. "This is a token. Keep it to remember our conversation. I picked it out because it resembles your dog at home. He's being taken care of, by the way."

As she reached out to grab it, Teddy lumbered forward and batted it out of her hand down the mountain. Shocked, she pointed to her bear to scold him, but he wore a gentle expression of innocence. Hannah started laughing. "Thank you, Uriel, but I already have a teddy bear. I'm content with exactly what I have. Plus, I don't think he wants any competition."

"I enjoyed our chat, young lady. You be careful on your way back down. I have a feeling that Cole's gonna have a surprise for you sometime today. Remember…you'll know when you're ready, and you'll know what to do. In the meantime, enjoy the adventure."

Hannah took her eyes off Uriel to give Teddy a few scratches behind the ears. "Thank you for the chat, Uriel…." She glanced up, but he was gone. "These are strange, strange times, Teddy," she sighed. She refilled her water bottle, unclasped her necklace, and tapped it on the rock, stopping the waterfall. She gave Teddy another pat on the head and said, "Let's go, big guy. It's time to go home."

●●●●● ◉ ●●●●●

Four Years Before the Discovery

After two days of mostly unproductive summit discussions, the political entourages from several Northern-African and Middle-

Eastern countries were dining in a private banquet facility in Piz Gloria. It was a 360 degree revolving restaurant which crowned the Schilthorn Peak, a 9744 foot high summit of the Bernese Alps overlooking the Lauterbrunnen Valley in the Swiss canton of Bern. A thirty-two minute cable car ride from the village of Mürren carried the political staffs to the mountain summit to enjoy a relaxing brunch with an unforgettable view.

After the meal, many of the satisfied diners made their way to the sightseeing platform outside the restaurant. They were provided with Zhumell binoculars with twenty times magnification. Israeli Prime Minister Edelstein and President Shalom shared theirs, while only five yards away, Jordanian King Adnan stood beside an invisible Cassiel, peering across the valley with his own pair. Cassiel steered the king to observe a very specific place.

Mesmerized by the beauty, Edelstein and Shalom sat silently for a few moments, but eventually Edelstein spoke. "This whole country is so peaceful. Do you think there'll ever be peace in our homeland, Elias?"

"Unfortunately, no, Binyamin. That's why we must continue to grow our defense. Our weapons, technology, and military must be second to none. Except for possibly the United States, there is no one we can truly trust." He lowered his voice and glanced away from Akmal-Adnan, who seemed absorbed with something he saw through his magnified lenses. "Especially him, Binyamin. He has changed, and there is an evil presence about him. You must be leery of him."

Edelstein, who respected his friend's wisdom, glanced at the King, who had become agitated and was focusing his binoculars and clearly trying to get a better view of something across the valley. The prime minister laughed. "Something has certainly gotten his attention."

Curious, Elias aimed his field glasses in approximately the same direction and began to peruse the mountainside. Because of some unusual reflections of light, it took him only seconds to locate what he was sure the king was seeing. There was a young girl seated on a flat mountain outcropping. She held a blue, gem-like staff while a large brown bear scraped a paw at the rocks behind her and shoveled something into its mouth. The staff seemed to emit a glow and occasionally caught the brilliant sunlight, reflecting it off the mountainside. She was either carrying on a conversation with the bear behind her, or she was talking to herself. The bear seemed to take no notice of her, nor did she seem concerned about her safety. Uriel was invisible to both men as they surveyed the scene across the valley.

Akmal-Adnan removed a phone from the pocket of his suit coat and placed a call. When it was answered, the king began speaking in Arabic. Elias took a couple of steps closer to eavesdrop.

"General, I've spotted her again….The girl! The girl with the staff! The same girl who used the staff to cause the earthquake that injured me!" he stated as he touched the scar on his face. "She's with a large grizzly bear. I'm sure it's her….No, I can't get to her. I'm on the sightseeing platform at Piz Gloria and she's up in the mountains on the other side of the valley." He used his cell phone to take a few pictures through the view lens, and finally seemed satisfied with at least one of the photos.

Elias focused his field glasses on the girl while he listened in on the conversation. She stood and tapped the end of the blue rod on the rock surface and water shot up like from a spring in an arc above the ledge and then fell into the rocks a hundred meters below. Continuing in Arabic, King Adnan exclaimed, "It's the Staff of Moses; I'm sure of it! She just drew water from a rock. The bear is drinking from it. General, that staff performs miracles, and I must have it. If she's in the valley, maybe we can locate her. Station men along the cable car route. If she's on foot, she can't get to Bern, but possibly she could take a cable car to one of the small villages. How hard will it be to find a young girl carrying a sapphire staff? Deploy some men who can blend into the mountainside villages and watch for her. I'll send you her picture."

After sending the photo, he ended his call and stomped in a huff back into the restaurant. The prime minister waited until he had passed by before commenting. "I wonder what that was all about. He seems genuinely flustered."

"He said the girl has the Staff of Moses."

"What girl? And since when do you know Arabic?"

"I was born in Jordan, Binyamin. My parents were from the tribe of Levi, and my father was employed many years in Tishbe—as we preferred to call it—in the Gilead Heights near the present city of Ajloon. I learned how to speak Arabic many many years ago."

"So you overheard Adnan say something about a girl with the Staff of Moses?" His curiosity was definitely piqued.

Elias moved behind his prime minister and carefully aimed the binoculars in the correct direction. "He was talking about that girl on the mountain ledge—the girl with the blue staff near the spring of water cascading down the mountain."

Binyamin scanned through the glasses for a few seconds before saying, "Oh, I see her now, but there's no waterfall and no staff. There is, however, a large, brown bear."

Elias took another glimpse, confirming what the prime minister had said. "I don't understand. I saw it myself. The king spoke of the staff causing an earthquake, and then I saw with my own eyes as the young girl used it to cause water to stream out from a rock. Adnan then made arrangements with one of his generals to blend-in in small mountain villages along the cable car route in hopes of finding her."

"Do you think the Staff of Moses really exists?"

"Aren't you aware of how the staff was buried with Moses on Mount Nebo before the Jews entered the Promised Land?"

"Not really, but you believe it still exists?"

"Well, the stories through the ages have always suggested that the staff was passed from one individual to another until the death of Moses when it was sealed in a tomb by God Himself...or possibly some of his angels. If it was sealed by a decree from God, then it still exists."

"You spoke of our national defense," alluded the prime minister. "Consider if we had that staff."

"And just think if the King of Jordan had it. I see no good coming from that," replied Elias. "No good at all."

• • • • ● • • • •

TWENTY-ONE

· · · · · · ● ● ● ● ● ● ● ● ● ● ● · · · ·

Cole roared the Kawasaki down the street with Lauren holding on tightly around his waist. The silver Infinity kept pace as Cole ran a stop sign and raced down Court Street toward Dort Highway. He slowed a little at each stop sign and stoplight to check for traffic and then accelerated rapidly down the street. Each time he slowed, the Infinity gained on him before losing ground once again.

The tires squealed around the corner at Dort Highway as they headed for the expressway. "You know your way around here?" Lauren yelled out from the back of the bike.

"Lived in the area most of my life!" he called back. When he slowed at a stoplight where cars were waiting for the signal to turn green, the Infinity caught up. The right-handed driver held a gun out of the window, but it was in his left hand, so the shots he fired missed and struck two random cars. "That was a little too close for comfort. Hang on!" he shouted as the Ninja roared back to life.

Cole weaved his way between cars while the shooter swerved out into the opposite lanes and passed the other vehicles. As he zoomed up the expressway entrance to I-69, Lauren asked, "How did you appear in that house, and how did we get through Shanice's door?"

The Infinity raced recklessly behind them as they merged onto the expressway. "Seriously? That's what you have on your mind right now? That guy's trying to kill you!"

Immediately, more shots rang out as the driver attempted to assassinate Lauren. Cole had the motorcycle racing at more than a hundred miles an hour, yet the car kept pace and shots were being randomly fired in their direction. "Yeah, because I was thinking now would be a good time to do it again and maybe if he can't find me, he can't shoot me."

"I can't just disappear. There's a good chance the guy would go back to Ms. Brown's house. We need to make sure he doesn't do that."

"Well, I hope I don't get shot while you're cooking up a plan!"

"Reach into the back of my pants, Lauren."

"Seriously? That's what you have on your mind right now? That guy's trying to kill me!"

More shots rang out as Cole steered wildly among several cars. "Yeah, because I was thinking now would be a good time for me to jump to a new spot on the expressway. Maybe if he doesn't see us, *you* could shoot *him*."

"Oh," she said as she grabbed the gun from the waist of his jeans. "I have it."

"Do you know how to use it?"

"'Course I do. Do you want me to turn and shoot back?"

"No, that would put others in danger. Hold on tight!"

All of a sudden, the riders disappeared from the road and reappeared behind the silver Infinity."

"Holy, crap!" Lauren yelled. "There he is in front of us!"

"When I pull up, empty the clip in his front tire....D'you understand?"

He didn't wait for her answer but instead whooshed quickly up beside the driver who had slowed somewhat while he craned his neck searching for the motorcycle.

"Now!" he yelled.

Lauren started shooting at the tire. Shot after shot rang out until the tire exploded and the car veered out of control. Police sirens sounded in the distance behind the drivers as the hitman swerved to the right and his wheels skidded uncontrollably on the shoulder of the road. The car turned and slid sideways down the road until the back tires dropped down an embankment, turning the vehicle another ninety degrees. The car began sliding back wheels first through the unmowed undergrowth before it rolled the rest of the way down the hill.

Cole and Lauren flashed past the tumbling car, but Lauren kept her eyes on the vehicle. "In the movies, it would have blown up by now!" Cole shouted, and precisely as the words escaped his mouth, the car exploded into a flaming ball. The confused police officer giving chase braked to a stop at the point of the explosion because the motorcycle had vanished. Cole teleported the bike off the expressway and slowed to a stop at the end of an exit. They had made it out alive.

●●●●●◉●●●●●

THURSDAY, JUNE 21
Five Days After the Discovery

Lauren removed her helmet, and after the moment it took to get her heart beating normally, she asked, "Where in this awful town is Grand Blanc?"

"Not far away. Why?"

"Because the doctor that delivered you is retired and living in the Bahamas, but the nurse who assisted is living in Grand Blanc. I plan to talk to her, and since we left my car—and I assume we're not going back for it—I need you to drive me there. Or maybe we can teleport and save time. We *really* teleported?"

"Yes. I'm a jumper," he explained as he removed his helmet. "Lauren, I was told to save you—the King of Jordan didn't take too kindly to your accusations, and that apparently earned you the privilege of a bullet in the head—so the best thing to do right now would be to get you out of here where no one can find and kill you."

"But I'm here to find out about *you*, so I can't leave until I know some more information."

"Why don't you just ask me?"

"Okay…why were you abandoned? Who is your mother and where is she? How did you end up inside Hurley Hospital? What about your father? Did either of them ever try to find you? How come you were never told you were adopted?"

She waited a few seconds, and when it became clear that Cole didn't know a single answer, she continued. "Since you don't know anything, take me to Grand Blanc and maybe we'll learn something. My assignment is to find out about you…but don't you think *you* deserve to know too?" she said softly, her dark brown hair blowing in the summer breeze, her curiosity strengthened by her sincere desire to help the man who had saved her life.

Cole rolled his eyes. "Is every female left in the world a pain in the neck? I'll take you, but then you're coming with me where I can hide you until I figure this all out."

"That's the spirit. Curiosity is a great motivator, isn't it?" She didn't say anything more as they replaced their helmets. Cole restarted the Kawasaki Ninja and smoothly drove away. As they picked up speed, she handed him an address and directions. "She lives on Oxford Lane." Cole nodded but didn't say anything. "Your father...? Carter? He's about as unlikable a person as I've ever met."

Cole turned his head a little so she could hear him. "He's a toad. He's lucky I only threatened to pound the crap out of him. But he knew I could do it any time, so he tried to stay away from me. I was pretty much parentless from the age of thirteen."

"I could see it in his eyes. He was responsible for your mother's death, wasn't he?"

"'Course he was. His drunk driving killed someone I loved, and *he* walked away scot-free. I, on the other hand, was defending myself from five muscle-bound dimwits when one died accidentally, and *I* went to prison for three years."

Confused, Lauren said, "I've investigated your life—two different paths, apparently—and there's no record of you going to prison. That's odd."

"Hard to explain," was his only response, and then there was silence until they neared their destination. "There's Oxford Lane." He took a left and found the house on the right, the third driveway down the street.

Lauren climbed off the bike, and then Cole stepped off as well. "Her name's Lillian Marsh. She's a retired nurse, but she was there at your birth. She must be home," Lauren declared after observing that the garage door was up and two cars were parked in the driveway. There was a stainless-steel screen door, but the front door was opened and curtains were blowing at the opened front window.

They removed their helmets before stepping onto the porch in front of the combination cream-vinyl-sided and brick ranch and rang the bell to the right of the metal door.

A chunky, curly-haired, blonde girl yelled, "I'll get it, Grandpa!"

She ran to the door and stared at the visitors without saying a word. "Is Lillian Marsh home?" Lauren asked the girl who appeared to be about eight or nine years old.

"You mean my grandma?" she replied.

"I don't know if she's your grandma, to be honest. I only know her given name."

"Who is it, Alexis?" hollered an irritated, male voice from the back of the house.

"Some people who wanna see Grandma!" she called back.

"Well, for the love of God…what is this? Grand Central Station? How many more people can stop by in one day?" he asked as he made his way to the door. He scrutinized his visitors for several long seconds before saying, "You're the Fox reporter that called Lily on the phone, aren't you?"

"Yes, sir, I am."

"Just a minute. She's in the bedroom watching soap operas is my guess. Come on inside. Invite 'em inside, Alexis, and I'll go get your grandmother."

The visitors stepped into the house when Alexis pushed the door open, but neither stepped past the threshold, and except for Cole's polite "thank you" to the young girl, neither spoke another word.

When the man came back, he was alone, but Cole could see the nervousness in his eyes. "She'll be right out," he stated unconvincingly. "Go ahead and have a seat there in the living room," he suggested. Lauren moved a couple of steps before she realized that Cole hadn't budged. She turned and eyed him curiously, but Cole's intense, unwavering gaze was on the man who had a hand behind his back.

He spoke directly to Cole. "You're the guy on the news report. The one who kidnapped the girl with the staff. The same guy who disappeared after that killing in Goodrich."

He lifted a gun from behind his back, but before he could even raise it parallel to the floor, Cole disappeared from his spot at the door and reappeared in front of the man. With a quick chop on the wrist, he knocked the gun free. Cole scooped it up, opened the chamber, and emptied the weapon onto the hardwood flooring. After kicking the bullets under the couch, he handed the gun back to the shocked man an instant before his wife walked into the room.

Lillian Marsh had lots of gray in her curly, brown hair and packed over two hundred pounds in her squat five-foot-five-inch frame, but it was her excitable voice that was most-memorable. "What are you doing with that gun, Leonard Marsh? Put it down right this minute! That's no way to welcome my guests!" To her "guests" she apologized. "I'm sorry. He's a retired policeman whose daily ambition is to make just one more arrest. And if he didn't have bad knees, a bad back, and a pot belly, he might be able to do it. Shame on you, Leo! Put that gun away!"

Leo was still visibly shaken, having been disarmed in under a second, but eventually, he set the gun on top of the piano that was against the wall nearest the door and stood sheepishly next to his wife, rubbing his sore wrist.

"He didn't kidnap anyone, Mr. Marsh," explained Lauren. "He rescued that girl, just like he saved my life a short time ago. And I don't believe for a minute he killed anyone in that fight." Then she gave her attention to Mrs. Marsh while Cole said nothing. He continued to carefully watch Mr. Marsh. "I'm hoping you can tell us about the baby boy I mentioned to you on the phone."

"Yes, of course," she replied. The volume of her voice reduced but the excitement remained. "Please sit down." Cole didn't move. "Young man! I believe I asked you to sit down!" The volume rose again to demonstrate her authority. "I've a story to tell, and my head doesn't spin on a swivel. You sit over there on the couch with Ms. Molina, and I give you my word that the retired old fart will refrain from any new feats of bravery." Her voice had softened somewhat, but she still managed to be authoritative when she said, "Get these young people some water, Leo. We have two celebrities in our home, and I've got a whopper of a tale to tell."

Only when Leonard left for the kitchen did Cole obey Lily Marsh.

"Mrs. Marsh, this is Cole Flint. He happens to be protecting me right now from the King of Jordan—believe it or not—but I persuaded him to bring me to you before he whooshes me off to the wild-blue yonder like he did Hannah Carpenter."

"I'm not surprised you got your way, Ms. Molina…"

"Please, call me Lauren."

"I certainly will." She focused her attention on Cole. "This lovely young lady probably already has you wrapped around her finger, doesn't she, Cole?"

"I mean no disrespect, ma'am, but I'd have to like her for her to have me wrapped around her finger. So far, she's been nothing but trouble." He voiced those words with a slight grin on his face that Lily didn't miss. Lauren tilted her head and glared down her nose at Cole, but he ignored her.

When Leo returned, he handed out the glasses of water and parked himself on a chair across the room, undoubtedly to "protect" his wife from the criminal, but when he studied Cole's eyes, he had to uncomfortably admit to himself that he was no match for his adversary.

"Mrs. Marsh, what happened in that hospital twenty-four years ago?" probed Lauren.

"Twenty-four years ago…my, my, time sure does fly! It was October nineteenth; that I remember because it was the day after my own birthday. Detective Dimwit over there forgot my birthday, and I was mad."

"You're *still* mad about that, Lily? I been makin' that up to you the whole rest of my life. I never forgot again, *did* I?"

"No, you didn't, but I put a sign up—'My birthday is October 18'—every year since. Men! Now let me get to the story, and quit interrupting me." She took a breath as if to settle herself down before continuing. "I was working second shift in Labor and Delivery. I'd finished arranging for a patient to be wheeled into Recovery, and when I finished my paperwork, I went back into the delivery room to get a bed ready for the next patient. There was no one on the bed when I bent to get a sheet, but when I turned back, a woman was there, and she was deep into labor." She paused and glared at her husband. "Don't you say it!" she demanded, her voice rising once again. "He doesn't believe me. Never has. Which is another thing besides him forgetting my birthday that I just can't seem to get over."

Leo shook his head like a broken man. "I told you I believed you, honey."

"Don't you 'honey' me!" she gasped. "If you believed me, I would see it in your eyes. Like Cole here. He believes me. I can see it in *his* eyes. You have striking eyes, young man—I find I can't help but say. Don't let this one get away, Lauren, 'cause I can see you already like him, and I don't see any ring on your finger."

"I just met him today…"

"Shush, young lady. I been matchmaking most of my life, and I know what I'm doing. Not including my marriage to Mr. Skeptic over there, my success rate is worth bragging about."

"Aww, come on, Lily! You know I've loved you for the whole thirty-one years of our marriage."

"It's been thirty-*three* years!" Her voice escalated once again. "You *do* know what year it is, right? My goodness, Leo, you should learn to keep that mouth of yours shut! Now, where were we?" she inquired while regaining some of her composure.

"You were in the delivery room when a woman in labor climbed into an unused bed," prodded Lauren.

"Climbed? Are you kidding? That's like saying Leo here could run a mile and live to tell about it. It's utterly impossible. The woman was already dilated to ten centimeters, and she was ready to push. There's no way she walked into the room and climbed into that bed."

"Then someone wheeled her in when you weren't looking," Lauren suggested.

"That's what I said!" chimed in Leo. "See? It's a plausible explanation!"

"You just said you believed me! I could see it in your lying eyes that you didn't." She refocused her attention from her husband. "How old are you, Cole? You're a handsome man and you haven't once yet rammed your foot up your mouth. Maybe it's time for me to be searching for a younger model since Lauren here won't admit that she likes you. No siree, Bob, she wasn't *wheeled* in. She flew in. Or she was beamed in by some futuristic science fiction thingamajig."

"That would be a transporter, Lily. And there's no such thing. Don't ya think we would've heard of another instance in all these years? Your idea's just nuts."

"It's less nuts than a woman with her baby's head pushing through her birth canal walking around a hospital and jumping into a random bed when I turned my back. How many babies you delivered, Doctor Marsh? None? That's what I thought!"

"So tell us about the delivery," Lauren interrupted, trying to save Leo from more humiliation.

"Well, soon as I saw her, I called out for help, and Dr. Stilburt arrived almost immediately. The girls and I believed he dropped an *h* from his name because who would go to an obstetrician/gynecologist named Stilburth? Lauren, honey, I would never have gone to that man anyway. He had the biggest hands I've ever seen… long, fat fingers. I'm telling you, before you choose an ob/gyn, look at his fingers. You'll be happiest with little, skinny ones. How in the world did a man with that name and those hands choose to be a baby doctor?"

"Somewhat ironic, I have to agree." Cole couldn't help but interject.

"Right you are, Cole. Are you sure you don't want an old, fat woman to take care of you? I can cook a mean meal. But I bet Lauren there can cook a mite herself, even though she could use some more meat on her bones."

"What about the baby, Mrs. Marsh?"

"Oh, yes, the baby. You're good at this interviewing thing, Lauren. Keeping me right on track, aren't you? You're simply adorable." She studied Cole and raised her eyebrows as if to say, "Don't you agree?" Then she continued. "Doc came in, took one glance and told her to push. The baby was delivered within five minutes. Cutest little thing. Never even cried."

"Tell us about the mother."

Lily glanced over at Cole again and smiled. "I don't remember her name… Elaine or Laney or Eleanor. Something like that. Man was she happy, that one. She called her baby Cole straight out." Lily paused…hesitated…considered Cole a moment…thinking. Finally she said, "She loved that baby. She cried and kissed him a thousand times at least. Kept saying 'I love you, Cole' over and over. That mother would never have abandoned her child…so I think she was abducted by aliens."

"Oh, Lord!" Leo exclaimed.

"You shut up over there! You don't know a thing! You weren't there. You were probably eating donuts and planning out your next speed trap—I hate that about cops. I spent thirty years of my life working in that hospital, and I know a happy mother when I see one."

"You don't have to defend her, Mrs. Marsh. It's okay."

"No, it's not! You're Baby Cole, aren't you? Another nurse took you away to clean you up, weigh you, measure you, take prints—you'll know all about that when *your* missus delivers a baby. Doc Stilburt had finished stitching your mother up and left, and I was there with her all by myself." She started crying. "I was cleaning up…talking to her…and doing my sad, old job the day after my own husband forgot my birthday! You don't ever forget the birthday of someone you love!" Her voice rose again as an embarrassed Leo repositioned himself in his chair. "And I turned around, and she was gone. I don't know what happened to her— and don't you tell me, Leo, that she could not've been beamed up into some spaceship or another—but now here you are, Cole, and you don't know your mama, do you?"

"No, ma'am. I thought I did, but I guess I was adopted. I never knew until today."

"That woman's looking for you, Cole. You can be sure of that. However it was she appeared and disappeared, it wasn't her own doing. You mark my words. That woman loved you and would never have abandoned you."

●●●●● ◉ ●●●●●

TWENTY-TWO

Linda "Linny" Laurinaitis was on a mission. Of all the rising names in politics, the senator from Michigan was on the most-meteoric of rises. She was the chairman of both the Senate Committee on Foreign Relations and the Committee on Homeland Security and Government Affairs. She also served on the Budget and the Appropriations Committees and was rumored as her party's overwhelming choice to run in the next election for the President of the United States. If any woman was fit to lead the country, it was Linny, but she found herself in the opposite political party as the president, who planned to run for a second term. President Stonehouse was not on the best terms with Senator Laurinaitis, so because she needed something handled, she went directly to Secretary of State Roland Bolander instead.

"Did you watch the president's farce of a press conference?" she asked the secretary of state.

"Farce? I think his speech was diplomatic and forceful. He showed concern and confidence, and he answered the questions honestly."

"Ever the confident politician, that one, Roland, but never the one to get anything done. He may have appointed you, and you may feel obligated to him, but you're better than him, and I'd have no problem reappointing you if I win the presidency. Get ahold of the Jordanian prime minister and find out if they're holding the Carpenter family or not. I want this resolved. You and I both know that our president is going to do nothing except interject some sound bites that make him seem concerned, but this is a *family* we're talking about, for heaven's sake. No one should be separated from or lose part of their family. Hannah Carpenter should know her family is safe, and the family shouldn't be sitting in some detainment cell wondering about Hannah. I lost a son over twenty years ago, and I still think about him every single day. I know how it feels to lose a child."

She put her hands on her hips and tapped her toe impatiently, glaring at Roland.

"Okay...okay." He gave in, picked up his phone, and made the request to his personal secretary. "Get Prime Minister Ghazi-Hazim on the line for me."

After several minutes of uncomfortable silence, his phone rang. "It's the prime minister, Mr. Bolander."

"Ghazi! How are you? Thank you for taking a few minutes out of your busy schedule....Well, yes she's fine. Thank you for asking. I'm sure she's at one of the kids' events as we speak....And your family?...That's great to hear. Listen, Ghazi, I don't want to take up too much of your time. I'm sitting here in front of Senator Linda Laurinaitis. After watching the president's press conference, she'd like to know what you know about Richard, Kristina, and Sarah Carpenter....Yes, they're the people that King Adnan detained on Mount Nebo...." He listened for nearly a minute as Linny sat with her arms crossed and her eyes staring lasers at the secretary of state. Finally, he added, "That's all you know? Surely there's more to tell? You were with the king when the family was arrested....Okay, 'taken in for questioning.' My apologies...Yes, I understand, Ghazi, but you must still be in the information loop. Do you know where they are now? If they're still in custody, do you have any idea where they would be?...The SOCOM facility in Jordan?...No, Ghazi, I have no plans to do anything. I'm just trying to ease a friend's mind. Certainly, if there's a concern, we'll be in contact with you....No, it's no problem. Thank you very much for your time."

As soon as he hung up the phone, Linny said, "Well?"

"He claims the family was simply taken in for questioning and released when it was obvious they weren't involved in the disappearance of the staff. He never saw where the family was taken, but he says since General Marid was involved in the detainment, they were probably taken to the SOCOM facility in Jordan, so if they're still in custody, they're probably still there."

"In other words, he doesn't know where they were taken, so he doesn't have any idea if they've really been released or not. And since there has been no word from them in three days, I think it's safe to say, they're still in custody, which means something needs to be done."

Secretary of State Bolander could do nothing more than nod his head in agreement.

"The family needs to be reunited, Roland. It was hard enough for me to lose one son. If someone took my other son, I'd move mountains to get him back. The Carpenters are in no position to be reunited with Hannah if they're incarcerated in SOCOM. They should be free to find their daughter. We need to start pushing the president to get them out of Jordan. And if he won't do it, we need to do it ourselves."

● ● ● ● ● **●** ● ● ● ● ●

THURSDAY, JUNE 21
Five Days After the Discovery
and Also Four Years Before
the Discovery

After saying their thank you's and goodbye's, Lauren and Cole reboarded the motorcycle and drove off. "Lily hugged you like a mother saying goodbye to her own son. What'd she whisper in your ear?"

"She said you're a good one, and I need to make sure you don't get away. You're not gonna try to escape are you?"

"Are you that naïve? She was still matchmaking."

"Yeah, I was kidding, Lauren."

"Oh." There was a hesitation. "She said more than that."

"She asked if I believed in aliens, transporters, and 'the wild blue yonder.'"

"Are you ever serious?"

"I'm serious about getting you to safety. I'm not as serious about finding the woman who abandoned me as the two of you are."

"Don't you think there has to be an explanation?"

"How about she didn't want me? Have you thought of that?"

Lauren was silent for a few seconds before she spoke. "I don't believe that." She hugged Cole a little tighter before asking. "Where are you taking me?"

"Well, have you been to Switzerland?"

"Just once....I went on the most-awesome hike ever in the Alps, starting in Mürren. It was about two years ago."

"I saw a sign to some cable cars leading to Mürren, but that was *four* years ago. Hang on."

Lauren secured her grip even more and closed her eyes tightly. She felt a whoosh, everything went still for a second, and then there was another gust of air as she felt a bump and sensed the motorcycle slowing to a quick stop. When she opened her eyes, she found herself in a gorgeous mountain valley in front of an isolated cabin.

"We're home," Cole announced.

They jumped off the bike, and Cole led the way into the cabin while Lauren tagged along, mesmerized by the scenic beauty. He opened the door and walked directly into chaos. Teddy had a couch cushion in his mouth and wildly shook his head. Cushion stuffing flew and floated all over the cabin. On the floor lay two other murdered cushions, and the third was well on its way to final decimation.

"It's a bear!" Lauren shrieked. She stepped back out of the door, holding it for Cole, but instead of coming out, he headed further inside—an act Lauren thought was unbelievably stupid.

"Teddy, stop that right now!" Cole yelled as he ran and jumped on the bear's back. With dust and debris still floating in the air, Cole and Teddy started wrestling on the floor. By pure surprise, Cole had the first advantage. The grizzly dropped the cushion and tumbled backward, only to wrap his legs around Cole, rolling right over on top of him.

In a moment of insanity, Lauren re-entered the house, grabbed the shovel that Cole had failed to return to the pantry, and smacked the bear on the shoulder with all her might, right as Teddy licked Cole in the face. The force of the swing probably didn't hurt the six-hundred-pound grizzly much, but it was done with enough strength that Teddy stopped slobbering on Cole and turned to see what just happened. When he saw Lauren, he let out a ferocious roar. Terrified, she stumbled backward onto the sofa, flipping it over on its back, her legs kicking wildly in the air as she tried to scramble off the cushionless couch.

Teddy moved to retaliate on his attacker, so Cole jumped off the ground and onto the bear's back, riding him around the room with his arm around Teddy's neck in a stranglehold. "No, Teddy! No! She's a friend!"

Lauren scrambled to her feet and ran to the kitchen where she faced the grizzly, her shovel brandished like a lance. Just as with prey in a trap, her dark brown eyes were wild with terror in the midst of the madness. With Cole on his back, yanking on his neck and yelling for him to stop, Teddy wasn't making much progress, but when Hannah stepped into the room, a towel wrapped around her head like a turban and another wrapped around her body, he stopped completely.

It wasn't that he recognized her because, well, she was hard to recognize, but it was her voice that got him to stop. "What are you *doing*, Cole? What is this mess?" And as she surveyed the chaos, she asked, "And who is *she*?"

Lauren was still in defensive posture behind her shovel, but it was clear that she was beautiful, and since Cole was bear wrestling to keep Teddy away, he must have brought her. Immediately, Hannah was self-conscious about her appearance, wrapped in towels with no make-up and pearly white skin compared to Lauren's natural dark complexion. Teddy tilted his head as if to say *I recognize that voice, but who's the fair-complexioned mummy speaking the words?*

"I thought you went after my parents, and I was *worried* about you. Instead you went out and picked up a *girl?*" She started crying, so Teddy shook Cole off his back and lay down right in front of her with his head planted directly on her bare feet. When she bent down to scratch his ears, the towel fell off her head, making her even more self-conscious as her wavy, reddish locks fell upon her face. Cole stared at her, speechless. He felt miserable, realizing how much she was worried about her family.

"You're Hannah Carpenter, aren't you?" Lauren finally spit out. "You have a pet bear? Cole, why didn't you tell me that she was here? Do you have the Staff of Moses? May I see it?"

Hannah glared jealously at Lauren before walking out of the room without a response.

When she re-entered the living room—about forty-five minutes later—she was fully dressed in tight-fitting jeans and a long-sleeved T-shirt, her hair styled attractively and make-up applied perfectly. Cole, with little-to-no help from Lauren, who couldn't go anywhere near Teddy without him growling at her, had cleaned up the entire mess. Even the couch cushions were restuffed, but they weren't much good in their torn condition.

Hannah sat down on one of the oddly-shaped couch cushions and glared at Cole. Teddy lay down at her feet. "What have you been doing today?"

"Hannah, I'm sorry I haven't gone for your parents yet. I'll go as soon as we talk. I was sent by an angel named Uriel..."

"I met him today."

"Good. So you'll believe me when I say he sent me to keep King Jordan—whatever his name is—from assassinating Lauren."

"Who's Lauren?"

"I'm a news reporter from F...." She stopped midsentence because Teddy had popped his head up and growled again.

"He doesn't like her," Hannah said to Cole.

"She whacked him with a shovel."

"Good one. Can't you see he's tame?"

"Not..."

The grizzly growled and cut her off again.

"He was kind of getting the best of me in a wrestling match," explained Cole. "I think she thought he was about to disfigure me instead of slobbering on my face. This bear of yours acts like a monstrous dog. Who would expect that?"

"And who again is she?"

"She's the reporter that recorded the events on Mount Nebo—including your family's arrest—and broadcasted my name and yours all over the news. It seems she ticked King Jordan off enough that he sent someone to kill her."

"Imagine that," uttered Hannah.

"Listen, Hannah. I'll go right now and see what I can do. You and Lauren can keep each other company, and I'll come back as soon as I can."

"I want to go with you. Teddy can babysit her and make sure she doesn't cause us any more trouble."

"You're not leaving me here with that bear. I'm going too," said Lauren, a demanding edge to her tone.

"You can't go. What're the chances that I can touch five people at the same time to transport you all out? What're the chances I can do *three* at once?"

Hannah's voice softened as she regarded Cole's eyes. "That's what I saw in your eyes. You're not afraid of those soldiers. You're afraid you can't get everyone out. I'm right, aren't I?"

All of a sudden, it was as if Lauren was no longer in the room. "I won't even be able to get to them, Hannah, unless they take me to them, and what if they aren't all in the same place, or what if they're in the same room but I can't get them all together where I can get them all out?"

"Then take me with you. I'll trade the king the staff for my parents."

"You know you can't do that, and there's no guarantee they'll let them out anyway...and then I'll have *four* of you to move. I need you to be safe."

"I have the Staff of Moses. It has to be good for more than dividing rivers and getting water from a rock."

"You divided a river?" Lauren questioned before Teddy growled again.

"You got water from a rock?" asked Cole.

"Yes," she replied as she continued to stare into Cole's eyes and ignore Lauren. "Maybe I can make some plague happen that will buy you some time or get us closer to my parents. I can help you."

"Hannah, if you were supposed to come, one of the angels would have told me. They're always one step ahead of me. It's like they're manipulating me—and you—to get something they want. We still don't know what that is, but they haven't steered me wrong yet." Cole's voice softened when he said, "I want you to be safe. I swear I'll do my best to get them out by myself."

Hannah grabbed his hand and nodded. Cole nodded back before handing his gun to Hannah and scanning a picture he'd removed from his back pocket. He smiled what he hoped would be a reassuring smile, and then he disappeared, reappearing at the front doors of the SOCOM facility in Jordan.

●●●●●●●●●●●

THURSDAY, JUNE 21
Five Days After the Discovery

When Cole arrived, he heard Arabic words that he couldn't understand; however, he was smart enough to infer that the best *modus operandi* would be to stand still while slowly raising his hands into the air—and maybe to keep his smart-alecky mouth shut.

Soldiers appeared from everywhere. Two scrambled inside the building, but the majority spread out around Cole with their rifles and handguns raised. When Cole failed to respond to their foreign questions about how he managed to get inside the secure property, a soldier kicked Cole behind his knees, dropping him to the ground. The intensity of the questions increased as he continued to remain silent.

When the SOCOM facility doors finally flew open again, General Jibril-Marid, stepped outside. He eyed Cole carefully before saying in English, "You're an American. Tell me who you are and what you want, and then we'll most likely shoot you as a trespassing spy."

"My name is Cole Flint." The general's eyebrows shot up in curiosity before Cole continued. He didn't miss the intensity in the trespasser's eyes, causing a sense of uneasiness. "I'm here to see the Carpenter family. Hannah Carpenter has the Staff of Moses, but she isn't willing to turn it over to you unless she's certain that her family is safe."

"You know where the staff is?" the general inquired.

"Yes. It's safe with Hannah. She's willing to trade it, but only if her family is safely released."

The general didn't respond. Instead, he gave an order in Arabic, and pivoted before returning inside the military facility. A gun rammed into Cole's back, and an order was sternly given. Cole took a cautious glimpse and interpreted from the soldiers' hand movements that he was to follow the general inside, so he stood and carefully walked up a few steps and into the building. He was led into a holding cell where he was patted down and locked inside without a word of explanation. About two hours later, he heard keys in the lock, and the cell door was pushed open. Two soldiers with handguns trained on Cole entered first, followed by a man in a William Fioravanti custom-made suit and the general to whom Cole had spoken earlier. The cell door closed behind them and relocked with a *click*.

Cole rose carefully and scrutinized the exquisitely-dressed man who seemed to be in charge. There was evil in his eyes, but his voice was courteous and pleasant. "Mr. Flint, I presume. I am King Akmal-Adnan. You are the young man who rode away with my staff."

"Hey there, Your Highness. It seems you're the old man who kidnapped Hannah Carpenter's parents. That's an awesome suit you have, by the way. I'm feeling *really* underdressed."

General Marid spoke. "How dare you speak to my king like that!" With a nod of his head he communicated a message to one of the soldiers who attempted to strike Cole in the face, but Cole coolly knocked the punch away with his forearm and jabbed a return punch into the man's throat. Gagging, the man dropped directly to the floor.

The second soldier readied his gun, awaiting an order to shoot.

"I really enjoyed that little scuffle, but I'm not here to shame your soldiers. I'm here to see your three prisoners. If they're fine, Hannah is willing to trade the staff for her family. Tell that one," he ordered with a confident nod of his head, "to lower his gun…I mean, I'm really terrified right now." By then, Cole had keenly evaluated each soldier and the general and had calmly taken mental note of their weapons.

The king's voice changed to a more sinister, demonic tone as Hoaxal began to take over. "You're in no position to make demands. I could have you killed on the spot. The staff is mine. Bring it to me, and I'll consider a negotiation for the family."

"Wow, that's a really creepy voice you have, Your Excellenciness. But apparently, you're under the delusion that the Staff of Moses belongs to you. It doesn't. It belongs to Hannah Carpenter. And since your SOCOM snipers already tried to kill Hannah and you tried to kill Lauren Molina *and* you've kidnapped three innocent Americans, I don't believe I can trust you. I say you take me to the family, so I can see that they're safe. Then we can talk about the staff."

The soldier rose from his knees hiding a knife he'd drawn from a sheath on his left hip. "And tell your soldier to put the knife down before I use it to kill him."

General Marid waited for his orders. "What do you say, my King?"

Akmal-Adnan calmly commanded, "Kill him."

Before the two syllables were out of his mouth, Cole had teleported behind the soldier with the gun. He wrapped his hand around the soldier's grip and quickly shot the man with the blade. In one smooth motion, he slid the shooter's knife from his sheath and sliced it across the man's neck. As he dropped dead to the floor, Cole kept a grip on the pistol, aiming it at the general who hadn't had time to move.

"Change of plans, oh Powerful Potentate. Have your general go get the Carpenters and bring them to me while I hold *you* hostage."

King Adnan was formerly the highest ranking Jordanian military officer and had created SOCOM, developing the unit into the "Arabian secret weapon." Considering his tactical options, he reached the experienced conclusion that Cole Flint was a cool yet dangerous adversary; the speed at which he took out two of SOCOM's best soldiers was beyond anything he'd ever witnessed.

Cole added. "I could shoot you now, but then you'll never know how I escaped, and that'll take away all the fun."

"I can send for the family, but you'll never get out alive."

"I got in, didn't I? You're not getting the staff if I can't confirm they're alive, and I can't confirm they're alive if I don't get out. General, bring me the family while I babysit your Monarch and think of more king synonyms."

Akmal-Adnan nodded his head, so Jabril-Marid headed for the door. Cole maneuvered so the king was between him and the general, and he kept his distance from the king whose evil eyes and demonic voice made him leery. The general ordered other soldiers who had gathered at the door to move away, and he left to collect the Carpenter family, the lock re-engaging behind him.

After a pause in which the king seethed with anger, he responded, "You have no idea who you're dealing with or how powerful I am."

"If being crazy and demon-possessed brings power, you're well on your way….Majesty…I just thought of another synonym. That's what I'll call you when I get out of here—Mad Majesty. It's got a really nice ring to it, don't you think?"

"I don't know who you think you are, Cole Flint, but there *will* be consequences for your lack of veneration to me."

"This whole situation seems pretty simple to me. You have innocent people in your custody. Let them go, and I'll bring you the staff."

"No. Bring me the staff, and I'll let them go."

"It seems we're at an impasse."

"It seems you underestimate me. There will be consequences for your flippant attitude and your contempt of my throne. Mr. Flint, I've now located her four times. I'm confident I can do it again."

"Four times? Unless you've invented a time machine, I really don't think so, Liege, and you should just be happy that I haven't shot you yet. You seem like a dangerous man. I have a feeling the world would be better off without you." Cole had a way with snappy banter, but the fact that Hannah had been seen by King Adnan in the past worried him considerably. If he'd seen her in Switzerland, it would *seem* that she'd escaped him, but the thought gave him a bad feeling that she could be in trouble. Time travel made little sense to him.

"You seem surprised that Miss Carpenter's circus performance on Mount Nebo wasn't the first time I've seen her with the staff. Maybe you don't know her as well as you think you do."

Before Cole could reply, the door unlocked and opened, and in walked Richard, Kristina, and Sarah Carpenter with General Marid close behind. Once again, he closed the door and the lock engaged. It was only the six of them and the two dead bodies in the room. All of the Carpenters recoiled in shock at the sight of the dead men, the two pooling circles of blood, and the young stranger who pointed a gun at the King. The general also had a gun in his hand.

"There you have it, Mr. Flint. I've kept them safe," said the King. "Until now...but as I informed you, you underestimated me. Today, one will die, and tomorrow another one, and the next day another...unless you bring me the staff....General, choose one to kill."

"Certainly," he responded with a smile. He grabbed Sarah. Kristina screamed, "*Nooo!* Please...please don't hurt her," she begged. "She's just a little girl!"

"No! Kill me instead," pleaded Richard. "Don't hurt her. I'll give myself up for her."

Everything had gone amazingly wrong in an instant. In an attempt to regain a position of strength, Cole said to the King, "If any of them die, you die." But his eyes were on the general as he spoke, and he failed to notice the king draw a weapon from under his suit jacket.

"Shoot her, General," the king ordered.

Cole reacted immediately. He time traveled and jumped to the general a mere two seconds before the order. He knocked the gun away from Sarah's head and shot the general in the temple, but before the general could even collapse to the floor, another gunshot rang out. Cole flinched, assuming he'd been shot, but when he felt no pain, he wondered if he had time traveled or entered some other dimension. A scream from Kristina brought him back to reality and the sight of Akmal-Adnan's smoking gun pointed in the direction of Richard Carpenter, who was lying dead on the floor. As the king began to turn toward the other three people, Cole placed his hands on the ladies, and all three instantly vanished from the evil man's sight. The next thing they saw was a ranch in Montana, five years in the past.

•••••●•••••

TWENTY-THREE

· · · · · · ● ● ● ● ● ⬤ ● ● ● ● ● ● · · · ·

Four Years Before the Discovery

Lauren saw Hannah Carpenter as the story of a lifetime. A cute, innocent girl of eighteen who was miraculously granted possession of one of the most-cherished relics in the history of the world. The Cole Flint story, she had to admit, was nearly as good. He was a great-looking, time-traveling fugitive teleporter who drove a cool motorcycle and was a fighter of super-hero affinity—and she liked him a lot—but the Staff of Moses could perform miracles and influence nations if it landed in the wrong hands. Whatever was going on, Hannah Carpenter with the miraculous staff and the grizzly bear was the better story, and Lauren needed information before Cole came back and interfered.

"I left Cole a note," Hannah mentioned as she climbed off the back of the Kawasaki Ninja that she and Lauren had borrowed to drive to the Schilthorn cable cars. "It's best if he knows where we are."

"You need to get your mind off him, and just take it easy for a while. I think this'll be a good way to get your mind off your worries. When I saw those pamphlets on the counter, I knew this was the thing to do. Two years ago—or two years from now, I guess—I took a hike up here that was the coolest thing I'd ever done. We'll take a cable car up to Mürren where there's a hiking trail to beat all trails. Be ready for the thrill of a lifetime."

"You keep saying that it's 'thrilling,' but what do you mean?"

"They'll put you in a helmet and body harness and strap you in with ropes and two carabiners which they'll hook to metal cables that are fixed to the mountain. It's a straight fall of a half mile to the valley floor, and we get to traverse the mountain wall and balance on wire ropes and metal suspension bridges over open gaps. It's similar to a high ropes course except about a half mile higher than you might be used to," she said with a smile.

They settled into the crowded cable car and watched in awe as it climbed over the Lauterbrunnen Valley's west wall before eventually making a short stop to switch cars at the peaceful hamlet of Gimmelwald which was set among meadows ablaze with wildflowers. It was at Gimmelwald that one of King Adnan's men and another older gentleman slipped unnoticed into the second cable car that would rise further to the car-free village of Mürren, set on a tranquil, elevated ridge of pasture that sloped down the sides of the mountain. It had the feel of a desert island, except the sea was replaced by infinite sky.

Lauren and Hannah stepped off the cable car with a sprinkling of other riders while the remaining passengers continued the breathtaking ride up to Birg and on to the Schilthorn Summit, nearly three thousand meters or ten thousand feet above sea level. They received directions to the hiking tour company and walked the smoothly-paved street along the mountainside, gawking at the beauty, wholly unaware that King Adnan's man had picked up a partner, and they were being tailed by two plain-clothed, Jordanian security officers.

Lauren paid for the equipment rental and their self-guided tour and read a pamphlet of touristy information aloud. "It says 'From Mürren, the valley floor is eight hundred meters straight down [one half mile], and the panorama of snowy peaks filling the sky is dazzling: You gaze across at the blank wall of the Schwarzmönch, with the great Trümmelbach Gorge slicing a wedge of light into the dark rock, while the awesome trio of the Eiger, Mönch, and Jungfrau are ranged above and behind in picture-perfect formation.'"

"Sounds fascinating," said Hannah dryly, her mind still on Cole, regardless of Lauren's excitement. "So are you gonna tell me why we're really doing this?" As she spoke and the women headed for the beginning of the tour and their final instructions, the Jordanian security officers paid for their own self-guided tour. "You're interested in Cole, right?" Hannah asked anxiously.

"I admit it. He would be quite a catch, but right now, I'm more interested in getting *your* story." Tour guides checked their equipment and explained that they were always, through the entire hike, to keep at least one carabiner attached to a guide wire, all of which were, in turn, securely fastened to the mountain wall.

Hannah kept quiet as Lauren led the way along an easily traversed path before bursting through a patch of trees into the open air where a view of the Lauterbrunnen Valley took Hannah's breath away. When they continued, the trees ceased to exist, and the path narrowed.

"Tell me how it felt to pull that staff from the stone mosaic, Hannah."

"I don't know…It was like it was meant to be, and I knew it, so I really wasn't surprised. It was actually kind of peaceful."

"Why you?"

"I don't know what you mean."

"Lots of people, including me, tried to pull that staff from the stone. It didn't budge. Why did it budge for you?"

They began to step onto artificial iron steps—metal ladder-like clamps protruding from the mountain rock. Several times along the way, they had already unhooked and reattached the carabiners, one at a time, to pass around a bracket holding the wire cables.

"I don't know. So far, I don't have any idea except that it's best that the King of Jordan *doesn't* have it."

They started climbing down a permanent metal ladder fastened to the rock wall. It was a tedious process as they each had to manipulate their ropes and hooks. Next, they tightroped on a narrow rock ledge that extended beyond the flat mountain wall. It was like walking a balance beam and concentration was needed. There was confidence in the safety of the harness and ropes, but they were balancing a half mile above ground, which was some-what disconcerting. At the end of the rock ledge was a waterfall that sprayed water on the iron steps, making them slippery.

"How long have you had a pet grizzly?"

"Two days. Or four years. Or maybe more."

"What?"

"Hard to explain."

"There're a couple of guys catching up behind us. Maybe we should pick up the pace," suggested Lauren.

"Or we could let them pass."

"Seriously? Where's the competitive spirit?"

Hannah smiled as they both increased their speed and rounded a corner. After a high intensity three or four minutes, the wall curved back out in the previous direction. They could see the men again, and somehow they had managed to be closer than before. "Holy cow! Are you sure you want to outrun these guys?" asked Hannah.

"I think they're trying to *catch* us. Why would someone...? Oh, no! We're in trouble, aren't we?"

●●●●● ● ●●●●●

Five Years Before the Discovery

Cole, Kristina, and Sarah reappeared outside a striking ranch home in Montana—the one in Cole's picture. As soon as their feet touched solid ground, the ladies separated from Cole, and somehow both stumbled backward, ending up seated in the dirt.

Cole, who still had a gun in his hand, realized the fear the women were experiencing. He slipped the gun into the waist of his jeans and raised both hands as if surrendering. "You're safe. Don't worry." He realized how hollow and preposterous his words must have sounded to two people who didn't know him and who had seen him kill a man only a moment earlier. Plus, they were sitting in the dirt in *Montana*. It was crazy to expect them to easily accept what had just happened to them.

Sarah wrapped her arms around her mother, crying.

"This'll be hard for you to understand, but I don't have time to explain details. You're in Montana, five years before Hannah pulled that staff from the church floor. You'll be safe here, but I have to go and leave you because that crazy king said he's seen Hannah several times before I took her away. I don't understand it, but I think she and another friend are in trouble, and I need to help them. I'll bring her here when I find them. This house is yours, I assume." After a pause, he apologized. "I'm very sorry about your husband, Mrs. Carpenter."

Kristina *didn't* understand, but she saw the pain, concern, and sincerity in his eyes. She nodded as she held Sarah, and before her very eyes, he vanished.

●●●●● ● ●●●●●

Four Years Before the Discovery

Cole reappeared in the Swiss valley cabin. It was empty. "Hannah! Lauren! Teddy! Is anyone here?" Immediately anxious, he made a quick tour of the cabin, and his fears were confirmed. They weren't there. On the counter, however, he found a note. It was from Hannah.

"Cole, Lauren and I have taken your motorcycle to the cable cars. We're heading to Mürren, where Lauren says she hiked two years from now. lol. Teddy's outside. It's 2:00. We should be back in a few hours."

"Crap!" Cole yelled. It was already 3:30, but before he could even begin to worry about how to find them, he found the pamphlet Lauren had discovered earlier, advertising the "car-free" town and the many outdoor tourist activities. He wasted no time teleporting immediately to the Alpine Adventure Trail Tour office pictured on the brochure.

A lady behind a counter glanced up with surprise at Cole's sudden emergence but didn't have time to ask a question before he blurted out, "Could you tell me if two young ladies came here to take a hike?"

"Several hikers paid for self-guided tours. Two women and three men."

"Lauren Molina and Hannah Carpenter? Do you have their names?"

She checked her activity book before confirming, "Yes, those were the ladies' names. Is there a problem?"

"Where's the trail?"

"It's marked outside." She pointed across the street toward the mountain precipice.

"Thanks," he said as he headed for the door.

"You'll need gear, and you have to pay if you're planning on taking a tour. You can't make that hike without safety gear."

"I can," Cole assured the woman before heading out the door on a dead run toward the trail.

●●●●● ● ●●●●●

TWENTY-FOUR

· · · · · · · · · ● · · · · · · · ·

Four Years Before the Discovery

Hannah and Lauren came to a gap between two cliffs. Strung across it were three wire ropes—two at shoulder height and one on which to walk. Pouring down beside the permanent metal cables was a waterfall, sprinkling a fine mist of water onto the wire. Lauren stepped out first to be the example for Hannah, who had never traversed such a thing. One at a time, she quickly snapped her carabiners onto the upper wires and stepped out onto the lower one to cross the gap. The wire wobbled slightly with each step.

Concerned, Hannah looked over her shoulder and saw the two men closing in, but behind them was something even more shocking. It walked prone on two legs like a human, arms gripping the guide wires, but it had wings like a bat and its legs appeared to be connected to each other by black, reptilian skin. The sight of the bearded, gray-haired man was so shocking that she immediately clipped her carabiners to the guidewire and stepped onto the unsteady wire behind Lauren. With both ladies navigating the high wire, it wobbled even more tremulously.

Lauren slowed noticeably due to the added difficulty, but she gritted her teeth, focusing on the impending, rocky lip, and she pressed on. Hannah teetered along with each and every step and was having a terrible time placing her feet firmly on the wire. Lauren managed to reach the other side without incident, but Hannah didn't. A boot landed inaccurately, and she fell with a scream.

As she dangled from the two upper cables, she beheld the ground a half mile below, and the resulting panic motivated her to start kicking her feet wildly, attempting to get one foot onto the shaking wire. It took several seconds before she was successful. In the meantime, the two security officers gained additional ground. "Hurry, Hannah! They're getting closer! Hurry!"

Hannah tried to regain her composure but was having trouble calming herself. Finally, she used her shoulders, strengthened from years of swimming, and pulled herself up high enough to place her feet back on the wire. With Lauren off, it didn't wobble quite as much, but her success was more hinged on her renewed focus. Step after accurate step was completed, and she walked off the metal cable just as her first pursuer stepped on.

The two girls reattached their carabiners and climbed down a metal ladder fixed to the rock. Once the descent was completed, they were forced to step closely along the mountain on more of the iron rung-like steps. The steps curved around the mountain and ended on a flat surface facing a bridge. The bridge had a metal walkway with ridges for surer footing, but it was basically a suspension bridge that hung from one mountain precipice to another. It sloped down to the middle and then back up to the other side. The bridge was strung across by two large, horizontal wire cables which were attached to the walking platform by dozens of vertical cables on each side, but there was only one shoulder-height cable for the walkers to attach to on the right.

Lauren, who was in the lead, hesitated. Somehow her cara-biners were clipped together in the most-recent exchange, and she struggled to get them unhooked. "Go!" she ordered. "I'll be right behind you."

Hannah hooked both of her clips on the cable and started walking ahead. The bridge was longer than the wire they had crossed, and there was much more wind in the larger open space. The metal walkway was additionally unsteady and difficult to negotiate. She held onto the support wire with her right hand, but with her left, she could only occasionally grab the vertical attachment wires. When she glanced over her shoulder, she real-ized Lauren wasn't going to make it. Hannah was close to halfway, and though her impulse was to continue to the other side, she stopped and tugged her necklace from her neck. As soon as she touched the sapphire, the entire staff grew in her hand. The weight caused the metal walkway to lean awkwardly and Hannah lost her balance, her feet slid, and she fell off the bridge.

Cole would look as far as he could safely see, and he would teleport to the next spot where he would grab ahold of the guide wire and consider his next jumping point. In so doing, he made quick progress, and soon he saw a man—or some otherworldly being—in a reptilian-like black suit. He appeared to have wings and two legs connected by some ghastly flap of skin. His next jump was to a spot close behind the thing, and when he landed, the creature glanced back at him. It wasn't an animal; it was the old, gray-haired man who had run over Russ Smallock with Cole's car. Whatever he was doing there on the mountain two years after the fight was more than he could comprehend; therefore, he jumped right past the man to the next sensible landing area that he could see.

From there, he could see the suspension wire strung over the gap in the rock. He jumped to the other side. There was a ladder down, so he teleported to the bottom. From there, he spotted the girls and the two men who were chasing them. On the suspension bridge, he saw Hannah turn, lose her balance, and fall.

The harness and attached ropes caught Hannah, but she scraped her stomach and chest on the metal walkway, and the pain caused her to release the staff which settled against two of the vertical wires, the tremendous weight tilting the walkway of the bridge several degrees. Too tired to haul herself back onto the walkway, she struggled to throw her leg and foot onto the bridge. By the time she finally got a leg up, Lauren was in the grip of one of the men.

Lauren fought to get away, but the man slapped her and threw her to the ground. He held her down as he glanced at his partner who held the guide wire with his right hand and was actually running—though at a careful pace—across the bridge. When he got to Hannah, she was still trying to pull herself up. He stepped on her hand causing her to lose her grip, and she toppled back over, dangling from the side of the bridge.

Hannah's attacker bent down and touched the blue staff gingerly with his hand. "Is this really the Staff of Moses?"

Hannah didn't respond, so he laughed. "I was told to bring you to King Adnan if I found you and you didn't have the staff, but here it is, so I no longer have to worry about your safety." He tried to pick it up, but it was too heavy. Speechless, Hannah stared at him as he called to his partner. "I have the staff. We have no more need for either of them. Kill her."

Both men took out knives, one intent on cutting Lauren's throat, the other intent on cutting through the rope that kept Hannah from falling to her death. As Lauren's abductor drew his knife, Cole appeared beside him and slammed his head into the side of the mountain. His knife fell as he crumpled to the ground unconscious. Cole picked it up and turned toward the bridge, ready to jump to Hannah's rescue, but Lauren caught him in a frightened hug.

From the ledge slightly above the metal ladder, the man in the creepy suit bent his knees and leapt forward into the open sky. He spread his arms and legs wide, catching the mountain air beneath his wingsuit. He flew straight for the bridge with what appeared to be practiced precision. As the second Jordanian officer began to cut away at Hannah's ropes, the winged man soared directly at him, grabbing his harness while flying overhead, pulling the officer into the air. The flying man tumbled and dropped straight down with the burden of the extra weight until he released his victim, letting the Jordanian fall the half mile to his death. Hannah was safe. The winged man repositioned himself and spread his arms and legs again, catching the breeze and flying away safely.

Hannah, still dangling from the bridge, observed Cole and Lauren in the midst of an emotional hug, and tears filled her eyes. Cole had witnessed Hannah's rescue, but he had saved Lauren instead of her.

●●●●●⬤●●●●●

TWENTY-FIVE

Four Years Before the Discovery

Take me home." Those were the first words Hannah spoke after she pulled herself onto the bridge and walked back to the mountain ledge. She clasped her newly shrunken staff back into her necklace and faced Cole, whose hand was held firmly in the grasp of Lauren's.

"Are you all right?" Cole asked, hurt clearly expressed in his eyes. He'd let her down, and he felt ashamed.

"I'll be having nightmares of me hanging from a rope a half mile off the ground while getting rescued by Batman, but my body's fine. Take me back to Missouri to my family." Cole didn't know how to break the bad news, so he didn't immediately respond. "You *did* rescue my family, right? You at least rescued *them*, didn't you?"

"They're not in Missouri. They're in Montana. At least your mom and sister are."

Hannah could see the pain in his eyes. Something had gone wrong. "Take me to them now."

To Lauren, Cole stated, "I need to get you out of here too. I'll take you home, but I need a picture to do it."

"I have pictures on my phone," she said as she scrolled to a picture of her apartment. Cole glanced at it, grabbed both girls by the arm, and dropped Lauren off in New York.

●●●●● ● ●●●●●

Five Years Before the Discovery

After dropping Lauren at her apartment in the present, they barely said goodbye before Cole delivered Hannah to her mom and sister in Montana where they had made their way into the house.

When they appeared in front of the house, Hannah simply asked, "Are they in there?"

"Probably."

She strode away without another word, and opened the door without knocking. Cole trailed behind like a lost puppy. When the door swung open, Kristina aimed a shotgun at her daughter, but as soon as she recognized Hannah, she dropped it and ran to her, holding her in a tight hug. Cole hung back, feeling lost and alone. In front of him, crying in a desperate hug, were two examples of people he'd let down. He hadn't asked for it, but his new ability to time travel had left him feeling more sadness than before.

"Where's Dad?" Hannah asked, tears in her eyes.

"He's not here, honey. He didn't make it."

Hannah tore herself away and scrutinized a sadly despondent Cole, but then Sarah made her way to her sister, sobbing.

Without saying goodbye, and with no real understanding as to why he did it, Cole traveled back to his former home in Goodrich, Michigan, leaving Hannah to grieve with her family.

"He's still a prisoner?" she asked Sarah hopefully.

"Daddy's dead, Hannah. The King of Jordan shot him. He murdered him."

"Cole couldn't stop him?"

"He stopped him from killing Sarah, honey. He saved Sarah's life, but he couldn't save them both." Kristina glanced away, hoping to speak with Cole, but he wasn't there. "Where did he go?"

Hannah rushed for the door, and stepped outside, but he was nowhere to be found.

●●●●● ● ●●●●●

FRIDAY, JUNE 22
Six Days After the Discovery

After spending a lonesome night soul-searching, Lauren finally checked her phone which had an inbox filled with messages and missed phone calls. She couldn't get her mind off her feelings for Cole, and she'd found it nearly impossible to put together the story about Hannah that she knew was so important.

She could tell by Cole's behavior that he felt horrible about what went wrong in Jordan, but on the morning news, there was no information about the Carpenter family. An Internet search about Flint, Michigan, uncovered news about a Middle-Eastern "terrorist" who was captured in a Flint neighborhood and additional information about a terrible accident on I-69 in which a rider and passenger on a blue motorcycle escaped a shoot-out and a police chase.

Finally, she called Liz, who had left about a dozen messages.

"Where have you been?"

"Good morning to you too, Liz. Um…Switzerland."

"Switzerland? You were just in Michigan yesterday. You're in Switzerland?"

"No, I'm in New York."

"You're not making any sense. What possessed you to go to Switzerland for the day? It better be good or I don't want to see it on your expense account."

"Cole Flint took me there, and except for some hiking rentals, there's nothing to claim."

"You met him?" Liz probed, her heart racing.

"And Hannah Carpenter…and her pet grizzly bear, Teddy… and two hitmen that tried to kill me in Michigan yesterday and two that tried to kill me and Hannah in Switzerland four years ago. Oh, and the King of Jordan murdered Richard Carpenter, but Cole saved Kristina and Sarah. They're in Montana, five years ago. I don't know where Cole is now."

"I've been worried sick about you, Lauren, and when you finally call me back, you feel the need to be sardonic and unprofessional? I'm not finding any humor in your sarcastic response."

"I was wondering how open-minded you'd be. At least I know now. And here's what else I know. Cole's mother miraculously appeared in Hurley Hospital in Flint, Michigan, and gave birth to a baby boy who she immediately named Cole. Then she just as inexplicably disappeared without her son, and she was never heard from again. The child was sent to Shanice Brown temporarily before being placed in a foster home under the care of Carter and Ellie Flint in Goodrich, Michigan. They dropped out of the foster care business, adopted the baby, and never told Cole he'd been adopted. Carter got his wife killed in a car wreck when Cole was thirteen and ignored him for the next five years before Cole got into a fight either in his school parking lot or at a gas station/Subway in town. Cole went to prison for three years, but for some reason, those three years of his life seem to be missing. Cole changed his name several times and he's now a teleporting time traveler whose mission seems to be to save damsels in distress, especially one with the Staff of Moses who has divided rivers and coaxed water from a rock."

Liz breathed an impatient sigh. "How much of what you said is really true?"

"However much you choose to believe. Why are you sending me on a wild goose chase in search of Cole Flint when Hannah Carpenter has one of the greatest relics known to man?"

Liz didn't answer right away, but Lauren gave her a moment. "It's because I want to know about him; that's all."

"Well, he's ruggedly handsome, and he's funny, strong, tough, courageous, and compassionate."

"You were serious about meeting him?"

"He saved my life twice," she clarified, once again recognizing the feelings she had for him.

"Your story's unbelievable, Lauren. But if I, for some reason, acted as if I believed you, could you tell me what's going on with those two?"

"I don't have the slightest idea, but the weird thing is, I don't think Hannah or Cole know either."

●●●●● ● ●●●●●

FRIDAY, JUNE 22
Six Days After the Discovery

Carter Flint stumbled into his home, still drunk after passing out in his car outside a bar. When he walked in, he saw Cole and fell to his knees. "It's you!" He held his arms and hands instinctively in front of his face as if he were afraid Cole was going to strike him. Perisa sat invisibly in a kitchen chair.

"Why didn't you ever tell me I was adopted?"

"Your mother made me promise, and after her death, I figured the least I could do was keep her secret." Carter started crying. "If you're here to hurt me, make it quick. My life ain't worth a darn anyway."

"Why did you never come to my trial or come see me in prison after that fight outside the school?"

"The fight was in town, Cole, and I never saw you since. I never knew you was in jail."

Cole remembered how he'd changed history, so his question became irrelevant.

"Why didn't Mom want me to know I was adopted?"

"Your mother was afraid she'd lose you, so she didn't tell nobody. And she wanted you to have a good life—a happy life. She didn't want you to know you was abandoned in that hospital, and she didn't want that lady to show back up and claim you."

"Why did you slap her? And why did you hit me?"

"'Cause I'm a no good piece of crap. I regretted that time I slapped your mom, soon's I did it. You, I didn't do nothin' to you that my old man didn't do to me. It's how I learned to discipline."

"You were nothing but a mean drunk, and you're responsible for her death."

Carter started crying again. "Maybe I was, but I didn't mean to do it. I loved her, son. I loved your mom."

"You don't know what it means to love, and if it wasn't for her, I wouldn't know either." Cole realized for the first time in a long time, he'd finally met people about whom he truly cared.

"You're here to hurt me, aren't you?"

"You're so pathetic." Cole took a deep breath. "I'm here to forgive you, *Dad*. I don't think I can ever forget what you've done, but you don't have to fear me." Cole sat in a chair and put his face in his hands.

Carter got off his knees, grabbed the handle of a frying pan from the kitchen counter, and walked slowly over to Cole, who had his eyes closed while rubbing his temples. Carter wound up and swung the pan as hard as he could, striking Cole on the side of the head with the metal edge. Cole fell to the floor bleeding, only semiconscious, but conscious enough to see his "dad" winding up for another blow. As Carter made his second swing, Cole time traveled only a few seconds into the past. He turned his head in time to relive Carter's "first" attempt to maim his own son. Cole reached up and caught his father's wrist, wrestling the weapon from his grasp.

With frying pan in hand, Cole's eyes blazed the intensity that had terrified his father for years. Carter, expecting retaliation, immediately fled, but Perisa had rolled up the edge of a kitchen rug in his pathway of escape. The drunk tripped and fell headlong into the kitchen wall, knocking a hanging calendar beside him onto the floor. Carter dragged himself from the tile, his nose broken and bleeding. A drop of blood fell with a splat on the calendar square that read "Friday, June 15." Cole stared at the date, an idea formulating in his mind.

"My nose is broke!" Carter wailed. "Look what you done! Get outta my house! You're no son of mine!" He reached up and wiped his nose and upper lip and flung blood droplets to the floor from his fingertips. Cole watched as the red liquid spattered the tile and the same "June 15" square on the calendar. Perisa smiled as she invisibly held the calendar with her right hand. The blood spatters weren't simply a coincidence, and Cole's idea solidified into a plan.

"Get out!" Carter demanded once again before wiping more blood with his sleeve.

Cole set the frying pan on the counter and headed for the door but stopped before exiting. He frowned at the pathetic man on the floor. "As pitiful as you are, I still forgive you, Dad. But you know…though I'll always miss Mom, I think I'll be fine without you." With that, he flung open the door, stepped outside, and jumped to Lauren's apartment. He had a plan in mind and needed some information.

•••••●•••••

TWENTY-SIX

When Cole appeared in the bathroom doorway, Lauren was blow-drying her hair, her clothes on the countertop and a towel wrapped around her body after showering. When she saw him in her mirror, she jumped and dropped the blow-dryer.

"Don't do that!" she complained, her hand over her heart. "I nearly had a heart attack."

"I'm sorry. It looks like I got here a few minutes late too." He smiled.

"You wish. Am I gonna have to worry about you popping in every time I take my clothes off?"

"You wish." Cole paused, gazing at her gorgeous face. He took a deep breath before he spoke again. "I need you to do something for me—two things, actually."

Lauren shut off her blow-dryer and considered his saddened eyes, but when she did, she also saw something more—hope.

"What is it?"

"I need you to find out if there's any event that happened in Jordan with the king on June fifteenth. I need to know where he was that day."

"There are people at the news station who could find that out. What else? You mentioned there were two things."

"I have no idea how you might do it, but I'd like you to help me find my mother."

"You saved my life twice, Cole. I'd love to help you *find* yours. I'll do what I can."

"I know. Thank you."

"Cole? What's going on with you and Hannah? I don't understand."

"That first day I time traveled, an angel told me that I needed to help her. That's what I've been trying to do ever since. I'm not doing so well."

"Do you know why you're helping her?"

"Not really. But everything points to the King of Jordan. I know he's evil, but I don't know what he's up to."

"I think I can help you with that. Hold on a minute." Lauren made a phone call to a friend at the news station, asking for details about the King of Jordan on June fifteenth. When she was done, she pushed Cole out of the bathroom and shut the door. Twenty-five minutes later, she finally emerged, more beautiful than Cole had ever seen her.

She smiled, and Cole grinned back at her. "From what I've learned, the King of Jordan has been trying to unify the Middle East. There is a lot of speculation that he has nuclear capability. He's signed a treaty with Turkey and Egypt already, and rumor has it that he wants one with Israel too before moving on to the oil producing nations. President Stonehouse and NATO have worked to stop him in his attempt to build nuclear power plants because Israel keeps providing evidence that he's really planning to build nuclear bombs. He's the man who built SOCOM and trained the first SOCOM soldiers who are comparable to our Navy SEALS. When his father died, he became king and he's built up his military exponentially. Certainly, he believes that the Staff of Moses belongs to him since it was discovered on Jordanian land. What he would do with it is anyone's guess."

"He's evil, Lauren. I saw it in his eyes…heard it in his devil-voice. Within only a few minutes, he ordered me to be killed, then Hannah's sister, and then he murdered Hannah's dad. He thought nothing of it. But I don't believe the staff would be useful to him in the least. It isn't meant for him; it's meant for Hannah."

Lauren's ring tone played, and she answered her phone. It was her contact at the news station. After listening and scribbling down some information, she said, "Just a minute, Tommy."

While regarding Cole, she recited, "Tommy says that on June fifteenth, a political contingent from Israel visited the Bosman Palace. It included the prime minister, the president, and the foreign affairs minister. It was King Adnan's initial attempt to persuade Israel to sign a treaty. Is there anything specific you need to know?"

"Yeah, ask him if he knows a specific time and the location of the meeting."

Lauren relayed the question and waited impatiently for an answer. When it came, she relayed the information to Cole. "He says the meeting was scheduled for 4:00 p.m., Jordanian time and was in the king's office at the Palace."

"Can I get a picture of the office?" Cole asked.

Lauren relayed the question and gave her home email address for the photo to be sent. She thanked Tommy, hung up, went to her computer, and opened up her email to wait for the picture. Cole seemed uneasy, so she asked him if he wanted to sit down. "Can I get you something to drink?"

"No, thank you."

"You're always so polite…" she observed. "How you talked to Shanice Brown and Lily Marsh…and how you treat Hannah." She didn't get any response. She sat down next to him on her couch and took his hand. "What are you thinking about?"

He smiled. "You mean besides *you*, right?"

"Yeah. Well, I figured you were thinking about me," she flirted, "but what about June fifteenth? What about Hannah?"

"It seems to me I've been watching over her until she's ready to face the King. We're being manipulated somehow to prepare us to meet him, but since she found that staff and you broadcasted it all over the world, I can't see how she'll ever be safe even if she somehow defeats him."

"I'm sorry. If I could undo it, I would. I swear."

"Well, you can't. But I think I can."

"How?"

"The staff was discovered on June sixteenth. If we can take him down before the staff is placed in that church, then maybe we can actually change history and the event on Mount Nebo will never happen."

There was a beep, notifying Lauren that an email had arrived. She went to her computer and downloaded the zip file. It had four separate views of Adnan's office. Cole examined them and chose one in the corner, away from a conference table. Lauren printed it and gave it to him. While he folded it and put it in his back pocket, she wrapped her arms around him and buried her head in his chest. Cole closed his eyes and placed his cheek on her head, inhaling the fragrance of her hair and perfume. He held her at her waist, his fingers touching the skin beneath her short shirt.

She lifted her head and met his eyes before gently kissing him. Cole took in her kiss and returned it. As much as Lauren wanted to keep him with her, her mind spun, and though she already knew the answer, she interrupted the kiss. "If you want to change the future, you'll have to take Hannah there, won't you? What if you fail and something happens to you?"

"We have to believe that everything that's happened has a purpose for good. I can't imagine that we've been selected only to fail. I believe our purpose is to stop the King of Jordan. I don't think he'll ever give up searching for that staff."

Lauren considered Cole's statement. "Well, if you have her placed back in time, how can he get to her?"

"He saw her on Mount Nebo, and everywhere I've placed her so far, he's found her. He told me he's located her four times already." There was a pause. "Oh, crap!"

"What?"

"After Mount Nebo, he found her in Tennessee and in Switzerland. Now she's in Montana. It's the only other place she's been since she found that staff, and he's seen her *four* times. She could be in danger again. I'm sorry, but I have to go."

●●●●● ● ●●●●●

Five Years Before the Discovery

Hannah, you're driving me crazy. You stand up, stomp around, sit down, and do it all over again. And you've been doing it for hours. And why do you keep watching out the windows?" her mother asked, her eyes still red from crying.

"Mom, I know you're gonna find this hard to believe, but I'm looking for Teddy."

"Your dog? Why in the world would he be here? Actually, he wouldn't even be alive if this is five years back in time like your boyfriend said."

"He's *not* my boyfriend, and I'm talking about my *bear*."

"If he's not your boyfriend, why are you so miserable?" asked Sarah, who should have known better than to ask because she was miserable herself.

"First of all, my *dad* was murdered. You *both* should understand how I'm feeling. Secondly, I miss my dog, but I keep expecting to see my bear—yes, I now have a pet bear. And thirdly, where *is* Cole? Isn't he supposed to be watching over me? He's probably with *Lauren*," she said with disgust.

"Maybe you should go get some air, honey. We're five years in the past on a remote patch of land in Northwest Montana. I can't imagine we could be safer. Go get some exercise. Everyone grieves in their own way. Sitting around doesn't seem to be what's best for you."

"Fine," she remarked as she yanked her hiking boots onto her feet. That was exactly what she wanted anyway. Teddy was probably wandering around out there somewhere, but even if he wasn't, being shut up in a house after all the recent adventures was driving her crazy. Plus, she needed to do something to get her mind off Cole.

Her hand instinctively reached for her sapphire necklace as she closed the door and started a hike into the landscape of rugged mountain peaks and alpine lakes cut by clear streams. Besides the picturesque mountains in the distance, Hannah saw giant red cedar trees, an array of wildflowers that she recognized such as violets and buttercups. Huckleberries and wild blackberries, and numerous small game were also visible. Far ahead, she could see a lake to her left and a flat patch with scattered trees to her right. It was in the scattered trees that she saw a grizzly. The bear was eating mushrooms and digging up some roots and tubers.

A sense of joy began to ease into her soul. She wasn't sure, but she had a good feeling that the grizzly was her Teddy. She slipped off her necklace and watched as her staff expanded to its full size. She planned to use it as protection if she was wrong. As she started toward the huge animal, however, she gasped in wonder. Lumbering up to its mother was a cub. She paused to consider what to do, and then in the distance, she saw a jeep driving toward the bears.

"Look," said King Akmal-Adnan as he perused the landscape with his field glasses. "A bear."

His hunting guide took a quick glimpse. "We could hunt black bears, but that's a grizzly. You can't shoot that. And it's a mother with her cub."

"We'll say we made a mistake."

"No way. You pay me because of my knowledge and expertise. The animal we're approaching has a dish-shaped face; small, rounded ears; and a shoulder hump. Clearly, it's a grizzly."

"Driver, make your way toward those trees. I would love to have a trophy bear head and a bearskin rug."

"Sir…Your Highness…you're here to hunt nothing more than mountain lions, antelope, or big horn sheep. It's against the law to hunt a grizzly here in Montana."

"Do you think I care about your laws? I paid a lot of money to have you guide me on this hunt, so I expect you to cooperate."

"There would be a huge fine, and I could lose my job. Sir, I'm pleading with you to reconsider."

"I am not concerned about your job or your country's petty fines. We will continue toward those trees, and I will shoot my prize as I wish."

"I have to forbid it, sir. You may not shoot a mother grizzly with a cu…"

Before he could finish his sentence, King Adnan bashed him in the side of the head with his hunting rifle, knocking him unconscious. Then he pointed his rifle at the driver. "Driver, you will continue toward that bear. You may tell your employers that I forced you…and your friend was rendered unconscious for his protests, but you *will* continue on as I say."

With fear in his voice, the driver replied, "Yes, sir. As you wish."

The jeep maneuvered to within fifty yards of the bears and stopped. King Adnan rose from his seat and aimed his rifle. The mother grizzly, sensing danger, rose onto her back legs—more than seven feet tall—and roared at the jeep.

"*No!!*" shouted Hannah, who ran in the direction of the impending disaster. "Don't shoot!!"

But there was no stopping the merciless king. A shot rang out…then another…and another. The bear was struck once before running toward the shooter in an attack. The second shot connected and then the third. The bear went down. The shooter reaimed his rifle at the cub…and Hannah lifted her staff before slamming it into the ground.

A rumbling growled from the earth, and the ground shook violently. The king took aim and fired, missing his mark. The earth continued to heave and buckle. The ground split open and divided like a canyon, Hannah and the cub on one side, the dead grizzly and the jeep on the other. The earth on King Adnan's side rose into the air and buckled again, throwing the jeep over backward. The vehicle crashed to the ground, its passengers violently tossed from it. King Adnan's head careened against a jagged rock, splitting his face open in a ghastly, laceration.

Out of nowhere Cole appeared beside the cub that was terrified as the land rolled in crazy bounces. He teleported it to Hannah a safe distance from the trees that leaned precariously before toppling to the ground.

There was Hannah, standing tall on a grassy mound with her sapphire staff glowing a remarkable blue. There also was King Adnan. Cole recognized him immediately. Blood streamed down his face, and he stared directly at Hannah and the bear cub with wonder and astonishment. Then the ground buckled one more time, throwing the king once again and raising a wall of rock which blocked him from view. Only then did Hannah stop glaring at the king and realize that Cole stood next to her with a small grizzly that had little, round ears making him look exactly like a teddy bear. In Cole's hand was a small bag of apples that he tossed to Hannah.

"I think we just found Teddy for the first time."

Hannah extracted an apple from the bag and offered it to the trembling cub. He sniffed it and regarded it as if asking Hannah for permission. Cole simply smiled.

"Eat it, Teddy," said Hannah. "That evil man just killed your momma, but I'll take care of you. I'll take care of you, Teddy." She began crying, and as the bear chomped on the apple, she hugged him around the neck. "Thank you for coming, Cole. You saved, Teddy."

"Hannah…that man. The one who was staring at you. That was the King of Jordan. He's the man who killed your father."

●●●●● ● ●●●●●

FRIDAY, JUNE 22
Six Days After the Discovery

Once Cole left, Lauren decided to head to the Fox News offices in hope of getting access to much more powerful computers than she possessed. She was determined to help Cole find his mother, but all she had were two facts and two theories. The first fact she knew was the time and date of the birth, and the second was that she knew the baby's name. Because she had been witness to actual time traveling and teleporting, her first theory was that maybe someone else could do it too. She figured if Cole's mother was a time traveler who abandoned her baby, she would probably never be found. But the other theory was that the mother was transported against her will—first-hand accounts seemed to verify that she loved and intended to keep her child—and if that was true, maybe a kidnapping was reported or maybe there would be medical records about a delivery without a baby. Maybe there would be a record of the mother searching for her child or a crazy report of a mother claiming an abduction.

She had some keywords for her computer search, and she had a computer whiz from the technology department helping—just in case. Frantically, she scribbled down information that they dug up. She expected a lot of frustration. She didn't expect to easily find a possible answer. She got what she *didn't* expect.

●●●●● ● ●●●●●

TWENTY-SEVEN

· · · · · · ●●●● ● ●●●● · · · · ·

Five Years Before the Discovery

Cole moved Hannah and Teddy into the mountains where the king would never find them if he attempted a search. Teddy calmed down while eating the apples and seemed very content being petted by two human beings.

"I'm angry," Hannah admitted.

"You have every right to be."

"He killed my dad. He tried to kill me and you and my little sister...."

"And Lauren."

Hannah didn't acknowledge Cole's comment. "Then he tried to kill Teddy. He's made this very personal."

Teddy seemed to sense Hannah's ire, so he picked up his paw and placed it on her lap.

"Maybe it's time we put an end to this, Hannah, and I think I know how." As Cole watched, Hannah lifted the staff and it shrank in her hand before she snapped it back into her necklace. "That was cool."

"Yep." She was focused and angry and not in the mood for Cole's off-topic comments. "Tell me your plan, and then we can both get on with our separate lives," she demanded.

"You're mad. You blame me for your dad, don't you?" The inner demons rose once again to the surface. It seemed to Cole that he was meant to be unhappy. Violence seemed to follow him wherever he went, and whenever he found good in his life, something bad seemed to inevitably snatch it away. Hannah was good, but his failure to save her dad would become a permanent impediment to their relationship, and the thought of that saddened him more than he ever would have thought.

"No, Cole, I don't. But yes, I'm mad. I'm mad at you, that Royal pain in my butt…and Lauren too. My life is complicated enough without her. Why does *she* have to be a part of all of this?"

"I don't know what to say. I don't have any answers for you. I still don't know why we're being put through all of this, but until it's over, the two of us are a team, Hannah. And it's high time we put an end to that evil man's reign. Let's end this thing together."

"Then I'll go back to my family and start over, and you can go off and do whatever it is that you want to do, separate from me. I'll no longer be a burden to you. What's the plan?"

Cole didn't like the way those words sounded, but it was the second time she'd used them. It seemed that she was ready to part ways. Hannah could see the hurt her words had caused, but at that moment, she didn't care. He could jump on out of her life and live happily ever after with whomever he chose, but she had her whole life ahead of her, and she was determined to make the most of it. Once King Akmal-Adnan was defeated, she'd move on.

Uncomfortably, Cole started. "I happen to know that King Adnan was in his office at 4:00 p.m. in Jordan on June fifteenth.

I have no doubt that if we crash that meeting, violence will break out. I'll kill him, Hannah, and then he'll never be on that mountain where you grabbed the staff. Maybe we'll change history enough so those angels who are manipulating us won't even plant the staff in that church. Maybe then we can live our lives free of people trying to track us down."

Hannah stared off into space, thinking. Cole waited. Finally, she said, "Let's do it, but there's one thing wrong with your plan."

"What's that?"

"You won't kill the king. *I* will."

● ● ● ● ● ● ● ● ● ● ●

Five Years Before the Discovery

Cole stood sheepishly across the room as Hannah and her mother argued.

"This has to end, Mom. I...*we* believe that the reason we were chosen and given the gifts we were given was for this moment. The King of Jordan is a possessed lunatic who won't stop until he gets what he wants. He wants to monopolize control of the whole Middle East, and he wants the Staff of Moses. I...*we* can't let him get either thing."

"It isn't safe; I can't let you do it."

"Mom, why do you write?"

"Because I was given the skills, the knowledge, and the creativity to do it. It's my gift, and I use it to the best of my ability."

"And why did Dad do his research?"

"Because he had a passion and a gift for it. He loved it, and that made him great at it."

"So what's *my* gift, Mom? What in the world have I ever had that made *me* special?"

Kristina hesitated.

"*Exactly*! You can't think of one thing."

"That's not true! You're special in lots of ways."

"On Saturday, June sixteenth, we sat in our kitchen and Dad told me I could save the world. You said to me that one day I would make my mark on the world….You did it. Daddy did it. Sarah's going to someday. So what do *I* have that makes it possible to make *my* mark?"

"Well," she struggled, "you have a grizzly bear as a pet…"

"You have the Staff of Moses," interjected Sarah. "She has the Staff of Moses, Mother. If anyone can make her mark, it's Hannah. And don't forget…she has that super hero over there to watch her back. Let her go, Mom. It's what she was meant to do."

Kristina was speechless. She looked at Cole whose eyes were filled once again with that burning intensity, but she could swear he was also admiring her daughter with pride. Maybe something more than pride. Finally, Cole assured Kristina. "I'll watch over her, ma'am. I'll protect her. I'll give my life for her if I have to." Hannah practically twirled around to face Cole. "I've got your back, Hannah. I promise to bring you back to your family."

"Mom…let her go," Sarah said. "If he says she'll be back, she'll be back."

Kristina wrapped her arms around Hannah. "I know. What kind of mother would I be if I didn't worry about you? You're right. Your gift is that staff…and the biggest heart of anyone I know. Do what you're meant to do."

Everyone gave hugs and tears flowed, but finally Hannah took her necklace from her neck. The staff grew to its full size, and she stepped next to Cole, grabbing his hand. It's time. Let's do it."

Cole had stared at the picture of Akmal-Adnan's office for so long he'd memorized it. He nodded, and they disappeared together from the room.

●●●●●●●●●●●

FRIDAY, JUNE 15
One Day Before the Discovery

When Cole and Hannah appeared in the king's office, they couldn't see a thing, but they heard, "Will you be *for* me or against me?"

There was a rustling sound around them that was so close they could practically feel it.

"Are we there?" Hannah asked.

"I'm not sure *where* we are."

"*Shhh!*" they heard. Only then did they realize that they were surrounded by three winged beings who were blocking their vision. Perisa and Uriel were two of the beings. The third Cole didn't recognize.

"Take us all to your grandfather's cottage," Perisa whispered, and without a second's hesitation, Cole, Hannah, and the three principalities disappeared and reappeared in Gaylord, Michigan, twelve years before.

●●●●●●●●●●●

Twelve Years Before the Discovery

The three angels no longer had wings. The one with the powerful-looking chest and firm, unsmiling jaw, Cassiel, spoke first. "Do not be concerned. We'll allow you to return to King Adnan's meeting. This detour was one of necessity."

"What happened to the wings?" Cole asked.

"The wings were essential so that we could hide you. They aren't something we often use," replied Uriel.

"Who are *you*?" Cole asked Cassiel.

"I am Cassiel, the leader of this band of principalities. We've been preparing you for your encounter in the Bosman Palace, but we first needed to preserve the timeline we've altered. We couldn't let you confront King Adnan yet. The king heard your voices in his office, so your original encounter has made its mark in history, but it will not influence what occurred on Mount Nebo."

Regardless of the questions he had, Cole couldn't help but tell Cassiel what was on his mind. "You're the one responsible for putting us through this crap? You suck."

"Cole?" Perisa said.

"Yeah?"

"We're never responsible for the evil, immoral decisions and actions that occur. You live in a fallen world. The people in your world make choices and take actions for which we are not answerable. *Occasionally*, we help right the wrongs that have occurred, but we do only what we're capable and *allowed* to do. You and Hannah are the vessels who are capable of influencing change on a human level."

"Okay," Hannah said, "so why did you take us away? Why couldn't we be discovered if we're the ones to cause the changes you so desperately want?"

Perisa explained. "You remember, Cole, when I took you from that meeting at your high school? When I did that, I didn't change your future—I changed your past. History now says you never went to prison, and you've been living life as a fugitive. The six years you lived between then and the fight in Florida were dramatically changed for you. But you're a time traveler. Those changes are inevitable for you. What we are attempting to do is to take advantage of your time-traveling abilities while not dramatically altering the histories of *other* people."

"And that has some correlation to our trip to the Bosman Palace?"

"Precisely," said Cassiel. "Each time you took Hannah back in time, she crossed paths with people—most notably the King of Jordan. Can you understand that the historical timeline you have been altering *must* include Hannah taking possession of the staff? If you had your confrontation with the King of Jordan on June fifteenth of this current timeline, Hannah would never take possession of the staff, and without the staff, none of your adventures would ever have happened. This whole undertaking would have been futile, and we'd have to start over again. I realize that you're having difficulty comprehending time, but what we're all trying to explain to the two of you is Hannah needs to go back to the church and gain possession of the staff once again."

"By taking you away when we did," continued Uriel, "the confrontation *you* had planned with the king didn't occur. Now, all the events on Mount Nebo can happen during this particular timeline, and Hannah can be there to take possession of the staff—*again*. If we didn't take you away and keep you from altering history, Hannah wouldn't have removed the staff from the rock. Now she will, and all that has happened to prepare you for your confrontation has been preserved."

"But if I kill him, and I *will* kill him, why won't *that* change history?" Hannah asked.

"It will…but only from June fifteenth on. Once you rewrite *that* historical timeline, there will be no need for you to take possession of the staff. You'll no longer possess it, and it'll be preserved and hidden until it's needed again."

"That's just spooky weird," said Cole. "I have to admit, I don't fully understand what's going on."

"Let me try to explain again." Cassiel hesitated. "Time—the way humans view it—is not the way it is perceived in the spiritual realm. As principalities, we can see the present and the past at the same time, and occasionally, when we have a task to accomplish, we are also given a glimpse of the future. Humans cannot comprehend that because you see time linearly. But one thing I hope you *can* comprehend is that there are no multiple timelines. Time cannot split with people living in parallel universes. This current timeline will be completed and re-established only when Hannah takes hold of the staff again. It was at that moment that you went back in time, and we started our work modifying and preserving history."

"What do you mean by that?" Hannah asked.

"Well," explained Perisa, "we modified it, for instance, by making sure King Adnan saw you everywhere Cole took you. And the people who died? All of them would have died whether you went back in time or not. All of them died under different circumstances because of the involvement of you two, but all along the way, we've preserved history."

"Like the Russ Smallock incident," interjected Cole.

"Exactly," she replied. "He died the same day except in a slightly different place and in a different way. The same people were involved and you were still blamed."

"So you pulled us away to avoid the confrontation in this timeline, but if we go back and take possession of the staff again, you'll let us return with it to face the King?" Hannah asked.

"That is correct," replied Cassiel.

"Is there anything else we might need to know before my head explodes?" asked Cole.

"There is," continued Cassiel. "King Adnan is possessed by the powerful demon, Hoaxal. As long as the demon occupies the king's body, Hannah will not be able to defeat him. Hannah needs to drive Hoaxal out so I can take care of him in the spiritual realm. Until she does it, King Akmal-Adnan is too strong for her."

"And how do I drive this demon out?" she asked.

"You have the Staff of Moses, Hannah," hinted Perisa. "The power to expel Hoaxal is in your staff. If you can contact him with it while it's in your hands, you can use its power to set the demon free. Once he's back in the spiritual realm, we'll take care of him and his minions."

"Is that what this is all about?" Cole asked. "Hoaxal and some demonic horde?"

"That is the part that *we* have the power to control. The result of your part is yet to be determined. Political, military, and economic issues are under our sphere of influence. But the human element is always unpredictable. The result of your involvement is yet to be determined. We've told you all that we're able to say," admitted Cassiel.

"And you think the two of us can handle this situation?" asked Hannah.

"It won't only be the two of you," said Uriel. "We'll be there... and you also have an additional ally. You'll know him when you see him—and he can be trusted."

After a lengthy pause, Perisa spoke up. "Hannah, you'll need to give us the staff for Cassiel to put back in the stone floor."

Without hesitation, Hannah handed it over.

"God bless you both," she said. "It's been my pleasure watching over you." She hugged them and slipped Cole a picture of the staff inside the Church of Moses. Uriel nodded at Cole and hugged Hannah as well.

Finally, Cassiel spoke confidently. "The Most High *will* be with you."

With that, the angels disappeared, leaving the cottage quiet and still.

Hannah eyed Cole curiously. "How come every time I look up, some attractive woman is giving you a hug?"

"What can I say? They find me irresistible....*You* must not feel the same way." He winked.

"Me?" Hannah asked, astounded that Cole would say such a thing.

"Yes, you." Cole walked over and gave Hannah the hug that *she'd* never offered him since they'd met. "Are you ready to go?"

"Do you think I'm ready?"

"I have every confidence you're ready to make your mark on the world, Hannah. You're more than just a 'Carpenter.' And I'll be there to help in any way I can."

Hannah smiled. "Then let's do it, and when we're done, we'll head back to the Pacific Northwest, and I'll become plain, simple Hannah Montana."

Cole smiled, appreciating her sense of humor. "Maybe we should wait and see what the future holds." He grabbed her left hand with his right before glancing at the picture Perisa had given him. Instantly, they were standing alone inside the Byzantine Church of Moses on Mount Nebo.

The Staff of Moses was entrenched firmly in the stone floor and a tremendous storm was raging outside the church walls. Hannah looked at Cole and smiled again. Then she reached forth and slid the staff from the rock. Cole squeezed her hand and smiled back. He formed a mental picture, and once again, they appeared in the corner of the king's office in the Bosman Palace. But this time, they could see where they were, and so could everyone else.

•••••●•••••

TWENTY-EIGHT

King Adnan roared, "*For* me or against me?"

Shaking with anger, Israeli Prime Minister Edelstein stood and directed his staff of men to follow. "As I said before, I will *never* sign a treaty. A pact with the devil…that's what it would be, and I refuse. Excuse us. We will be leaving now." He ripped the treaty in two and let it flutter to the floor.

Everyone watched Binyamin Edelstein's actions, but as the document fell and the prime minister moved toward the door, all eyes were diverted to the young American couple standing in the corner of the room. Cole Flint's intense eyes blazed toward the king, and beside him was Hannah Carpenter with her blue sapphire staff glowing in her hand.

Finally, when no one spoke, the king shouted, "It's you!" His hand went to his face, trailing an outline of the scar on his cheek from the earthquake in Montana.

Cole, always the cautious one, glanced quickly around the room. There were trophies of the king's gaming kills displayed, one of a grizzly bear which was surely Teddy's mother. There were swords mounted on the walls. All of the eight people appeared to be unarmed, but the general, who stood beside the king in a gesture of protection, almost certainly had quick access to a gun. Cole recognized one of the men, President Elias Shalom of Israel, as the man who had killed Russ Smallock six years before and who had saved Hannah's life in the Swiss Alps. Elias smiled, and Cole instantly recognized him as the ally of whom Cassiel had spoken.

"Did you know, young lady, that the prophet Moses was buried on Mount Nebo in Jordan? His staff is a historical relic that belongs to the nation of Jordan—of which I am king. That means the staff which you have been flaunting for the last five years is mine."

"I don't think so. It belongs to me. As long as I'm living, I believe it'll be mine."

"I see." The king's voice took on a demonic quality, the tone of which caused the hairs on Hannah's arms to stand. "Then you best be careful, for I am more than willing to kill you."

Cole slid his gun from the back waist of his jeans and commandeered a sword from the wall. He prepared himself for the violent action that was sure to develop.

"If you give it to me, I will let you live," the king continued.

"If you can lift it, I'll give it to you."

The king confidently approached Hannah and extended his hands. With one end sitting on the floor, Hannah pushed the other end to the King. He caught it with both hands, but the weight toppled him over onto his back. Everyone leaned forward for a better view of the king who struggled under the tremendous weight—everyone except General Marid, who slipped his own gun from his suit's coat pocket. Hannah stood over the king who strained to lift the staff. She grabbed one end and lifted, but kept the other end planted firmly on the king's chest. He could barely breathe. Hannah had no idea what to say, so she simply winged it. "Evil, creepy king, I say it's time to let your demon buddy go." Nothing happened right away, so Hannah tried again. "*Get out!*"

With an earsplitting scream, the invisible demon tore itself away. Because of the convulsion that the king experienced and the calm that immediately settled over his body, Hannah was sure the demon was exorcised. She lifted the staff and backed away, wondering if her work was done, waiting to see if three angels would appear and tell her to go home, but no such thing happened.

The king rose to his feet as Hannah stepped back, and the room was filled with silence. Anger settled into his features, and finally, as he glared hatred toward the young girl, he shouted, "Kill her!"

The general raised his gun, but before he could shoot, Cole teleported beside him and with his sword, slashed Jibril-Marid's hand clean from his wrist. The gun fell to the table, the general's hand still squeezing it. The king's special assistant lunged for the weapon as the king removed a gun of his own from his suit jacket and aimed it at Hannah, who began twirling the staff like a baton. The king unloaded all fifteen rounds at Hannah while everyone ducked. Hannah's staff deflected them all as it spun in blazing circles, one deflection killing the Israeli foreign affairs minister and another wounding the Jordanian prime minister.

With the general's amputated hand still grasping the gun, Cole wrestled it from the assistant and heaved it behind the king's desk, but at the sound of the king's shots, all of the security personnel who were waiting in the lobby outside the office burst through the door. Chaos ensued.

As Hoaxal rose from King Adnan's body, there in front of him was Cassiel, his glistening sword in hand. Uriel and Perisa hovered back to back, at least a dozen demonic minions surrounding them. Hoaxal produced a huge, double-bladed sword and floated confidently facing Cassiel. "So we finally meet. You shall regret meddling in my affairs," he boasted.

Cassiel's eyes briefly met Uriel's and Perisa's. Then he smiled and said, "I don't think so."

He swung his sword at Hoaxal, whose blade deflected the swing. A fiery spark illuminated the office and floated toward the floor before dissipating.

The demonic minions attacked Uriel and Perisa, who blocked their thrusts. Smaller sparks lit the air, and the fight was on.

The king threw his gun at Hannah as General Marid howled in pain, blood flowing from the stump of his wrist. Sparks floated in the air above as soldiers and security personnel flooded the room, grabbing swords off the walls. Elias Shalom grabbed the king's assistant by the shoulder and back of the head and pounded his forehead into the desk until the man was unconscious. One Jordanian soldier killed an Israeli bodyguard, and the king tugged the sword from the dead man's grasp. He swung it at Hannah, who blocked it with the staff, sending a jarring pain through the king's arm. He swung again, but the staff knocked the sword from his grip. Hannah twirled the staff back into the king's hip, sending him flying to the floor.

One of the soldiers swung his sword at Hannah, but Elias blocked it, then spun and sliced him open. The Israeli prime minister slid into the corner behind the king's desk and peeled off General Marid's hand from the gun. He tried to keep out of harm's way, but his secretariat wasn't so lucky, falling victim to a Jordanian soldier.

As the demons attacked Uriel and Perisa, they retaliated with precision. They both weilded two swords and each blocked a swing with one sword and sliced a demon open with the other. The two demons dissipated into smoke, a stench of sulfur the only other sign of their passing. As the demon hoard continued to attack, more sparks lighted the room and more remnants of sulfur floated to the floor. Uriel blocked, twirled, and sliced; Perisa deflected a sword and thrust. Smoke rose, traces of sulfur fell, and sparks flew.

Hoaxal roared in anger as Cassiel parried expertly, once succeeding with an offensive jab, slicing the demon's arm. Hoaxal spun and sliced a blow toward Cassiel's head, but it was blocked, and another spark flew from the swords. Hoaxal used his powerful arms to send blow after blow toward Cassiel, who backed away and parried skillfully, eventually slicing a deep wound across Hoaxal's shoulder. The tired demon continued pressing, however, fueled by his tremendous rage.

Eight of the twelve minions were nothing but smoke, but the strongest ones waited until the end, hoping to tire the angels before they got involved. They managed to separate Uriel and Perisa, fighting two against one, but the angels continued to frustrate the demons' attempts.

King Adnan again picked up his sword, irately using it to kill an Israeli fighter before he faced Hannah once more.

As sparks burned the air and the sulfuric smell grew more noticeable, Cole threw a table over onto a fighting soldier, driving his head into the wall and knocking him out of commission. The wounded Jordanian prime minister drew back his sword to attack Cole, but Elias intervened, killing him with one quick stroke. Only Hannah, Cole, President Elias, King Adnan, General Marid, and Prime Minister Edelstein were left standing.

The general held a sword in his left hand, his face white from pain and loss of blood, but he was determined to defeat Cole Flint or die trying. Cole blocked his swing and retaliated with a punch in the general's face. "I already killed you once, General. But I'm perfectly willing to do it again."

"That's impossible!" he roared. The general rotated his hips and pressed a second attempt, but Cole ducked and pierced his sword into the general's thigh.

"It *is* odd, but it happens to be true." The general swung wildly again, but the blow was sidestepped and Cole drove his sword into Marid's left shoulder, rendering him nearly defenseless, but the soldier weakly thrust again. Cole deflected it, then spun and sliced him deeply across the throat. He fell to the floor and died.

All four demons began spinning at a phenomenal speed causing the air to churn, stirring up the sulfur that had settled onto the floor. Uriel held his sword out level and glanced at Perisa who did the same thing. "I guess word doesn't travel well in the demonic world. Abigor died trying this same maneuver."

"Are these Tasmanian Devils, by chance?" asked Perisa. "The velocity is impressive."

Uriel shrugged his shoulders, but he refocused as the demons began their move. Instantaneously, a bolt of lightning shot out of each of the angels' swords, dividing in two and dematerializing the spirits instantly into sizzling, smoky vapors. The lightning bolts, however, ignited some of the sulfur, and as it settled, several small fires began in the king's office.

King Adnan thrust his sword frantically at Hannah, but she used her impressive flag corp twirling skills to thwart each attempt. The staff was so heavy that each clash with the sword sent a jarring pain through the King, and his arms became like lead. For a second time, Hannah blasted him with her staff and sent the king crashing to the floor. When he dragged himself back to his feet, he bowed his head and lied. "I surrender. I give up. Please, have mercy on me. My demon is exorcised. Only now can I rule my country as I should."

Hannah didn't know what to do. She thought she would need to kill him, but now it appeared that he desired a second chance. She lowered the staff with grace in her heart, but as she did, the king unexpectedly charged again. Twirling the staff once more, she knocked the sword from his hand as she snapped both his radius and ulna in two. She spun her weapon one final time, striking him in the forehead, cracking his skull and sending him sprawling to the floor. The King of Jordan was dead.

Uriel, Perisa, and Cassiel surrounded Hoaxal. Exhausted, he frantically swung his sword in a futile attempt to escape. Uriel struck his back, Perisa his leg. Cassiel continued his defensive tactics, matching Hoaxal blow for blow as sparks showered King Akmal-Adnan's office and additional fires began to light. Uriel and Perisa weakened their adversary more with two additional cuts to his shoulder and lower leg.

Finally, Cassiel sensed the end was near. "Your time on earth is finished Hoaxal. You'll be heading to the Underworld for eternity. You've failed!" With that statement, Cassiel finally took the offensive. He slashed the demon's arm and his chest before his final blow that decapitated the demon's head. Hoaxal's body erupted into ghastly smoke and dropped the last demonic sulfur to the floor.

Immediately, the three angels focused their attention on the fires, ensuring that their charges remained safe.

"We need to get out of here!" Hannah yelled, the staff still held firmly in her right hand. "He's dead, Cole. We've done what we came to do."

Elias spoke. "This fire is the perfect cover-up. You two get out of here, and the prime minister and I will spread the story. No one will know what happened here today."

"I'll know!" Edelstein shouted. "She's not leaving with that staff!"

He raised the gun in his hand and aimed at Hannah, but before he could shoot a single shot, Cole nearly emptied his clip into the prime minister's chest. He dropped dead as the curtains of a nearby window burst into flames.

Cole, with that sadness filling his eyes, calmly stated, "I told you I had your back." He hurried to a confused-looking Hannah who was standing with her empty palms held out while looking frantically all around her. He took a hand in his own. "What's wrong?"

"The staff...I had it in my hand, but now it's gone....It's gone, Cole!"

A new sadness tugged at Cole's heart, but there was no time to console her. The fire flared to a dangerous level.

He turned quickly to the gray-haired man with a question he needed to ask. "Who are you?"

"I'm Elias Shalom, President of Israel," he explained, "but my real friends over the centuries call me Elijah. I'm a time traveler, just like you."

"Elijah...the prophet? The one who was translated into Heaven?" asked Hannah.

Elias simply winked at her and said to Cole, "Get her out of here."

●●●●●●●●●●●

TWENTY-NINE

Five Years Before the Discovery

When Cole and Hannah arrived, Kristina jumped up from the couch where she was reading. "Hannah's back, Sarah! She's safe!"

Sarah came running from a back room with Teddy trailing behind her.

They both gave Hannah a hug, but Teddy pushed his way between them and sat down, staring up at his owner.

Hannah bent down and hugged her cute bear cub.

"You weren't gone long at all. Is it over?" Kristina nervously asked.

"I'm not sure, Mom, but Cole will go back to the future to see what's changed. I *think* it's over, though. That evil king is dead… and the staff is gone. It'll be hidden again, and we should be safe.… Mom? Are you reading *To Kill a Mockingbird*?"

"Yeah, it was here, lying on the lampstand when I sat down. I've always wanted to read it."

"You actually finished it before we left for Jordan."

"I did? I don't recall. Did I enjoy it? It's pretty good so far."

"Uh huh. You did. You said it was possibly the best book you'd ever read, but I guess you now get to read the book again for the first time. Not many people get to have that experience."

"Hannah?" asked Sarah. "Practically everything we own is here in this house somehow, but I can't find my shirt that says 'I kick butt and take names.' I was going to give it to you when you came back."

"You already gave it to me…when my luggage was lost at the airport."

"You lost your luggage, honey? I'm so sorry," said Kristina.

"You don't remember…? Mom…? Sarah?" Both just shrugged their shoulders. "Well, apparently there're some things you don't remember and some that you do. This time-traveling thing is beyond my understanding."

"I'm sure you're light years ahead of *us*, Hannah. Regardless, I'm *so* relieved you're back home safely. Thank you, Cole, for keeping your word."

"Mrs. Carpenter, I'm not sure she needed me. You have one special daughter, and she held her own. You can be very proud of her too."

"You're proud of me?" Hannah asked.

"Of course I am." Cole seemed somewhat uncomfortable when he said, "Hannah, I still have some things to do, but I'll be back; you can count on it."

Hannah stopped petting her bear and put her arms around Cole. "There. *I* hugged you now too."

"See? Beautiful women find me irresistible." He winked and disappeared.

●●●●●⬤●●●●●

FRIDAY, JUNE 22
Six Days After the Discovery

When Cole time traveled to Lauren's apartment, she was engrossed in a search of the Internet. She jumped when he spoke.

"What are you doing?"

"Stop surprising me like that! You're gonna give me a heart attack." She got up and put her arms around him. It felt good to be in her arms, but he had questions that he needed answered. Lauren sensed it immediately. "Something else is on your mind, isn't it?"

"I'm really happy to see you...*really* happy, but I came here to see what effect we had on the past. King Adnan is dead."

"I already know." She sat back down at the computer. "He died a week ago in a fire in the Bosman Palace along with his prime minister and the head of SOCOM. The Israeli prime minister and foreign affairs minister also died along with nine others. The only survivor of the fire was Israeli President Elias Shalom who wasn't in the meeting room when the fire started."

"Is there other news about Shalom?"

"He had some minor burns and a few cuts from trying to get to the others, but there were no major injuries. The man is known for his political wisdom, and he's managed to ease the anxiety the death of the prime minister has caused. Now they're focusing on *him* as the potential next prime minister of the country. All seems to be well in Israel."

"Is that so?" Cole smiled. "What about the Staff of Moses?"

"Cole, is Hannah all right? Since you left me to work out your plans, I've been monitoring the news, wondering what effect you would have. I can no longer find any evidence that the staff was ever discovered. I can't find evidence that the Carpenters ever went to Jordan either. But four years ago, two Jordanian men died during a hiking accident in the Swiss Alps. And June fourteenth, two SOCOM soldiers and an escaped convict were found floating in the river by some hikers in the Smoky Mountains. I can't find any records of an arrest outside Shanice Brown's house or any shooting or car explosion on the expressway in Flint; however, two suspected Jordanian terrorists died in a shooting with police the same day we had our run-in with the assassins. I never even made a news report of the staff's discovery, Cole....And get this— I wasn't in Jordan on June sixteenth. I was in Washington, D.C., reporting on President Stonehouse's new budget proposal.

"We never met with Shanice Brown or Lillian Marsh. I called them and asked, and even Carter Flint has no memory of meeting me. I felt totally stupid that they didn't know what I was talking about. There wasn't even a treaty between Jordan, Egypt, and Turkey. One thing that *has* remained the same is that the Israelis were meeting with the King of Jordan before the building burned down."

"What about Hannah's father?"

"He reported his family missing five days ago. I haven't managed to contact him yet. I'm afraid he'll show up in a morgue eventually."

There was a pause as Cole sorted his thoughts. Finally, he said, "Okay, we changed history. The staff was never found, but our activities before June fifteenth are set in time. Events after the fifteenth have disappeared, except big incidents like people dying still managed to happen in a different way. I guess that makes sense. What doesn't make sense to me is why *you* remember everything. I don't get it."

"Besides the fact that I experienced quite a bit of the adventure and lived to tell about it, I have a theory—two theories, actually."

"Okay?"

"Theory one is just me being a smidgeon egotistical, but maybe I was allowed to remember because I'm needed in some way in the future. Since I know there are time travelers, maybe I can help somehow, you know?"

Cole smiled. "It's possible," he admitted. "You have another theory?"

Lauren got a sly smile on her face. "Theory two is that I had this piece of paper in my pocket which connected me to you in a way that allowed me to remember."

"What is it?"

"It's some notes from some research I did on June twenty-second—today—but the *first* June twenty-second *before* you did whatever you did to the king a week ago. And you're not going to believe what it says. It says that I know who your mother is."

● ● ● ● ● ● ● ● ● ● ●

THIRTY

• • • • • • • • • ● • • • • • • • •

So you've never been to Washington, D.C., before?" Lauren asked.

"Never. But I watched *National Treasure* and the *Night at the Museum* movies, so I've seen all the sights."

"You knew nothing about the Capitol Building...I now know that, so I'm sure you don't know about the congressional office buildings. This one's the Hart Building. I was told your mother was doing an interview, but she agreed to meet us when she was done."

After checking in and receiving visitor's badges, they headed to the second floor where they were asked to go for their meeting.

Finally, an attractive lady in her late-forties walked up to Lauren. "Lauren, what are you doing here? I got a message that you needed to meet with me. I don't understand."

"It's important, and I think you'll be glad you met us. This is my friend, Cole Flint."

"Cole? That's a name I've always liked. It's nice to meet you."

"Thank you. It's nice to meet you too."

"So tell me what's so important, Lauren, that you came here all the way from New York on a Saturday."

"Well, let me begin by saying that eight days ago, I covered a story that has literally changed the world."

"I don't know what you're talking about."

"No, you wouldn't. But on that day, a girl by the name of Hannah Carpenter took possession of the Staff of Moses on Mount Nebo. Before the King of Jordan could capture her, she was rescued. Her rescuer, Cole Flint, became a household name."

"How could I miss a story like that?"

"You didn't, but you've forgotten it—because history was changed—but it's true nonetheless. The news station investigated Cole and learned that he was born nearly twenty-five years ago on October nineteenth at Hurley Hospital in Flint, Michigan. I was asked to investigate his history."

"Why don't you sit down, ma'am?" Cole asked as he held a chair out for her. "There's quite a bit to the story."

Lauren continued as Cole's mother sat in the chair. "What I found out was that Cole's mother inexplicably appeared in a delivery bed moments before he was born, and shortly thereafter—just as mystifyingly—she disappeared. Before she did, she told the nurse, Lillian Marsh, that the baby's name would be Cole. When the mother didn't return after three days, the baby was placed in the care of Shanice Brown, a foster mother in Flint. Three days later, Cole was transferred to Carter and Ellie Flint, where he was adopted and lived until he was eighteen years old."

"Cole Flint," the woman remarked, giving Cole her attention. "Was it a good family?" she asked.

"I was never told I was adopted," Cole explained. "My father had a lot of flaws, but my mother loved me and raised me well until I was thirteen when she died in a car accident. My father and I never saw eye-to-eye after that, and I basically raised myself from that point on."

"I didn't understand why researching Cole was so important," Lauren interrupted, "until I started considering things from the other point of view. Who was the mother? Who was the father? I figured that if Cole wasn't literally abandoned—and Lily Marsh's story had me convinced that the mother had no intention of abandonment—then there must be a mother out there who claimed to have been abducted or claimed that her baby was kidnapped. Because I had the date and the time of birth, the baby's name, and a strange theory, I ran across an odd story about a hysterical lady who showed up pregnant in Mount Sinai Hospital in Queens. The doctors agreed that she was in the process of delivery, and then somehow she was lying there claiming to have delivered a child that didn't exist. A doctor even wrote an article in *The New England Journal of Medicine* explaining that the mother without question delivered a baby but there was no child to behold. One second she was dilated and instructed to begin pushing, and the next second she was stitched up and there was no baby. The woman's name was…"

"Elizabeth Desmond," Liz cut in, her face a pale white.

"Yes, Liz. It was you that told me to investigate Cole, and when I did, he found *me*. He saved my life two separate times. At first, I was confused why Hannah Carpenter and the Staff of Moses wasn't your primary interest, but once I began having feelings for Cole, and I learned about his adoptive mother dying, I wanted to find his real mom. It wasn't as hard as I thought it would be."

"I don't know anything about the Carpenter girl and the Staff of Moses, but I swear that I committed my entire life to finding my son. You're my son?" she asked Cole.

"Lauren says we have the same eyes," Cole said with a smile.
"And the same smile—if and when the two of you ever smile."

"You're my son?" she asked again, this time with tears flooding her eyes. "I didn't have any idea how to find you," she apologized. "I worked my butt off for the exact job I have at Fox News with the idea that I'd have the resources to find you, but I never could. I didn't even know if you would be named Cole."

Liz had risen from her chair but didn't appear to know what to do, so Cole took the initiative and went to her. He hugged her, and tears filled his eyes too. It was the hug of a lifetime, but finally, Liz asked Lauren, "Do you have any idea what happened?"

"I do," said Cole. "I know a few angels who are pretty good at manipulating circumstances. I think you were teleported from one hospital to another, so I could end up with the Flints."

"Teleported? But that's impossible."

"Really? You know it isn't because it happened to you, Liz," clarified Lauren. "And I know it isn't impossible because Cole is able to teleport too."

Elizabeth stepped back and focused on Cole for answers.

"A little over a week ago, I time traveled for the first time in my life. I met an angel who told me that I had to help a girl—Hannah Carpenter—who would gain possession of the Staff of Moses. Over the past week, we were responsible for taking down the King of Jordan, but to do it, we had to change history. You don't know about it because history has been changed."

"The King of Jordan died in a fire at his palace in Jordan."

"No, that's not what happened exactly," mentioned Cole, "but it's what history says happened. And I believe those same angels put Lauren in my life, so I could be reunited with you."

"I love him," admitted Lauren to Liz.

"You do?" Cole seemed surprised.

"Yes, now shut up; I'm talking to my boss. It's not going to be some kind of conflict of interest for me to be dating your son, is it?"

"Do I have any say in this?" Cole asked with a smile on his face.

"Not now, Cole. This is important."

Elizabeth smiled a huge grin too, and sure enough, the smile mirrored her son's.

"You're gonna be a nightmare, aren't you?" Cole asked.

"I'd like some time to get to know my son. You're not planning on interfering are you?" she joked.

"I wouldn't dream of it. I'm the one who got you two together, remember?"

Cole smiled the biggest, most-genuine smile he'd smiled in years before he grabbed both ladies' hands and said, "Speaking of together time, let's get out of here. We have lots of catching up to do, but this place reminds me of a courthouse. Have you ever been to the Grand Canyon, Mom? You're gonna love it."

● ● ● ● ● ⬤ ● ● ● ● ●

Five Years Before the Discovery

There was a knock on the door that had the whole Carpenter family curious. There had been no hint of people since they took possession of the Montana house. Hannah ran to the door, and when she opened it, there was Cole with a huge smile on his face. Hannah hugged him and invited him in.

After they said their hellos, Kristina addressed Cole. "We were planning on a memorial service later today. Would you consider attending?"

"Thank you for the invitation, Mrs. Carpenter, but I'm going to have to decline."

Hannah's jaw dropped in confusion. "What? Seriously? You have other plans that are more important...plans you can't time travel to later today?"

"Hold on, Hannah. You don't understand. Yes, I have other plans, but you're all going to be part of them. The service will have to wait. I'm gonna take you to the future...*all* of you."

"What's going on?" Kristina asked.

"The staff was never discovered. The king and everyone else who was a danger to Hannah and your family are either dead or are now unaware of your existence. I'm gonna move you back to the future where you ought to be. And I have a surprise for you."

"Are we taking Teddy?" Sarah asked.

"Nope. He's already there. Gather around. We can come back and get your things later if you need them."

All the ladies bunched around Cole in a huddle. He put his arms around them all, and seconds later, they arrived five years into the future at their home in Montana.

●●●●● ● ●●●●●

SUNDAY, JUNE 24
Seven Days After the Discovery

When they arrived, they were no longer inside the cottage, but rather outside, standing next to a giant grizzly bear that was lying on his stomach, staring at the homestead.

"Teddy!" Hannah squealed. "You're full grown! Did you find him in Tennessee, Cole?"

"Actually, he was here—waiting." Cole said.

"Is this the surprise?" asked Sarah.

"No, not exactly...I have some explaining to do. Hannah, remember when I was out trying to change my past while you were being attacked in the Smoky Mountains?"

Hannah looked over her shoulder at him with her eyebrows raised in the "Duh...how could I forget that?" look on her face.

"Well, Perisa gave me a picture of your house in Missouri. I never had any need to go there during the whole adventure, but I've been thinking about it ever since. It seemed to me that the angels were always a step ahead of us. They always had a plan that we didn't quite understand, so I got to wondering if maybe I was *supposed* to make a visit. I went there this morning, and when I showed up, Perisa and Uriel were there."

"They were expecting you, weren't they?"

"Yep. Made a few unnecessary comments about how slow I am to figure things out, but there they were—and they had three things for me to give you."

"Teddy! You brought me Teddy?"

"You know there are names for pets other than Teddy," Cole wisecracked.

"Is he inside?" Hannah asked impatiently, ignoring Cole completely. "Uriel said he was being taken care of," she proclaimed as she immediately starting heading toward the house.

"Hannah, wait!" Cole called out as the grizzly followed in her steps. "You can't go in there with that bear."

"Listen to him, Hannah," said Sarah. "Your dog is, like, bite-sized for that huge bear."

"I'll stay with Teddy," Cole volunteered. "The three of you can go inside." Cole started wrestling the bear, his heart happy for what the Carpenter women were about to see. When they made it to the front door, both Cole and Teddy sat still and watched.

Hannah threw open the door, and standing on the threshold with a brace on his neck, a cast on one arm, and a small shih tzu in his other was Richard Carpenter.

●●●●● ● ●●●●●

SUNDAY, JUNE 24
Seven Days After the Discovery

They sat bundled in a blanket up at a peak of the Cabinet Mountains. After some tranquil gazing at the scenery, Hannah finally broke the silence. "So all that 'righting wrongs' and 'occasionally interfering' when they're 'allowed' to and 'preventing things from happening' jazz was some sort of clue to you?"

"Comments like those and the nagging realization that Perisa gave me a picture of your house in Missouri so I could jump there. And then the fact that Lauren couldn't find any evidence that he had died—all those things left a nagging thought in my head. I finally figured out that Perisa wanted me to go there. When I did, they were there waiting. They protected him from a fatal car accident that would have happened the day he was shot in Jordan. He was at the hospital overnight because of a minor neck injury, and they had casted his broken arm."

"Finding him slightly battered was a lot better way of spending my Sunday than doing a memorial service. Thank you."

"You're welcome, but Perisa's the one who 'interfered' and protected him. Lauren would have tracked him down sooner or later, but sooner is better."

"You're together with Lauren, aren't you?" Hannah said so dishearteningly that Teddy lifted his head up from her lap and regarded her curiously. "It's okay, Teddy. I'm happy and sad at the same time." Teddy put his head back in her lap, and Cole grabbed her hand.

"After all that's gone on, I understand how you might feel."

"It's just…I knew she liked you. I mean, who *wouldn't*? But now I don't have to worry about it anymore."

"Worry about what?" Cole asked, playing stupid.

Hannah's face got red. She was embarrassed, but one thing she'd learned during her adventures with Cole was that she could be confident in herself, and her newly obtained self-assurance inspired her to actually say what she felt. She concentrated on Cole's striking eyes and admitted, "Worry about how you feel about me...because if the truth be told, I think I was falling in love with you."

Cole hesitated, which made Hannah nervous. "You know, Lauren said she loved me, and when she said it, all I could think of was you. I didn't know how I was gonna tell you, but I *needed* to tell you that I had feelings for her too." Cole paused. "You're nothing short of exceptional, Hannah. You're strong and courageous. They picked you because you're special. It took me a while to recognize it, but you kind of grew on me." He smiled his awesome smile. "All these things that happened to me over the years...I'm convinced were to prepare me to meet you. And your loving, pure heart prepared me to meet my mom and Lauren."

Teddy let out a lonesome howl-like sound as if he felt Cole had left someone—or something—out.

"And all these unbelievable things make it possible for me to accept that a grizzly bear can be a pet. You're a good boy, Teddy."

He stopped his whining and put his head in Cole's lap instead of Hannah's.

"But mostly, Hannah, I learned to love again. I love you...I really do." He leaned over the bear to give her a gentle kiss, and it was sure to be a memorable one for Hannah—except for the grizzly that stuck his nose between their faces and started licking like a gigantic dog. They both wiped away the slobber and laughed. "Maybe someday we'll get a do-over," suggested Cole.

"I have some growing up to do," admitted Hannah. "My family's back together...and I don't have to worry about protecting the staff anymore or fighting off bad guys because I have it.

But if we can use a do-over to defeat the King of Jordan, I'll keep my fingers crossed that I'll get a second chance with you too."

"Speaking of the staff...I said I was given *three* things to bring to you. Your tiny dog was one—are you sure that pipsqueak can be considered a real dog...?"

She slapped him on the shoulder. "Of course he can...but the name thing is gonna be an issue...." She steered the subject back on topic. "My dad was the second, I assume, so what's the third thing?"

Cole took a small, sapphire jewel out of his pocket and presented it to Hannah. "Perisa guaranteed that it'd fit in your necklace. She said it's a reminder to you of our adventure, but also that when the time is right, you need to be ready to wield the staff once again. We may just get that do-over."

Hannah smiled and snapped the stunning, blue stone into her necklace. "Thank you. And I'll be ready. I don't know if we'll be in Montana or Missouri, but I'll be ready when you come for me."

They both put their hands on Teddy's shoulders, and he settled his head back down on Hannah's lap while the two people he loved surveyed the gorgeous mountains and smiled.

•••• ● ••••

EPILOGUE

SUNDAY, JUNE 24
Seven Days After the Discovery

The Rocky Mountains in Banff National Park in Alberta, Canada, covered over twenty-five hundred square miles. Moraine Lake lay against a mountain backdrop in the Valley of the Ten Peaks, a chain of ten mountain peaks, all more than ten thousand feet tall. Three rays of light spotted the rock, grew, and transformed into three solid bodies. Characteristically, Cassiel met with Uriel and Perisa at one of the world's most-enchanting mountain views.

"Thank you for meeting with me again," began Cassiel.

"You pick the loveliest locales for our meetings," replied Perisa. "It's a pleasure to be here."

"The lake...would you describe that color as turquoise?" asked Uriel. "I can't decide if the lake is more breathtaking or that jagged line of mountains." They all admired the serene beauty in silence for a moment before Uriel asked, "I suppose we're here for a new assignment?"

"No, actually, I just thought it would be a pleasant place to debrief and celebrate a job well-done. All told, I think things worked out rather well," said Cassiel.

"Quite a nice list of accomplishments...I have to agree," added Perisa. "Hoaxal is out of our hair for good...that was a bonus."

"Plus the King of Jordan's evil plans were thwarted. With or without Hoaxal, he would've always been up to no good. I'd say eliminating him was another fabulous bonus."

"I agree, Uriel," continued Cassiel. "And I'm happy to see Cole Flint united with his mother and able to love again. He's been put through a lot over the years. That was a good idea getting Lauren Molina involved, Perisa."

"Thank you, friend. We also managed to keep the staff out of the world news and save Richard Carpenter. Hannah proved to have the courage and faith of a hero, and now she'll be safe with her family until she's needed again. "All along, the jumper thought he was helping Hannah, but in reality, she was helping him," interjected Perisa.

"And before we're done, both she and Cole *will* be needed again, but until then, we should take this moment to celebrate the *real* victory," said Cassiel. "Earlier today the one-hundred-twenty-member Knesset of Israel voted unanimously on their new prime minister. By setting the stage for Cole to kill Binyamin Edelstein, we've managed to rid Israel of his poor, failing leadership, and we've installed the prophet Elijah in his place. Elias Shalom is the new Prime Minister of Israel. We accomplished *exactly* what we intended at the beginning of this adventure."

Each of the principalities smiled in acknowledgment of a job well-done.

"Elias is only the first piece to the puzzle, Cassiel. What comes next?" asked Uriel.

"We've had time travelers throughout history, but never before have we had to make more use of them than now. It's time to prepare for part two of our plan."

"Which time traveler? The girl?" asked Perisa.

"Yes, the planer. She'll be needed soon. Until we meet again, continue to watch over her closely, Perisa. Times are perilous, yet with the time travelers, there is always hope. We did well this time, but we have much, much more to accomplish. Until we meet again, my friends, may the Most High be with you both."

●●●●● ● ●●●●●

ABOUT THE AUTHOR

Jeff LaFerney has been a language arts teacher and coach for more than twenty years. He earned his English and teaching degrees from the University of Michigan-Flint and his master's degree in educational leadership from Eastern Michigan University. He and his wife, Jennifer, live in Davison, Michigan. Both of their kids, Torey and Teryn, are currently college students. *Loving the Rain* (a suspense novel) and *Skeleton Key* and *Bulletproof* (mysteries) all include Clay and Tanner Thomas. Each novel stands alone and can be read in any order.

Made in the USA
Charleston, SC
11 October 2013